THE
WALKING
DEAD

By Robert Kirkman and Jay Bonansinga

The Walking Dead: Rise of the Governor
The Walking Dead: The Road to Woodbury
The Walking Dead: The Fall of the Governor, Part One
The Walking Dead: The Fall of the Governor, Part Two

THE
WALKING
DEAD

THE FALL OF THE GOVERNOR

PART ONE

ROBERT KIRKMAN
AND JAY BONANSINGA

TOR

First published in the US 2013 by Thomas Dunne Books,
an imprint of St Martin's Press

First published in the UK 2013 by Tor
an imprint of Pan Macmillan, a division of Macmillan Publishers Limited
Pan Macmillan, 20 New Wharf Road, London N1 9RR
Basingstoke and Oxford
Associated companies throughout the world
www.panmacmillan.com

ISBN 978-0-330-54138-1

9 8

A CIP catalogue record for this book is available from the British Library.

Printed and bound by CPI Group (UK) Ltd, Croydon, CR0 4YY

To Sheri Stearn, my constant reader and other mother,
and to Diego for the mechanics of death and destruction
—Jay Bonansinga

ACKNOWLEDGMENTS

A very special thank-you to the man, Robert Kirkman, who never fails to pull magic out of his hat; to Andy Cohen, my career compass; to Brendan Deneen, my editor and best dude; to Christina MacDonald for the best line editing ever; and to David Alpert, who holds it all together. Also a huge thanks to Kemper Donovan, Nicole Sohl, Stephanie Hargadon, Denise Dorman, Tom Leavens, Jeff Siegel, and my boys, Joey and Bill Bonansinga. Last but not least, my undying love and gratitude to the woman who changed my life and made me a better writer and man, Jill Norton Brazel.

—Jay Bonansinga

PART 1

The Gathering

So when the last and dreadful hour
This crumbling pageant shall devour,
The trumpet shall be heard on high,
The dead shall live, the living die,
And Music shall untune the sky.
                        —John Dryden

ONE

Writing in pain on the ground, Bruce Allan Cooper gasps and blinks and tries to catch his breath. He can hear the gurgling, feral growls of a half-dozen biters coming for him, moving in for a feeding. A voice in his brain screams at him: *Move, you fucking idiot! You pussy! What are you doing?!*

A big African American with an NBA forward's physique, a shaved, missile-shaped head, and a grizzle of a goatee, he rolls across the scabrous earth, barely avoiding the clawing gray fingers and snapping jaws of an adult female biter with half a face.

He covers maybe five or six feet until a dagger of pain shoots down his side, radiating fire across his ribs, seizing him up in paralyzing agony. He lands on his back, still gripping his rusty fire ax. The pick head is caked in blood and human hair and the black, viscous bile that has come to be known among survivors as walker-droppings.

Momentarily thunderstruck, his ears ringing, one eye already closing up from the swelling of a broken nose, Bruce wears the tattered army fatigues and mud-caked jackboots of the unofficial Woodbury militia. He can see the Georgia sky above him—a low canopy of filthy dishwater-gray clouds, inclement and nasty for April—and it taunts him: *You're nothing but a bug down there,*

Brucey-boy, a maggot on the carcass of a dying earth, a parasite feeding off the scraps and ruins of a vanishing human race.

All at once the panorama of the sky above him is eclipsed by three alien faces—dark planets slowly blocking out the heavens— each one snarling stupidly, drunkenly, each pair of milky eyes geeked perpetually open. One of them, an obese adult male in a soiled hospital smock, drools black mucus-gunk that drips on Bruce's cheek.

"GOD-*DAMMMMMMM*!"

Bruce snaps out of his stupor, finding an unexpected reserve of strength. He lashes out with his ax. The pointed end arcs upward and impales the fat biter in the soft tissue under the jaw. The lower half of the thing's face detaches and jettisons, a gristly phalanx of dead flesh and glistening cartilage pinwheeling upwards of twenty feet in the air before coming back down to earth with a splat.

Rolling again, scrambling to his feet, Bruce executes a one-eighty spin—fairly graceful for a big man in excruciating pain— and hacks through the putrid neck muscles of another female biter coming at him. The head falls to the side, wobbling for a moment on threads of desiccated tissue before breaking free and tumbling to the ground.

The head rolls for a few feet, leaving a leech trail of black spoor, while the body remains upright for an agonizing moment, twitching with insensate arms outstretched in horrible blind instinct. Something metallic lies coiled at the thing's feet as it finally sinks to the ground.

Bruce then hears the strangest thing that can be heard—muffled in his traumatized ears—following in the wake of the carnage: *cymbals crashing*. At least, that's what it sounds like to Bruce's ringing ears—a throbbing, metallic crashing noise in his brain— coming from the near distance. Backing away with his weapon at his side, spurred on by the sound, Bruce blinks and tries to focus on other biters shambling toward him. There are too many of them to engage with the pickax.

Bruce turns to flee, and without warning runs directly into another figure blocking his path.

"WHOA!"

The other figure—a thick-necked white man built like a fire-plug, his sandy hair cut in an old-school flattop—lets out a war cry and swings a mace the size of a horse leg at Bruce. The spiked club whizzes past Bruce's face, passing within centimeters of his broken nose. Bruce instinctively rears backward, tripping over his own feet.

He topples to the ground in an awkward display that sends up a cloud of dust and elicits another series of cymbal crashes from the hazy middle distance. The ax goes flying. The sandy-haired man takes advantage of the confusion and roars toward Bruce, the mace poised for action. Bruce grunts and rolls out of range at the last minute.

The mace head slams down hard, stick-pinning into the earth mere inches from Bruce's head.

Bruce rolls toward the fallen weapon that lies in the red dirt about ten feet away. He gets his hand around the wooden shank, when suddenly, without warning, a figure lurches out of the haze to Bruce's immediate left. Bruce jerks away from the biter, which is crawling toward him with the languid twitches of a giant lizard. Black ooze issues from the female's slack mouth—its sharp little teeth visible—its jaw snapping with reptilian vigor.

Then something else happens that brings Bruce back to reality.

The chain holding the female in place suddenly clangs, the monster reaching the limits of its bondage. Bruce lets out an instinctive gasp of relief, the dead thing only inches away, flailing impotently at him. The biter growls with inchoate frustration, the chain holding fast. Bruce feels like digging the thing's eyeballs out with his bare hands, like chewing through the neck of this useless piece of rotting shit-flesh.

Again, Bruce hears that weird cymbal-crashing noise, as well as the voice of the other man, barely audible under the noise: "C'mon, man, get up . . . get up."

Bruce gets moving. He grabs the ax and struggles to his feet. More cymbal-crashing noises . . . as Bruce spins, and then swings the ax hard at the other man.

The blade barely misses Flattop's throat, slicing through the collar of the man's turtleneck sweater, leaving a six-inch gouge.

"How's that?" Bruce mutters under his breath, circling the man. "That entertaining enough for ya?"

"That's the spirit," the stocky man murmurs—his name is Gabriel Harris, Gabe to his cronies—as he swings the club again, the nail-studded head whispering past Bruce's swollen face.

"That all you got?" Bruce mumbles, jerking away just in time, and then circling around the other way. He lashes out with the ax. Gabe parries with the club, and all around the two combatants, the monsters keep growling and gurgling their watery ululations, straining against their chains, hungry for human flesh, stirred into a feeding frenzy.

As the dusty haze on the periphery of the battlefield clears, the remnants of an outdoor dirt-track arena come into focus.

The size of a football field, the outer edges lined with cyclone fencing, the Woodbury Veterans Speedway is surrounded by the relics of old pit areas and dark cavernous passageways. Behind the chain link rise latticed bench seats, sloping up to huge, rusted-out light stanchions. The stands are now filled with scores of cheering Woodbury residents. The cymbal-crashing sounds are, in fact, the wild applause and jeering voices of the crowd.

Out in the miasma of dust swirling around the infield, the gladiator known as Gabe mutters under his breath so only his adversary can hear, "You're fighting like a goddamn girl today, Brucey"—the wisecrack punctuated by a roundhouse swing of the club at the black man's legs.

Bruce vaults into the air, executing a dodge that would be the envy of a World Wrestling Entertainment star. Gabe swings again and the club goes wide and strikes the head of a young male biter in ragged, greasy dungarees, a former mechanic perhaps.

The nails embed themselves in the thing's cadaverous skull, sending ropy strands of dark fluid into the air, before Gabe has a chance to dig the mace out and mumble, "Governor's gonna be pissed with your bullshit performance."

"Oh yeah?" Bruce counterstrikes with the handle of the ax, slamming it into Gabe's solar plexus, driving the stocky man to the ground. The ax arcs through the air and comes down within centimeters of Gabe's cheek.

Gabe rolls away and springs to his feet, still muttering under his breath. "Shouldn't have had that extra serving of cornbread last night."

Bruce moves in for another swing of the ax, whizzing the blade past Gabe's neck. "You should talk, fat boy."

Gabe swings the mace again and again, driving Bruce back toward the chained biters. "How many times have I told ya? Governor wants it to look *real*."

Bruce blocks the onslaught of mace blows with the ax handle. "You broke my fucking nose, motherfucker."

"Stop your bellyaching, dickweed." Gabe slams the mace down again and again until the nails stick into the ax handle. Gabe pulls the mace back and wrenches the ax out of Bruce's grip. The ax goes flying. The crowd cheers. Bruce dives away. Gabe goes after him. Bruce cuts and runs the other way, and Gabe lunges while simultaneously swinging the mace under the black man's legs.

The nails catch Bruce's fatigue pants, tearing a swath and

superficially lacerating flesh. Bruce stumbles and goes down hard. Thin tendrils of blood loop across the pale, dusty daylight as Bruce rolls.

Gabe soaks up the frenzied, frantic applause—the clapping is almost hysterical—and he turns toward the bleachers, which are filled with the bulk of Woodbury's post-plague population. He raises his mace *Braveheart*-style. The cheers swell and rise. Gabe milks it. He turns slowly with the mace over his head, an almost comical look of macho victory on his face.

The place erupts into pandemonium . . . and up in the stands, amid the waving arms and whooping voices, all but one onlooker seems transported by the spectacle.

Sitting in the fifth row, way off on the north end of the bleachers, Lilly Caul turns away in disgust. A faded linen scarf wound tightly around her swanlike neck to ward off the April chill, she is dressed in her customary ripped jeans, thrift-shop sweater, and hand-me-down beads. As she shakes her head and lets out an exasperated sigh, the wind blows tendrils of her toffee-brown hair around her once-youthful face, which now bears the lines of trauma—the wrinkles nested around her aquamarine eyes and along the edges of her mouth—as deep as the grain in burnished cowhide. She isn't even aware that she's mumbling under her breath, "Fucking Roman circuses . . ."

"What was that?" The woman next to her glances up from an insulated cup of tepid green tea. "Did you say something?"

Lilly shakes her head. "No."

"You okay?"

"Fine . . . just peachy." Lilly keeps gazing off into the distance as the rest of the crowd yelps and hollers and emits hyena howls. Still only in her early thirties, Lilly Caul looks at least ten years older than that now, her brow perpetually furrowed in consternation. "You want to know the truth, I don't know how much more of this shit I can take."

The other woman sips her tea thoughtfully. Clad in a dull-white lab coat under her parka, her hair pulled back in a pony-tail, she's the town nurse—an earnest, soft-spoken girl named Alice—who has taken a keen interest in Lilly's tenuous place in the town's hierarchy. "It's none of my business," Alice says finally, speaking softly enough to go unheard by any nearby revel-ers, "but if I were you, I would keep my feelings to myself."

Lilly looks at her. "What are you talking about?"

"For the time being, at least."

"I'm not following."

Alice seems vaguely uncomfortable talking about this in broad daylight, in plain sight of the others. "He's watching us, you know."

"What?"

"Right now, he's keeping tabs."

"You gotta be—"

Lilly stops herself. She realizes that Alice is referring to the shadowy figure standing in the mouth of the vaulted stone pas-sageway directly to the north, about thirty yards away, under the defunct scoreboard. Draped in shadow, silhouetted by the cage lights behind him, the man stands with hands on his hips, watching the action on the infield with a satisfied gleam in his eyes.

Of average height and build, clad in black, he has a large-caliber pistol holstered on his hip. At first glance, he appears al-most harmless, benign, like a proud land baron or medieval noble surveying his manor. But even at this distance, Lilly can sense his serpentine gaze—as cunning as a cobra's—scanning every corner of the stands. And every few seconds, that electric gaze falls on the spot at which Lilly and Alice now sit shivering in the spring winds.

"Better if he believes everything is just fine," Alice murmurs into her tea.

"Jesus Christ," Lilly mutters, staring down at the littered cement floor beneath the bleacher seats. Another surge of cheers and applause rises up around her as the gladiators go at it some more on the infield, Bruce going postal with his ax, Gabe getting boxed in by a cluster of chained biters. Lilly pays little attention to it.

"Smile, Lilly."

"*You* smile. . . . I don't have the stomach for it." Lilly looks up at the grisly action on the field for a moment, the mace tearing through the rotten craniums of the living dead. "I just don't get it." She shakes her head and looks away.

"Don't get what?"

Lilly takes a deep breath and looks at Alice. "What about Stevens?"

Alice gives her a shrug. Dr. Stevens has been Alice's lifeline for almost a year now, keeping her sane, teaching her the nursing trade, and showing her how to patch up battered gladiators with the dwindling storehouse of medical supplies stored in the network of catacombs beneath the arena. "What about him?"

"I don't see him playing along with this hideous shit." Lilly rubs her face. "What makes him so special—that he doesn't have to play nice with the Governor? Especially after what happened in January."

"Lilly—"

"C'mon, Alice." Lilly looks at her. "Admit it. The good doctor never shows up at these things, and he's constantly grumbling about the Governor's bloodthirsty freak shows to anyone who'll listen."

Alice licks her lips, turns, and puts a warning hand on Lilly's arm. "Listen to me. Don't kid yourself. The only reason Dr. Stevens is tolerated is because of his medical skills."

"So?"

"So he's not exactly a welcome part of the Governor's little kingdom."

"What are you saying, Alice?"

The younger woman takes another deep breath, and then lowers her voice even further. "All I'm saying is, nobody's immune. Nobody's got job security around here." She tightens her grip on Lilly's arm. "What if they find another doctor, one who's a little more gung ho? Stevens could very easily end up out *there*."

Lilly pulls herself away from the nurse, rises to her feet, and glances out at the ghastly action on the infield. "I'm so done with this, I can't take it anymore." She shoots a glance at the figure silhouetted in the shadow-bound cloister to the north. "I don't care if he's watching."

Lilly starts toward the exit.

Alice grabs her. "Lilly, just promise me . . . you'll be careful. Okay? Keep your head down? As a favor to me?"

Lilly gives her a cold, enigmatic little smile. "I know what I'm doing, Alice."

Then, Lilly turns, descends the stairs, and vanishes out the exit.

It's been over two years since the first of the dead reanimated and made themselves known to the living. In that time, the larger world outside the rural backwaters of Georgia gradually winked out with the slow certainty of metastasizing cells, the pockets of survivors groping for purchase in abandoned office parks, deserted retail outlets, and derelict communities. As the walker population incubated and multiplied, and the dangers increased, tribal alliances among humans formed themselves in earnest.

The township of Woodbury, Georgia, in the county of Meriwether, situated in the western part of the state, about seventy miles south of Atlanta, has become a virtual anomaly in the realm of survivor settlements. Originally a small farming village of about a thousand people, spanning a six-block stretch of main drag and railroad crossings, the town has been completely fortified and buttressed by the makeshift matériel of war.

Semitrucks retrofitted with fifty-caliber machine gun placements have been canted across the outer corners. Old railroad cars have been wrapped in concertina wire and positioned to block points of egress. Down through the center of town, walled ramparts surround the central business district—some of the barricades just recently completed—within which people live their forlorn lives clinging to memories of church socials and outdoor barbeques.

Making her way across the central walled area, striding purposefully down the cracked paving stones of Main Street, Lilly Caul tries to ignore the feeling that she gets whenever she sees the Governor's goons strolling the storefronts with AR-15s cradled high across their chests. *They're not just keeping the walkers out . . . they're also keeping us in.*

Lilly has been persona non grata in Woodbury for months now, ever since her ill-fated coup in January. It was obvious to Lilly, even back then, that the Governor had gotten out of control, his violent regime turning Woodbury into a death carnival. Lilly had managed to recruit a few of the town's saner denizens— including Stevens, Alice, and Martinez, one of the Governor's right-hand men—to snatch the Governor one night and take him for a ride out into walker country for a little tough love. The plan was to accidentally-on-purpose get the Governor eaten. But walkers have a way of gumming up the works of the *best*-laid plans, and in the midst of the mission, a herd had formed out of nowhere. The whole enterprise reverted to a survival struggle . . . and the Governor lived to rule another day.

Oddly, in some kind of Darwinian twist, the assassination attempt only served to solidify and strengthen the Governor's power base. To the residents already under his spell, he became Alexander the Great returning to Macedonia . . . Stonewall Jackson coming back to Richmond, bloodied but unbowed, a badass pit bull born to lead. Nobody seemed to care that their leader was obviously—at least in Lilly's mind—a pure sociopath. *These are brutal times, and brutal times call for brutal leadership.* And for the conspirators, the Governor had become an abusive parental figure—teaching "lessons" and meting out his petty punishments with relish.

Lilly approaches a row of little redbrick two-story edifices lined up along the edge of the commercial district. Once quaint little landscaped condo complexes, the buildings now bear the marks of plague shelters. The picket fences have been wrapped in razor wire, the flowerbeds fallow and stony and littered with shotgun shells, the bougainvillea vines over the lintels as dead and brown as frayed cables.

Gazing up at all the boarded windows, Lilly wonders once again, for the millionth time, why she stays in this horrible, desolate, dysfunctional family known as Woodbury. The truth is, she stays because she has nowhere else to go. Nobody has anywhere else to go. The land outside these walls is rife with walking dead, the byways clogged with death and ruin. Lilly stays because she's afraid, and fear is the one great common denominator in this new world. The fear drives people into themselves, it triggers base impulses, and leeches out the worst of the feral instincts and behavior lying dormant in the human soul.

But for Lilly Caul, the caged-animal experience has drawn out something else that has lurked deep within her for most of her life, something that has haunted her dreams and lurked in her marrow like a recessive gene: *loneliness.*

An only child growing up in middle-class Marietta, she usually ended up alone: playing alone, sitting alone in the back of the cafeteria or the school bus . . . always alone. In high school, her brittle intelligence, stubbornness, and sharp wit set her apart from the pom-pom-girl social scene. She grew up lonely, and the latent weight of this loneliness has dogged her in the post-plague world. She has lost everything that has meant anything to her—her father; her boyfriend, Josh; her friend, Megan.

She has lost everything.

Her apartment sits at the east end of Main Street, one of the shabbier redbricks in the complex. Dead kudzu clings to the west wall like mold, the windows veined in black, shriveled vines. The rooftop sprouts bent antennas and ancient satellite dishes that most likely won't be receiving any signal ever again. As Lilly approaches, the low ceiling of clouds has burned off and the midday sun, as pale and cold as a fluorescent light, blazes down on her, making perspiration break out on the back of her neck.

She steps up to the outer door, fishing for her keys. But she pauses suddenly, something catching her attention out of the corner of her eye. She turns and sees a tattered figure slumped on the ground across the street, a man hunkered against a storefront. The sight of him sends a jolt of sadness down her midsection.

She puts her keys away and crosses the street. The closer she gets to him, the more clearly she can hear his ragged breathing—clogged with phlegm and misery—and his low, wheezing voice, mumbling incomprehensible exhalations in his drunken stupor.

Bob Stookey, one of Lilly's last true friends, lies curled in a fetal position, shivering, passed out in his threadbare, reeking, navy pea coat, pushed up against the door of a derelict hardware store. The window above him bears the ironic, sun-faded advertisement in cheerful multicolored letters: SPRING CLEAN-UP SALE. The pain etched on the army medic's deeply lined, leathery face—which is pressed against the pavement like wet trash—breaks Lilly's heart.

The man has spiraled since the events of the past winter, and now he may be the only other resident of Woodbury who is more lost than Lilly Caul.

"Poor sweet thing." Lilly speaks softly as she reaches over to a ratty woolen blanket bunched at his feet. The stench of body odor, stale smoke, and cheap whiskey wafts toward her. She pulls the blanket over him, an empty booze bottle rolling out of the fabric and cracking against the breakfront beside the door.

Bob gurgles. ". . . gotta tell her . . ."

Lilly kneels beside him, stroking his shoulder, wondering if she should clean him up, get him off the street. She also wonders if the "her" he's babbling about is Megan. He was sweet on the girl—poor guy—and Megan's suicide pulverized him. Now Lilly pulls the blanket up to his wattled neck and pats him softly, "It's okay, Bob . . . she's . . . she's in a better—"

". . . gotta tell . . ."

For the briefest instant, Lilly jerks at the sight of his fluttering eyes, revealing the bloodshot whites underneath. Has he turned? Her heart races. "Bob? It's Lilly. You're having a nightmare."

Lilly swallows the fear, realizing that he's still alive—if one could call this alive—and he's simply writhing in a drunken fever dream, probably reliving the endless rerun of stumbling upon Megan Lafferty dangling at the end of a rope coiled off a broken-down apartment deck.

"Bob . . . ?"

His eyes flutter open, just for an instant, unfocused but glazed with anguish and pain. "Gotta—*tell* her—what he *said*," he wheezes.

"It's Lilly, Bob," she says, softly stroking his arm. "It's okay. It's me."

Then the old medic meets her gaze, and he says something else in that halting mucous wheeze that makes Lilly's spine go cold. She hears it clearly this time, and she realizes the "her" is not Megan.

The "her" is Lilly.

And the thing that Bob Stookey has to tell her will haunt Lilly for a lifetime.

TWO

That day, in the arena, Gabe delivers the final blow that ends the contest at just after three o'clock Eastern standard time, a full hour into the fight. The nail-studded head of the mace slams into Bruce's ribs—his midsection protected with body armor concealed under his army fatigues—and Bruce goes down for the count. Exhausted from the rough-and-tumble charade, the black man stays down, veiled by a dust cloud, breathing hard into the dirt.

"WE GOT A WINNER!"

The amplified voice startles many in the stands, the crackling noise issuing forth from giant horns positioned around the arena, powered by generators rumbling underneath the grounds. Gabe does his strut, waving the mace in his best William Wallace impersonation. The jeers and applause mask the low communal growling of living dead chained to posts all around Gabe, many of them still reaching for a morsel of human flesh, their putrid mouths working and pulsing and drooling with robotic hunger.

"STICK AROUND, FOLKS, FOR AN AFTER-SHOW MESSAGE FROM THE GOVERNOR!!"

On cue the speakers crackle and thump with the downbeat of a heavy metal tune, a buzz-saw electric guitar filling the air, as a battalion of stagehands floods the infield. Most are young men in hoodies and leather jackets, carrying long iron pikes with hooked ends.

They circle around the walkers. Chains are detached, collars hooked, voices raised, orders given by foremen, and one by one—in a thunderhead of dust—the workers begin leading the monsters across the infield toward the closest portal. Some of the creatures bite at the air as they are ushered back down into the shadows beneath the arena, others snarling and flinging gouts of black drool like reluctant actors being dragged offstage.

Alice watches this from the stands with silent distaste. The other spectators are on their feet now, clapping along with the headbanger tune, hollering at the horde of undead being led away. Alice reaches down to the floor beneath her and finds her black medical bag under the bench. She grabs it, quickly struggles out of her section, and then hurries down the steps toward the infield.

By the time Alice makes it to track level, the two gladiators— Gabe and Bruce—are walking away, heading toward the south exit. She hurries after them. Out of the corner of her eye, she senses a ghostly figure emerging from the shadows of the north portal behind her, making a dramatic entrance that would rival King Lear treading the boards at Stratford-Upon-Avon.

He comes across the infield in his leathers and studs, his stovepipe boots raising dust, his long coat flapping in the breeze behind him. He looks like a grizzled bounty hunter from the nineteenth century, his pistol banging on his hip as he lopes along. The crowd surges with excitement as they see him, a wave of applause and cheers. One of the workmen, an older man in a Harley T-shirt and ZZ Top beard, scuttles toward him with a hard-wired microphone.

Alice turns and catches up with the two exhausted warriors. "Bruce, hold up!"

Walking with a pronounced limp, the big black man reaches the edge of the south archway, pauses, and turns. His left eye is completely swollen shut, his teeth stained in blood. "Whaddaya want?"

"Let me see that eye," she says, coming up to him, kneeling down, and opening the medical bag.

"I'm fine."

Gabe joins them with a smirk on his face. "What's wrong, Brucie got a boo-boo?"

Alice takes a closer look, dabbing the bridge of his nose with gauze. "Jesus, Bruce . . . why don't you let me take you down to see Dr. Stevens."

"It's just a busted nose," Bruce says, pushing her away. "I said I'm fine!"

He kicks the medical bag over, the instruments and supplies spilling across the dirt. Alice lets out an exasperated groan and bends down to pick up the pieces, when the music cuts off and the sound of a low, velvety, amplified voice rings out over the winds and noise of the crowd.

"LADIES AND GENTLEMEN . . . FRIENDS AND FELLOW RESIDENTS OF WOODBURY . . . I WANT TO THANK ALL OF YOU FOR ATTENDING THE SHOW TODAY. IT WAS A BARN BURNER!"

Alice glances over her shoulder and sees the Governor standing center field.

The man knows how to work a room. Sizing up the crowd with fire in his gaze, grasping the hand mike with the puffed-up sincerity of a megachurch minister, he has a weird, charismatic aura about him. Not a huge man, not especially handsome—in fact, upon close scrutiny one might even call him a bit scruffy and malnourished—Philip Blake still gives off an air of preternatural confidence. He has dark eyes that reflect the light like geodes, and his gaunt face is festooned with the handlebar whiskers of a third-world bandit.

He turns and nods toward the south exit, stiffening Alice's spine as she feels his cold gaze on her. The amplified voice crackles and echoes: *"AND I WANT TO SEND A SPECIAL SHOUT OUT TO OUR FEARLESS GLADIATORS, BRUCE AND GABE! SHOW 'EM SOME LOVE, Y'ALL—GIVE 'EM A HAND!"*

The cheers and whooping and hollering climb several registers, ringing off the metal stanchions and far awnings like a hungry pack of barking dogs. The Governor lets it play out, a conductor patiently prodding a symphony. Alice closes her medical bag and stands.

Bruce waves heroically to the crowd, and then follows Gabe into the shadows of the cloister, vanishing down the exit ramp with the formality of a religious ritual.

Across the infield, Philip Blake lowers his head, waiting for the wave of cheers to wash back out to sea.

In the gathering silence, he lowers his voice slightly, speaking softly, his velvety voice carrying over the wind: *"NOW . . . GETTING SERIOUS FOR A MINUTE . . . I KNOW OUR SUPPLIES HAVE BEEN GETTING A LITTLE LOW. MANY OF YOU HAVE BEEN SCRIMPIN' AND RATIONING. MAKING SACRIFICES."*

He looks up at his flock, making eye contact as he continues.

"I FEEL THE CONCERN GROWING. BUT I WANT Y'ALL TO KNOW . . . RELIEF IS ON ITS WAY. GONNA BE MAKING A SERIES OF RUNS . . . FIRST ONE TOMORROW . . . AND THESE RUNS ARE GONNA YIELD ENOUGH PROVISIONS TO KEEP US GOING. AND THAT IS THE KEY, LADIES AND GENTLEMEN. THAT IS THE MOST IMPORTANT THING. WE WILL KEEP ON KEEPIN' ON! WE WILL NEVER GIVE UP! EVER!"

A few spectators applaud, but the majority of them remain silent, skeptical, ambivalent in their hard, cold seats. They have lived off the sour, metallic well water and rotting fruit of the untended orchards for weeks. They have given their children the last of the canned meats and the moldy remains of smoked game birds.

From the center of the infield, the Governor holds them in his gaze.

"LADIES AND GENTLEMEN, A NEW COMMUNITY IS BEING

BUILT HERE IN WOODBURY . . . AND IT IS MY SACRED MIS-SION TO PROTECT THIS COMMUNITY. AND I WILL DO WHAT HAS TO BE DONE. I WILL SACRIFICE WHAT HAS TO BE SAC-RIFICED. THAT'S WHAT COMMUNITY IS ALL ABOUT! WHEN YOU SACRIFICE YOUR OWN NEEDS FOR THE NEEDS OF THE COMMUNITY, YOU WALK WITH YOUR HEAD HELD HIGH!"

This gooses the applause meter a tad, some of the spectators finding Jesus and letting out yelps. The Governor pours on the sermonizing.

"YOU FOLKS HAVE HAD TO SUFFER IMMENSELY DUE TO THE PLAGUE. YOU HAVE BEEN ROBBED OF EVERYTHING YOU HAVE WORKED SO HARD FOR YOUR ENTIRE LIVES. MANY OF YOU HAVE LOST LOVED ONES. BUT HERE . . . IN WOODBURY . . . YOU HAVE SOMETHING THAT CANNOT BE TAKEN AWAY FROM YOU BY MAN NOR BEAST: YOU HAVE EACH OTHER!"

Now some of the residents spring to their feet and put their hands together, while others pump their fists. The noise builds.

"LET ME BOTTOM-LINE IT FOR Y'ALL: THE MOST PRE-CIOUS POSSESSION WE HAVE IN THE WORLD IS OUR OWN PEOPLE. AND FOR THE SAKE OF OUR PEOPLE . . . WE WILL NEVER GIVE UP . . . NEVER FALTER . . . NEVER LOSE OUR NERVE . . . AND NEVER LOSE FAITH!"

More spectators stand. The cheering and applause rises up into the sky.

"YOU HAVE A COMMUNITY! AND IF YOU HOLD ON TO THIS, THEN THERE IS NO FORCE IN THE WORLD THAT CAN TAKE IT FROM YOU! WE WILL SURVIVE. I PROMISE YOU. WOODBURY WILL SURVIVE! GOD BLESS Y'ALL . . . AND GOD BLESS WOODBURY!"

Across the arena, Alice carries her medical bag out the south entrance without even looking back.

She's seen this movie before.

After the post-game show, Philip Blake makes a stop in the men's room at the end of the arena's litter-strewn portico. The narrow enclosure reeks of dried urine, black mold, and rat turds.

Philip relieves himself, splashes water on his face, and then gazes for a moment at his cubist reflection in the cracked mirror. Way in the back of his mind, in some far-flung corner of his memories, the sound of a little girl crying echoes faintly.

He finishes up, and then bangs out the door, his metal-tipped boots and long belt-chain jangling. Down one long cinder-block corridor, down a flight of stone steps, down another hallway, and finally down one last flight of stairs, and he finds the "pens"—a row of rolling garage doors riddled with dents and ancient graffiti.

Gabe stands in front of the last door on the left, reaching into a metal oil drum and tossing something wet through a broken-out window. The Governor approaches without a word, pausing in front of one of the windows. "Nice work out there today, sport."

"Thanks, boss." Gabe reaches down into the drum and pulls out another morsel, a human foot severed raggedly at the ankle, glistening with gore. He casually tosses it through the jagged aperture.

Philip gazes through the dirty glass at the blood-speckled tile enclosure. He sees the swarming mass of undead—a small orgy of pale-blue faces and blackened mouths, the two dozen surviving walkers from the day's event gobbling at body parts on the tile floor like a drove of wild pigs fighting over truffles—and he stares and stares, enthralled for a moment, fascinated by the spectacle.

At length, Philip tears his gaze away from the abomination and nods at the bin full of fresh remains. "Who is it this time?"

Gabe looks up, his tattered black turtleneck torn over one

pectoral, bulging at the belly with body armor, his underarms stained with the telltale sweat-spots of exertion. He wears rubber surgical gloves that drip with fresh blood. "Whaddaya mean?"

"The chum you're tossing in, who is it?"

Gabe nods. "Oh . . . this is that old codger, used to live by the post office."

"Natural causes, I hope?"

"Yeah." Gabe nods, and tosses another piece through the opening. "Asthma attack last night, poor dude. Somebody said he had emphysema."

The Governor lets out a sigh. "He's gone to Glory now. Gimme an arm. From the elbow down. And maybe one of the smaller organs . . . a kidney, the heart."

Gabe pauses, the ghastly wet noises of the feeding frenzy echoing down the corridor. Gabe gives the Governor an odd look, a mixture of sympathy, affection, and maybe even duty, like a Boy Scout about to help his troop leader. "Tell you what," Gabe says, his husky voice softening. "Why don't you go home, and I'll bring 'em to ya."

The Governor looks at him. "Why?"

Gabe shrugs. "People see me carrying something, they don't even give it a second thought. You carry something, they'll want to help . . . maybe ask you what it is, wonder what you're doing."

Philip stares at the man for a moment. "You got a point there."

"Won't go over well."

Philip gives a satisfied nod. "All right then. We'll do it your way. I'll be at my place the rest of the night, bring it around back."

"Copy that."

The Governor turns to leave, and then pauses for a moment. He turns back to Gabe and smiles. "Gabe . . . thanks. You're a good man. Best I got."

The thick-necked man grins. A merit badge for the top Scout. "Thanks, boss."

Philip Blake turns and heads for the stairs with a very subtle change in his gait, a vague yet pronounced bounce to his step.

The closest thing Woodbury has to an executive mansion is the three-bedroom apartment spanning the top floor of a large condo building at the end of Main Street. Heavily fortified, the front door guarded at all times by a rotating crew of machine gunners manning the turret across the street, the building is clean yellow brick, nicely tuck-pointed, free of graffiti or grime.

Philip Blake enters the foyer that evening, whistling happily, passing the large bank of metal mailboxes that haven't seen postal service in over twenty-eight months. He climbs the stairs two at a time, feeling good and righteous and full of affection for his small-town brethren, his extended family, his place in this new world. At his door at the end of the second-floor hallway he pauses, fishes for his keys, and lets himself in.

The place would never make the pages of *Architectural Digest*. The carpeted rooms are mostly unfurnished, a few armchairs here and there surrounded by boxes. But the place is clean and well organized, a macrocosm of Philip Blake's compartmentalized, ordered mind.

"Daddy's home," he announces cheerfully as he enters the living room. "Sorry I'm so late, sweetie pie . . . busy day." He unbuckles his gun, sheds his waistcoat, and sets his keys and his pistol on the sideboard by the door.

Across the room, a little girl in a faded pinafore dress has her back turned to him. She softly bumps against the large picture window, a goldfish compulsively trying to escape its bowl.

"How's my little princess doing?" he says as he approaches the child. Momentarily lost in the domestic bliss of a normal life, Philip kneels down behind her and reaches out as though expecting a hug. "C'mon, babydoll . . . it's your daddy. Don't be afraid."

The little thing that was once a girl suddenly whirls around to face him, straining against the chain hooked to her iron collar. She lets out a guttural growl, gnashing her rotten teeth at him. Her face—once that of a lovely blue-eyed cherub—now bears the pallid fish-belly color of the dead. Her eyes are empty, milky-white marbles.

All the joy drains out of Philip Blake as he sinks to the floor, sitting cross-legged on the carpet in front of her, just out of her reach. *She doesn't recognize me.* His mind races, his thoughts returning to their dark, brooding default setting: *Why the fuck doesn't she recognize me?*

Philip Blake believes that the undead can learn, can still access dormant parts of their memories and past. He has no scientific proof of this theory, but he has to believe it, he *has* to.

"It's okay, Penny, it's just your daddy." He offers her his hand as though she might hold it. "Give me your hand, honey. Remember? Remember when we used to hold hands and take long walks up to Lake Rice?"

She fumbles at his hand, tries to pull it to her mouth, her tiny piranha-like teeth clamping down.

He jerks his arm back. "Penny, no!" He tries again, attempts to gently take her hand. But she tries to take another bite out of it. "Penny, stop it!" He struggles to control his anger. "Don't do this. It's me . . . it's your daddy . . . don't you recognize me?"

She grabs at his hand, her blackened, decomposed mouth chewing at the air, noxious, fetid breath puffing out on a watery snarl.

Philip pulls away. He stands. He runs his hands through his hair, his stomach clenching with anguish. "Try to remember, sweetie." He pleads with her with a catch in his throat, his voice wavering as though verging on a sob. "You can do it. I know you can. Try to remember who I am."

The girl-thing strains against her chain, her mouth working involuntarily. She cocks her ruined head at him—her lifeless eyes registering nothing so much as hunger, and maybe even a trace of confusion—the confusion of a sleepwalker seeing something that doesn't belong.

"Goddamnit, child, you know who I am!" Philip clenches his fists, towering over her. "Look at me!—I'm your father!—Can't you see that?!—I'm your daddy, goddamnit!—Look at me!!"

The dead child growls. Philip lets out a roar of anger, raising his hand instinctively to give her a slap, when all at once the sound of knocking breaks the spell. Philip blinks at the noise, his right hand still poised to deliver a blow to the child.

Someone is knocking on the back door. He looks over his shoulder. The sound is coming from out in the kitchen, where the rear storm door opens out over a ramshackle back deck over-looking a narrow alley.

Letting out a breath, Philip flexes his hands and sniffs back the rage. He turns away from the child, and takes slow, deep breaths as he heads across the apartment. He goes to the back door and yanks it open.

Gabe stands in the shadows, holding a cardboard box spotted with oily wet-stains. "Hey, boss. Here's that stuff that you said you—"

Philip reaches for the box, grabs it, says nothing, and goes back inside.

Gabe stands there in the darkness, vexed by the brusque reception, as the door slams in his face.

That night, Lilly has a horrible time falling asleep. Clad in a damp Georgia Tech T-shirt and panties, she lies on the bare mattress of her futon, trying to find a comfortable position, staring at the cracks in the plaster ceiling of her squalid garden apartment.

The tension in the back of her neck, her lower spine, and her joints grips her like electric current jolting intermittently through her. This must be what electro-convulsive treatments feel like.

She had a therapist once who suggested ECT for her alleged anxiety disorder. She had declined. But she always wondered if the treatments would have helped.

Now all the shrinks are gone, the couches overturned, the office buildings decimated and scoured out, the pharmacies ransacked, the entire field of psychotherapy gone the way of health spas and waterparks. Now Lilly Caul is on her own, alone with her excoriating insomnia and circular thoughts haunted by memories of the late Josh Lee Hamilton.

Mostly Lilly is thinking about what Bob Stookey uttered to her earlier that day in his inebriated catatonia on the sidewalk. Lilly had to bend down close to hear his strangled wheeze, the words coming out with laborious urgency.

"Gotta tell her what he said," Bob had muttered into her ear. "Before he died . . . he told me . . . Josh told me . . . it was Lilly . . . Lilly Caul . . . it was her . . . the only one he had ever loved."

Lilly had never believed it. Ever. Not then. Not when big Josh Hamilton was alive. Not even after Josh had been murdered in cold blood by one of Woodbury's thugs. Was there a wall around Lilly's heart because of guilt? Was it because she had led Josh on, had used him mostly for protection?

Or was it because Lilly simply didn't love herself enough to love someone else?

After hearing it being blurted out by a catatonic drunk on the sidewalk that day, Lilly had stiffened with horror. She had backed away from the old man as though he were radioactive, and then made a mad dash all the way back to her apartment, locking herself inside.

Now, in the eternal darkness of her lonely apartment, the restlessness and angst making her flesh crawl, she longs for the medication she routinely popped like candy during the old days. She would give her left ovary for a tab of Valium, a Xanax, maybe some Ambien . . . hell, she would even settle for a stiff drink. She stares at the ceiling some more and finally gets an idea.

She climbs out of bed and fishes through a peach crate of dwindling supplies. Amid the two tins of Spam, the bar of Ivory soap, and the half-used roll of toilet paper—in Woodbury, toilet paper is now acquired and distributed with the ruthlessness of gold bullion being traded on the New York Stock Exchange— she finds a nearly empty bottle of NyQuil.

She chugs the rest of it and gets back into bed. Rubbing her eyes, she takes shallow breaths and tries to clear her mind and listen to the white noise of the generators across the street, their ubiquitous, droning rumble becoming like a heartbeat in her ears.

A little less than an hour later, she sinks through the sweaty mattress and into the clutches of a vivid, terrifying nightmare.

It could be partially due to the NyQuil acting on her empty stomach, or partially because of the gruesome residue of the day's gladiator fights clinging to her mind's eye, or maybe it's a result of her unresolved feelings for Josh Hamilton, but for whatever reason, Lilly finds herself wandering a country cemetery, in the dark of night, desperately looking for Josh's grave site.

She's lost, and she hears the sound of feral growling in the dark forest behind her, on either side of her. She can hear twigs snapping, gravel crunching, the lumbering footsteps of the walking dead—hundreds of them—coming for her.

She passes gravestone after gravestone in the moonlight . . . searching for Josh's final resting place.

At first, the rhythmic banging sounds creep into the narrative of the dream subtly, from a distance, their echoes faint, drowned by the rising noise of the dead. Lilly isn't even aware of the noise for quite some time. She's too busy frantically searching for the one important grave marker, weaving through a forest of gray, weathered headstones. The biters close in.

At last, she sees a fresh grave off in the distance, on a steep slope of stony earth and skeletal trees. It lies in the shadows, a bone-white marble tombstone all by itself, the pale glow of moonlight reflecting off its surface. It stands at the head of a large mound of moist, ruddy earth, and as Lilly approaches, the name engraved on its face becomes visible in the moonbeams:

JOSHUA LEE HAMILTON
B. 1/15/69 – D. 11/21/12

The banging noises register in Lilly's ear as she approaches the grave site. The wind whispers. The walkers surround her. Out of the corner of her eye, she can glimpse the pack closing in on her, the putrid bodies emerging from the woods, dragging toward her, tattered burial clothing flagging in the wind, scores of dead eyes in the darkness like shiny coins.

The closer she gets to the tombstone, the more prominent the banging noises become.

She climbs the slope and approaches the grave. The banging noises reveal themselves to be muffled knocking sounds—a fist pounding against a door, or perhaps the *inside* of a coffin—the noise dampened by layers of earth. Lilly can't breathe. She kneels by the headstone. The knocking sounds are coming from *inside* Josh's grave. They are so loud now that the loose earth across the surface of his grave trembles and skitters across the mound in tiny avalanches.

Lilly's terror mutates. She touches the shivering mound of earth. Her heart goes cold. Josh is down there, knocking on the inside of his coffin, a horrible entreaty to be freed from death, to be loosened from this prison.

The walkers are coming for Lilly, she can feel their foul breath on the back of her neck, their long shadows sliding up the hill on either side of her. She is doomed. Josh wants out. The knocking rises. Lilly looks down at the grave, her tears tracking down her cheeks, dripping off her chin. Her tears flood the earth. The rough-hewn planks of Josh's simple coffin become visible in the mud, something moving inside the slats.

Lilly weeps. The walkers surround her. The knocking rises to a thunderous beat. Lilly sobs, and she reaches down and tenderly touches the coffin, when all at once—

—Josh bursts out of the wooden enclosure, tearing through it as though it were made of matchsticks, his hungry mouth chewing the air, an inhuman groan coming out of him. Lilly screams but no sound comes out of her. Josh's big square face churns with bloodlust as he goes for her neck, his eyes as dead and shiny as Buffalo nickels.

The impact of his rotting teeth hitting her jugular wakes her up in a spasm of horror.

Lilly jerks awake, soaked in feverish sweat, the morning light vibrating with the sound of someone knocking on her apartment door. She gasps for breath. She blinks away the nightmare, the sound of her own scream still ringing in her ears. The knocking continues.

"Lilly? You okay?"

The familiar voice, muffled outside the front door, barely registers in her ears. She rubs her face, taking deep breaths and trying to get her bearings.

At length, the room comes into focus, and her breathing returns to normal. She drags herself out of bed, the dizziness washing over her as she searches for her jeans and her top. The knocking gets frantic.

"Coming!" she blurts in a strangled voice as she pulls on her clothes.

She goes to the door. "Oh . . . hey," she mumbles after opening the door and seeing Martinez standing on her porch in the pale light.

The tall, rangy Latino wears a bandanna pirate-style around his head, and he has muscular arms, which poke through the cutoff sleeves of his work shirt. He has an assault rifle slung over his broad shoulder, and his handsome face furrows with concern. "What the hell's going on in there?" he says, giving her the once-over, his dark eyes shining with worry.

"I'm fine," she says, a tad unconvincingly.

"Did you forget?"

"Um . . . no."

"Get your guns, Lilly," he says. "We're going on that run I told you about, and we need all hands on deck."

THREE

"Morning, boss!"

A squat, middle-aged, bald man named Gus greets Martinez and Lilly out by the farthest semitruck, which blocks the exit gate on the north side of town. With his rhino-thick neck and oil-stained sleeveless T-shirt stretched taut by a rotund belly, Gus gives off the impression of a blunt instrument. But what he lacks in intelligence, he makes up for in loyalty.

"Morning, Gus," Martinez says as he walks up. "You mind grabbing a couple of them empty gas containers, in case we hit pay dirt on the trip?"

"Right away, boss."

Gus whirls and trundles off with his pistol-grip 12-gauge under his arm like a newspaper he hasn't gotten around to reading. Martinez and Lilly watch the little troll vanish around a corner.

Lilly glances to the east and sees the early morning sun peering over the crest of the barricade. It's not even seven yet and already the unseasonable chill of the previous week has burned off. In this part of Georgia, spring can be a tad bipolar—coming in cool and wet, but turning as warm and humid as the tropics without warning.

"Lilly, why don't you ride in back with the others." Martinez nods toward a big military cargo truck in the middle distance.

"I'll put ol' Gus up in the shotgun seat with me, in case we have to pick off anything on the way."

Idling under a canopy of swaying live oaks, the heavy-duty truck sits perpendicular to the semitruck. It features enormous mud-speckled tires and a mine-resistant, riveted hull as durable as a tank—a recent acquisition from the neighboring National Guard station. The rear hatch is draped in a tarp.

As Martinez and Lilly approach, an older man in a baseball cap and silk roadie jacket comes around the front of the truck, wiping his hands on a greasy rag. A weather-beaten, rail-thin sixty-something with cunning eyes and an iron-gray goatee, David Stern has the vaguely regal, hard-ass bearing of a college football coach. "She was down a quart," he says to Martinez. "I put some recycled oil in her . . . ought to keep her going a while. Morning, Lilly."

Lilly gives the man a groggy nod and mumbles a drowsy greeting.

Gus returns with a pair of battered plastic gas containers.

"Throw them in back, Gus." Martinez circles around the rear of the truck. Lilly and David follow. "Where's the little lady, David?"

"In here!" The tarp flaps open, and Barbara Stern sticks her graying head out. Also in her mid-sixties, she wears a denim jacket over a faded cotton muumuu, and has the wild, silver tendrils of an aging earth mother. Her deeply lined, sun-browned face is animated with the rapier wit that has presumably kept her husband on his toes all these years. "Trying to teach Junior here something. It's like pulling teeth."

The "Junior" to which she refers suddenly peeks out of the cargo hold next to her.

"Nag, nag, nag," the young man says with a rascally smirk. A boyish twenty-two, with long, dark, espresso-brown curls, Austin Ballard has deep-set eyes that sparkle with mischief. In his leather bomber jacket and multiple strands of bling around his neck, he affects the air of a second-tier rock star, an incorrigible bad boy. "How the hell do you stand it, Dave?" he says.

"Drink heavily and agree with everything she says," David Stern cracks wise from behind Martinez. "Barbara, stop mothering the boy."

"He was trying to light up in here, for Chrissake," Barbara Stern grumbles. "You want I should let him smoke and send us all to kingdom come?"

"Okay, everybody, can it." Martinez checks his ammo magazine. He's all business, maybe even a little jittery. "We got a job to do. Y'all know the drill. Let's get this done with a minimum of bullshit."

Martinez orders Lilly and David to get in back with the other two, and then leads Gus around to the cab.

Lilly climbs up and into the rank atmosphere of the cargo hold. The airless chamber smells of old sweat, cordite, and must. A caged dome light shines down dully on shipping containers lined along either side of the corrugated floor. Lilly looks for a place to plant herself.

"I saved a seat for ya," Austin says to her with a lascivious little grin, patting the unoccupied trunk next to him. "C'mon, take a load off . . . I won't bite."

Lilly rolls her eyes, lets out a sigh, and sits down next to the young man.

"You keep your hands to yourself, Romeo," Barbara Stern jokes from the opposite side of the gloomy enclosure. She sits on a low wooden crate next to David, who grins at the twosome across the cargo hold.

"They do make a good pair, though, don't they?" David says with a gleam in his eyes.

"Oh please," Lilly murmurs with mild disgust. The last thing she wants to do is get involved with a twenty-two-year-old, especially a kid as annoyingly flirty as Austin Ballard. Over the past three months—since he drifted into Woodbury from the north, arriving malnourished and dehydrated with a ragtag group of ten—he's hit on just about every single woman not yet in menopause.

If pressed, however, Lilly would have to concede that Austin Ballard is what her old friend Megan would call "easy on the eyes." With his curly mane and long lashes, he could easily kindle Lilly's lonely soul. Plus there seems to be more than meets the eye about the kid. Lilly has seen him in action. Underneath the pretty-boy looks and roguish charm lies a tough, plague-hardened young man who seems to be more than willing to put himself on the line for his fellow survivors.

"Lilly likes to play hard to get," Austin prods, still with that sideways grin. "But she'll come around."

"Keep dreaming," Lilly mutters as the truck vibrates and rumbles.

The gears kick in, and the cargo hold shudders as the vehicle slowly pulls forward.

Lilly hears a second engine—a big diesel—revving outside the hatch. Her stomach clenches slightly at the sound as she realizes that the exit is opening.

Martinez watches the semitrailer slowly backing away from the breach, its vertical stack spitting and spewing exhaust, opening up a twenty-five-foot gap in the barricade.

The woods adjacent to Woodbury reveal themselves in the pale sun a hundred yards away. No walkers in sight. Yet. The sun, still low in the sky, streams through the distant trees in hazy motes, burning off the predawn fog.

Pulling forward another twenty feet, Martinez brings the truck to a stop and rolls down his window. He peers up at two gunners perched on a cherry picker, which is pushed up against the corner of the wall. "Miller! Do me a favor, will ya?"

One of the men—a skinny African American in an Atlanta Falcons jersey—leans over the edge. "You name it, boss."

"While we're gone, keep the wall clear of biters. Can you do that for me?"

"Will do!"

"We want an easy entryway back in. You follow me?"

"We're on it, man! No worries!"

Martinez lets out a sigh, rolling his window back up. "Yeah, right," he mumbles under his breath, slamming the truck into gear and then stepping on the gas. The vehicle rumbles away into the dusky morning.

Just for an instant, Martinez glances through the driver's side window at the side mirror. Through veils of dust stirred up by the massive tires, he sees Woodbury receding into the distance behind them. "No worries . . . sure. What could possibly go wrong?"

It takes them half an hour to get to Interstate 85. Martinez takes Woodbury Road west, weaving through the abandoned carcasses of cars and trucks littering the two-lane, keeping his speed between forty and fifty miles per hour in the unlikely event some errant biter tries to lumber out of the woods and latch on to them.

As the cargo truck intermittently swerves between wrecks, the rocking motion keeps the folks in back holding on to their seats. Feeling nauseous, Lilly studiously avoids brushing up against Austin.

En route to the interstate, they pass Greenville, another little farming community along Highway 18 that is practically the mirror image of Woodbury. Once upon a time, Greenville was the county seat, a quaint little enclave of redbrick government buildings, white capital domes, and stately Victorian homes, many of which were on the historic registry. Now the place lies demolished and drained of all life in the harsh morning sun. Through the flapping rear tarp, Lilly can see the rubble—boarded windows, broken colonnades, and overturned cars.

"Looks like Greenville's been picked clean," David Stern comments morosely as they stare out the back at the passing devastation. Many of the windows bear the telltale spray-paint mark—a big capital D in a circle, meaning DEAD, meaning "Don't bother"—which adorns many of the buildings in this part of the state.

"What's the plan, Dave?" Austin asks, cleaning his fingernails with a hunting knife, an affectation that annoys Lilly immensely. She can't decide whether it's a genuine habit or strictly for show.

David Stern shrugs. "I guess the next town over—Hogansville, I think it is—has a grocery store that Martinez thinks is still viable."

"Viable?"

Another shrug from David. "Who knows . . . it's all process of elimination."

"Yeah, well . . . let's just make sure *we* don't get eliminated in the *process*." He turns and pokes an elbow gently against Lilly's ribs. "Get it, Lilly?"

"Hardy-har-har," she says, and then glances back out the rear.

They pass a familiar access road snaking off the main two-lane, a tall roadside sign glaring in the morning sun. The trademark logo, with its gold sunburst, leans to one side, the big blue letters cracked and faded and strafed with bird shit:

Walmart ☀
Save money. Live better.

A cold trickle of dread sluices down Lilly's midsection as she remembers the events of the previous year. At this very Walmart, she and Josh and their contingent from Atlanta first stumbled upon Martinez and his goons. In flashes of woozy memories, Lilly remembers finding guns and supplies . . . and then running into Martinez . . . the standoff . . . Megan freaking out . . . and then Martinez doing his sales pitch . . . and finally Josh agonizing over whether or not they should try Woodbury on for size.

"What's wrong with *this* joint?" Austin jerks his thumb toward the defunct retail outlet as they roar past the lot.

"Everything's wrong with it," Lilly murmurs under her breath.

She sees stray walkers wandering the Walmart's parking lot like hellish revenants, the overturned cars and scattered shopping carts so weather-beaten and fossilized they now have weeds growing up through their guts. The gas station islands are blackened and scorched from the fires that ravaged the place back in February. And the store resembles an ancient ruin of broken glass and sagging metal, empty cartons and boxes vomited out of gaping windows.

"Place got picked clean of food and supplies long ago," David Stern laments. "Everybody and their brother had a go at it."

As they pass the Walmart, Lilly gets a glimpse through the fluttering tarp of the rural farmland north of the property. The shadows of walkers—from this distance as small and indistinct as bugs under a rock—inch back and forth beneath the foliage and behind the dead cornstalks.

Since the advent of the herd last year, walker activity has picked up, the population of living dead growing and spreading into the backwaters and desolate farmlands that once lay fallow and deserted. Rumors have circulated that ragtag groups of scientists in Washington and underground labs out West are developing behavioral models and population forecasts for the reanimated dead, and none of it is promising. Bad news hangs over the land, and it hangs right now in the dimly lit cargo hold of the transport truck, as Lilly tries to push dark thoughts from her mind.

"Hey, Barbara." Lilly shoots a glance at the gray-haired woman sitting across from her. "Why don't you tell us the famous story again?"

Austin gives a good-natured roll of the eyes. "Oh, God . . . not this again."

Lilly gives him a look. "You be quiet. C'mon, Barbara, tell us the honeymoon story."

Austin rubs his eyes. "Somebody shoot me."

"Shush!" Lilly pokes Austin, then looks at the older woman and manages a smile. "Go ahead, Barbara."

The gray-haired woman grins at her husband. "You want to tell it?"

David puts his arm around his wife. "Sure, this'll be a first . . . me doing the talking." He looks at the older woman with that glimmer in his eye, and something passes between the two of them that reaches out across the dim enclosure and squeezes Lilly's heart. "Okay . . . first of all, it was back in the prehistoric days when I still had black hair and a prostate that worked."

Barbara gives him an amused punch in the arm. "Can you just cut to the chase, please? These people can do without your entire urinary history."

The truck rumbles over a railroad track, rattling the cargo hold. David holds on to his perch, then takes a deep breath and grins. "The thing is, we were just kids . . . but we were madly in love."

"Still are, for some reason . . . God knows why," Barbara adds with a smirk, giving him a loaded glance.

David sticks his tongue out at her. "So anyway . . . we found ourselves headed to the most beautiful place on earth—Iguazu, Argentina—with nothing but the clothes on our backs and about a hundred bucks in pesos."

Again Barbara chimes in: "If memory serves, 'Iguazu' means 'the Devil's throat,' and it's basically a river that runs through Brazil and Argentina. We read about it in a guidebook, and we thought it would be the perfect adventure."

David sighs. "So, anyway . . . we get there on a Sunday, and by Monday night we had hiked all the way upriver—maybe five miles—to this incredible waterfall."

Barbara shakes her head. "Five miles?! Are you kidding me? It was more like *twenty*-five!"

David winks at Lilly. "She exaggerates. Trust me . . . it was only like twenty or thirty kilometers."

Barbara playfully crosses her arms across her chest. "David? How many kilometers are in a mile?"

He sighs and shakes his head. "I don't know, honey, but I'm sure you're about to tell us."

"Like one point six . . . so thirty kilometers would be about twenty miles."

David gives her another look. "Can I tell the story? Is that all right with you?"

She looks away petulantly. "Who's stopping you?"

"So we find this amazing waterfall, and I mean, this is the most beautiful waterfall on earth. From a single point, you're practically surrounded, three hundred and sixty degrees, and the water's roaring all around you."

"And rainbows!" Barbara marvels. "Everywhere you look. It really was something."

"So then," David goes on. "Lover-girl here decides to get frisky."

Barbara grins. "I just wanted to give him a little hug, that's all."

"And she's feeling me up with the water rushing all around us—"

"I wasn't feeling you up!"

"She was all over me. And all of a sudden, she goes, 'David, where's your wallet?' And I feel the back of my jeans, and sure enough, the thing's gone."

Barbara shakes her head, reliving the moment for the millionth time. "My fanny pack was empty, too. Somebody had ripped us off somewhere along the line. Passports, ID, everything. We were stuck in the middle of Argentina and we were stupid Americans, and we had no effen clue what to do with ourselves."

David smiles to himself, holding the moment in his memory like a precious heirloom he keeps in a drawer. Lilly gets the feeling that this is something essential for the Sterns, something unspoken but as powerful as the motion of the tides or the gravitational tug of the moon. "We get back to the closest village and make a few calls," David continues, "but there's no embassy for miles and the cops are about as helpful as a poke in the eye."

"We're told we have to wait for our ID issues to be sorted out in Buenos Aires."

"Which is like eight hundred miles away."

"Kilometers, Barbara. Eight hundred *kilometers* away."

"David, don't start."

"Anyway, we have a few centavos left in our pockets—the equivalent of what, Barbara? A buck fifty? So we find a little village and talk a local guy into letting us sleep on the floor of his barn for fifty centavos."

Barbara smiles wistfully. "It wasn't exactly the Ritz but we made do."

David grins at her. "Turned out the man ran a little restaurant in town, and he agreed to let us work there while we waited for our passports to be ironed out. Babs waited tables while I worked in back, slinging chorizo and making menudo for the locals."

"Funny thing was, it turned out to be one of the best times of our lives." Barbara lets out a pensive sigh. "We were in such a different environment, and all we had to rely on was each other, but that was . . . it was . . . *nice.*" She looks at her husband and for the first time, her wrinkled, matronly face softens. A look comes over her—just for an instant—that obliterates time, erases all the years, and turns her back into a young bride in love with a good man. "In fact," she says softly, "it was even kinda sorta terrific."

David looks at his wife. "We were stuck there for—what? How long was it, Babs?"

"We were there for two and a half months, waiting for word from the embassy, sleeping with the goats, living off that god-awful menudo."

"It was . . . an experience." David puts his arm around his woman. He softly kisses her temple. "Wouldn't have traded it for all the tea in Tennessee."

The truck shudders over another series of bumps, and the noisy silence that ensues weighs down on Lilly. She had expected the story to lift her spirits. She had expected it to distract her, soothe her, maybe even put a salve on her brooding thoughts. But it has only served to pick at the scab that she has grown over her heart. It has made her feel small, alone, and insignificant.

Dizziness courses over her and she feels like crying . . . for Josh . . . for Megan . . . for herself . . . for this whole upside-down nightmare gripping the land.

At last, Austin breaks the spell with a confused furrow of his brow. "What the fuck is menudo?"

The cargo truck bangs over a series of petrified railroad tracks and enters Hogansville from the west. Martinez keeps both hands on the wheel as he scans the deserted streets and store-fronts through the windshield.

The mass exodus has left the small village overgrown with prairie grass and ironweed, boarded up tight, and littered with cast-off belongings across the roadway—moldy mattresses, loose drawers, and filthy clothing clogging every gutter. A few stray walkers as ragged as scarecrows wander aimlessly in the alleys and empty parking lots.

Martinez applies the brakes and slows the truck to a steady twenty miles an hour. He sees a street sign and consults a page torn out of an old phone book, which he has taped to the dashboard.

The location of the Hogansville Piggly Wiggly seems to be on the west side of town, about a half mile away. The tires crunch over broken glass and detritus, the noise drawing the attention of nearby walkers.

From the passenger seat, Gus pumps a shell into the breech of his 12-gauge. "I got this, boss," he says, rolling down his window.

"Gus, wait!" Martinez reaches down to a duffel bag stuffed between the seats. He finds a short-barrel .357 Magnum with a silencer attached, and hands it to the portly bald man. "Use this, I don't want the noise drawing more of 'em."

Gus puts the scattergun down, takes the revolver, opens the cylinder, checks the rounds, and then clicks it shut. "Fair enough."

The bald man aims the revolver out the window and picks off three corpses with the ease of a man playing a carnival game. The blasts—muffled by the noise suppressor—sound like kindling snapping. The walkers fold one by one, the tops of their crania erupting in bubbles of black fluid and tissue, their bodies sagging to the pavement with satisfying wet thuds. Martinez proceeds west.

Martinez makes a turn at an intersection blocked by the wreckage of a three-car collision, the burned-out husks of metal and glass tangled in a crumpled mess. The cargo truck skirts the sidewalk, and Gus takes down another pair of walkers in tattered paramedic uniforms. The cargo truck continues down a side street.

Just past a boarded strip mall, the Piggly Wiggly sign comes into view on the south side of the street, the mouth of the deserted parking lot crowded with half a dozen walkers. Gus puts them out of their misery with little fuss—pausing once to reload—as the truck creeps slowly into the lot.

One of the walkers topples against the side of the truck, a fountain of oily blood washing across the hood before the body slides under the wheels.

"Fuck!" Martinez blurts as he pulls up to the front of the store.

Through the blood-smeared windshield, he can see the disaster area that is the former Piggly Wiggly. Broken paving stones and overturned flowerpots spray across the storefront, the windows all broken out and gaping jaggedly, rows of rusted-out carts lying either on their sides or smashed by fallen timbers. Inside the shadowy interior of the store, the aisles are ransacked, the shelves empty, the fixtures hanging by threads and slowly turning in the wind. "Fuck! Fuck!—Fuck!—Fuck-fuck-fuck!"

Martinez rubs his face, leaning back against the driver's seat.

Gus looks at him. "So what now, boss?"

The tarp snaps open, the harsh light of day flooding the cargo hold. The glare makes Lilly blink and squint as her eyes adjust.

She rises to her feet and gazes down at Martinez standing outside the rear of the truck, holding the tarp open with a dour expression on his dark features. Gus stands behind him, wringing his hands. "Good news and bad news," Martinez grumbles.

The Sterns stand up, Austin also slowly rising and stretching like a sleepy cat.

"Grocery store's been trashed, cleaned out," Martinez announces. "We're S-O-L."

Lilly looks at him. "What's the good news?"

"There's a warehouse out behind the store, no windows, locked up tight. Looks like people have left it alone. Could be a gold mine."

"What are we waiting for?"

Martinez levels his gaze at Lilly. "Not sure how safe it is in there. I want everybody locked and loaded, and on their toes. Bring all the flashlights, too . . . looks like it's pretty dark in there."

They all reach for their weapons and gear. Lilly digs in her rucksack. She pulls out her guns—a pair of Ruger .22 semiautos—and checks the ammo magazines. She has two curved clips, each one loaded with twenty-five rounds. Bob taught her how to use the high-capacity mags, which make the pistols slightly unwieldy but also give her staying power if things get hectic.

"Austin, I want you carrying the duffels," Martinez says, tipping a nod toward the pile of canvas bags in the corner. "Keep 'em open and ready."

Austin is already standing over the bags, gathering them up and slinging them over his shoulder. The others check their ammo supplies, holstering their weapons in quick-release rigs on their hips and belts. Barbara shoves a Colt Army .45 down the back of a sash wrapped tightly around her thick midriff, David handing her two extra clips.

They work with the practiced concentration of veteran bank robbers. They've done this many times. Still, there's a certain tension crackling around the dim enclosure as Martinez takes one last look through the open tarp. "Gonna pull around back," he says. "Be ready to rock and roll, and watch your backs on the way in . . . the noise of the truck's already drawn more biters."

A quick succession of nods around the cargo hold, and Martinez vanishes.

Lilly goes over to the rear hatch and braces herself on the jamb as the sound of the cab doors slamming is followed by the revving engine. The truck lurches out of there and then rumbles around the side of the supermarket.

Forty-five seconds later, the air brakes hiss and the truck jerks to a stop.

Lilly takes a deep breath, draws one of the Rugers, pushes the tarp open, and hops out.

She lands hard on the cracked pavement, the sun in her eyes, the wind in her face, the smell of burning rubber wafting in from some far-off cataclysm. Martinez is already out of the cab, the .357 with the silencer holstered and banging on his thigh, Gus hustling around the front of the truck. The bald man climbs behind the wheel.

The warehouse sits off to their right, on the edge of the back lot, nestled in a jungle of weeds and razor grass, an enormous corrugated metal box the size of three movie theaters. Lilly sees the unmarked metal door at the top of a small flight of stairs, situated right next to the loading dock, and two huge rolling garage doors in the shadows of the overhang. Everything looks congealed and petrified with age, rusted shut, scarred with graffiti.

She glances over her shoulder and gets a glimpse of a cluster of walkers, a hundred yards away, out by the busted Piggly Wiggly sign, slowly turning toward the commotion and starting to shamble in their direction.

Austin comes up behind Lilly. "Let's go, let's go," he mutters, lugging the duffel bags. "While we're young and in one piece!"

David and Barbara come up fast behind Austin, the older couple staying low, with eyes wide and alert. Martinez gives a hand signal to Gus, pointing off toward the loading dock. "Back it up, Gus, and keep the radio open and an eye on things outside."

"Roger that." Gus revs the engine, then starts to put the truck into gear.

"We'll be coming out the loading dock side," Martinez informs him. "So keep the engine running and be ready to roll at a moment's notice."

"Got it!"

Then things get moving very quickly, very efficiently, as Gus backs the truck up to the dock while the others swiftly and silently creep toward the unmarked side door, moving with the cold competence of a SWAT team. Martinez climbs stairs, pulls a long metal shim from his belt, and starts working on the padlock, pounding the shim with the butt of his gun. The others huddle behind him, glancing over their shoulders at the encroaching dead.

The lock snaps, and Martinez pries the door open on squeaking hinges.

They plunge into darkness and overwhelming stench—rotting meat, acrid pukelike smells, ammonia odors—the door slamming behind them, making them jump. A single skylight way up above the cobwebbed gantries provides barely enough illumination to reveal silhouettes of aisles and overturned forklifts scattered between the high shelves.

Each one of the intruders—including Lilly—pauses to smile as their eyes adjust enough to see all the canned goods and packaged food rising to the rafters. It is, indeed, the gold mine Martinez had hoped for. But as instantly as they all register their good luck, they hear the noises building in the deeper shadows, as if on cue with their arrival, and one by one their smiles fade—

—as they glimpse the first of the shadowy figures emerging from behind well-stocked shelves.

FOUR

On Martinez's signal, they start firing, the collective snapping of silencers and flickering muzzle flashes lighting up the dark warehouse. Lilly gets off three quick blasts, and takes down two at a range of about fifty feet. One of the targets—an obese man in tattered work clothes, his flesh the color of earthworms—jerks against a shelf, his skull gushing cerebral fluids as he knocks over a row of canned tomatoes. The other biter—a younger male in greasy dungarees, perhaps a former forklift operator—collapses in a cascade of blood jetting out of the fresh hole in his skull.

The dead keep coming, at least two dozen or more, from every corner of the warehouse.

The air thumps and crackles with strobelike light, as the shooters stay clustered tight near the door, their gun barrels fanning out and blazing. Austin drops the duffels and starts working with his Glock 19, another acquisition from the National Guard depot, featuring a noise suppressor and an attachment below the barrel that sends a narrow thread of red light across the darkness. David picks off a female in a stained Piggly Wiggly uniform, sending the dead girl spinning against a rack of stale bagels. Barbara hits an older male in a blood-speckled dress shirt, clip-on tie, and name tag—maybe the former store manager—knocking the

creature down in a red mist that paints a light fixture in poin-
tillist profusion.

The dampened gunfire emits a surreal racket, like a round
of mad applause, accompanied by a fireworks display ripping
through the fetid stillness, followed by the jangle and clank of
spent shells hitting the floor. Martinez edges forward, leading
the group deeper into the warehouse. They pass perpendicular
aisles and fire at lumbering figures with milky white eyes coming headlong toward them—former machinists, stock clerks,
assistant managers, cashiers—each one collapsing in gushing
baptisms of blood. They lose count by the time the last one sinks
to the floor.

In the echoing silence, Lilly hears the metallic squawk of Gus's
voice coming through Martinez's walkie-talkie. "—the hellfire is
going on?! Y'all hear me?! Boss?! Y'all copy? What is *going on*?"

At the end of the main aisle, Martinez pauses to catch his
breath. He grabs the radio clipped to his belt. "We're good, Gus,"
he says into the walkie's mouthpiece. "Ran into a little welcom-
ing party . . . but we're clear."

Over the air, the voice sizzles: " 'Bout gave me a heart attack!"

Martinez thumbs the TALK button: "Whole fucking staff must
have hid out in here when the shit went down." He looks around
at the carnage behind veils of blue smoke, the air stinking now of
cordite. He thumbs the button. "You just be ready to roll, Gus.
Looks like we're gonna be loading the truck to the gills with
goodies."

The voice returns: "That's good news, boss. Copy that. I'll be
ready."

Martinez thumbs off the radio, puts it back, and turns to the
others. "Everybody okay?"

Lilly's ears ring, but she feels steady, alert. "All good," she says,
thumbing the catch on each of her Rugers, dumping the spent
magazines, the clips clattering to the floor. She pulls fresh mags
from the back of her waistband and slams them in place. She

scans the aisles on either side of her, where the remains of walkers lie in gore-drenched heaps. She feels nothing.

"Keep an eye out for stragglers," Martinez orders, glancing around the shadowy aisles.

"Damn this thing!" David Stern is complaining, shaking a flashlight. His gnarled hands tremble. "I checked the battery just last night."

Barbara rolls her eyes in the darkness. "The man's hopeless with technology." She takes the flashlight from him. "I thought these batteries might be a little iffy." She unscrews it and fiddles with the C-cells. It doesn't help; the thing will not come on.

"Wait a second," Austin says, shoving his Glock back behind his belt. "Got an idea."

He goes over to a shelf on which bundles of firewood are stacked alongside sacks of charcoal briquettes, cans of lighter fluid, and packages of wood chips. He pulls a long piece of hardwood loose, pulls a bandanna from his pocket, and wraps it around the end of the log.

Lilly watches him with interest. She can't quite figure this kid out. He seems older than his years somehow. She watches him douse the fabric with lighter fluid. He pulls a Bic and sparks the bandanna, and all at once a plume of brilliant orange light illuminates the center aisle in a radiant nimbus. "Very moody," Lilly says with a smirk. "Nice work, Huckleberry."

They split up into two groups. Martinez and the Sterns take the front of the building—a maze of shelves brimming with packaged goods, household supplies, dry goods, condiments, and kitchen staples—and Lilly and Austin take the rear. Martinez orders everybody to move quickly, no fucking around, and if they see something they're not sure about, leave it. Take only the items with a shelf life.

Austin leads Lilly down a side corridor lined with deserted

offices. They pass door after door, each of them locked and showing empty darkness behind their windows. Austin walks slightly ahead of Lilly, holding the torch high in one hand, the Glock in the other. Lilly has both her guns out, ready to rock at a moment's notice.

In the flickering yellow light, they move past rows of propane tanks, garden supplies, sacks of fertilizer, cords of firewood, coils of garden hoses, and useless ephemera like bird feeders and garden gnomes. The skin on the back of Lilly's neck prickles with goose bumps as she hears the echoing whispers and shuffling footsteps of the Sterns and Martinez coming from the darkness behind her.

At the end of the main aisle, against the back wall, they make a turn and discover a large hydraulic pallet jack sitting amid the rakes, shovels, and tools. Austin pulls the thing into the aisle—it's a big greasy hand truck with heavy iron wheels and twin forks that protrude at least eight feet—and he tests it by pumping the huge hand jack. "This might just come in handy," he speculates.

"Do me a favor, hold the torch up for a second." Lilly indicates the shadows along the back wall. Austin raises the torch and reveals, in the dancing glow of torchlight, a pile of empty pallets.

They move quickly, slamming the forks under the closest pallet.

Then they head back down the dark center aisle, the wheels squeaking noisily on the filthy cement floor. They start loading the pallet, Austin pushing and holding the torch, and Lilly grabbing the essentials. They grab fifty-gallon jugs of drinking water, cartons of seeds, sharp-edged tools, coils of rope. They make another turn and head down an aisle of canned goods. Lilly starts working up a sweat stacking shrink-wrapped cartons of peaches, corn, beans, collards, tins of sardines, tuna, and Spam.

"Gonna be heroes, comin' back with all this shit," Austin grunts as he shoves the jack along the aisle.

"Yeah, maybe you'll finally get laid," Lilly cracks, stacking the heavy trays with a groan.

"Can I ask you a question?"

"What."

"Where's this attitude come from?"

Lilly keeps working, her guns digging into the back of her belt. "I have no idea what you're talking about."

"C'mon, Lilly . . . I noticed it right away . . . ever since I met you . . . you got a chip on your shoulder about something."

They work their way toward the end of the canned goods aisle. Lilly slams another carton of cans on the pallet and grumbles, "Can we just get this thing done, and get the hell outta here?"

"Just making conversation," Austin says as he shoves the dolly around the end of the aisle with a grunt.

They head down another aisle stacked with crates of rotted fruit. They pause. Austin holds the torch up and reveals the blackened, shriveled peaches and bananas in their maggot-infested crates. The fruit has decomposed into slimy black lumps.

Lilly wipes the sweat from her face, her voice coming out low and hoarse. "The truth is, I lost some people very close to me."

Austin stares at the rotten fruit. "Look . . . I'm sorry I brought it up . . . I'm sorry." He starts shoving the dolly deeper into the aisle. "You don't have to—"

"Wait!"

Lilly grabs him, holds him still. A faint metallic tapping noise straightens her spine, and she whispers, "Shine the torch over there."

In the flickering glow, they see a row of freezer doors along the left side of the aisle. The stench of rancid meat hangs in the air. Lilly pulls her guns. The last door on the left is intermittently jiggling and creaking, the rusty hinges loose.

"Stay behind me, hold the torch up," Lilly whispers, thumbing the hammers on both her Rugers, creeping toward the last door on the left.

"Walker?" Austin grabs his Glock and moves in close behind her.

"Just shut up and hold the torch up."

Lilly moves past the jiggling door, pauses, stands with her back against the freezer. "On three," she whispers. "You ready?"

"Ready."

Lilly grabs the latch. "One, two, *three!*"

She rips the freezer door open, and both barrels go up, and her heart skips a beat. There's nothing there. Nothing but darkness and a reeking stench.

The odor engulfs Lilly, making her eyes water as she steps back, lowering the pistols. The black, oily death-rot clings to the inside of the dark freezer. She hears a noise, and looks down at something small and furry scuttling past her feet. She lets out a pained breath as she realizes it was just a rat making all the noise.

"Fuck me," Austin comments breathlessly, lowering the Glock and letting out a sigh of relief.

"C'mon," Lilly says, shoving her guns back in her belt. "We got enough. Let's head back, get the truck loaded, and get the fuck outta here."

"Sounds good to me," Austin says, yanking the dolly back with a smile, then pushing it back down the aisle, following Lilly toward the front of the warehouse. Behind him, a large figure lurches out of the freezer.

Austin hears it first, and only has time to turn around and see the massive male in dungarees and mangled face barreling toward him. Mandibles clenching and unclenching, eyes the color of sour milk, the biter stands well over six feet tall and is covered with a film of white mold from being shut in the freezer for so long.

Jerking away from it, reaching for his Glock, Austin trips over the corner of the dolly.

He falls down, his gun slipping out of his hand, the torch rolling across the cement. The huge biter looms over him, drooling black bile, the torchlight now shining up at a surreal angle. Flames flicker and reflect off the corpse's shimmering, milky eyes.

Austin tries to roll away but the biter gets its gigantic dead fingers around Austin's pant legs. He lets out an angry howl, kicking at the walker, cursing it. The thing opens its mouth, and Austin slams the heel of his boot into the maw of black, sharklike teeth.

The crunch of the lower jawbone hardly slows the thing down.

The creature goes for the flesh of Austin's thigh. The weight of the thing is unbearable, like a house pressing down on him, and just as the thing is about to bite down on Austin's femoral artery—the blackened teeth only centimeters away—the snapping of two silenced .22 caliber rounds rings out.

Only a few seconds have transpired from the moment the biter first appeared, but that's the exact amount of time it has taken Lilly to hear the commotion, stop in her tracks, spin around, jack the hammers, raise the guns, take careful aim, and intercede. She hits the biter dead center between the eyes, just above the bridge of the nose.

The huge corpse whiplashes backward in a cloud of blood mist that looks like smoke in the darkness, the top of its skull splitting open and gushing.

It lands in a wet heap at Austin's feet as the young man squirms away from it and gasps for breath and edges backward on his ass on the cold cement for several frenzied moments. "Fuck!—Jesus!—FUCK!"

"You okay?" Lilly comes over, kneels, and inspects Austin's legs. "You all right?"

"I'm—yeah—I'm—fine, *fine*," he sputters and stammers, catching his breath. He stares at the massive lump of corpse lying at his feet.

"C'mon, let's—"

"YO!"

The sound of Martinez's voice coming from the front of the warehouse penetrates Lilly's ringing ears. "Lilly! Austin! You two okay?!"

Lilly hollers over her shoulder, "We're good!"

"Get your shit and come on!" Martinez sounds nervous. "The noise is drawing more of them out of the woodwork! Let's go!"

"C'mon, pretty boy," Lilly mutters to Austin, helping him up.

They get up, and Austin retrieves the torch before it has a chance to set anything on fire, and they get the hand dolly moving. The thing weighs a ton now, and it takes both of them, huffing and puffing, to roll it down the aisle.

They all meet at the loading dock. The Sterns and Martinez have filled the duffels as well as half a dozen large cardboard boxes with a plethora of packaged goods, including cartons of Ramen noodles, gourmet instant coffee, two-liter bottles of juice, packages of flour, boxes of Rice-A-Roni, several pounds of sugar, gallon jars of pickled vegetables, and shrink-wrapped cartons of Crisco, Hamburger Helper, macaroni and cheese, and cigarettes. Martinez radios Gus, and tells him to back the truck up as close to the loading dock as possible, and be ready to roll when the garage door comes up. Austin, still breathless and shaky from the attack, pushes the pallet up to the corrugated metal hatch.

"Gimme that hammer you found back there," Martinez says to David.

The older man steps up and hands the hammer over to Martinez. The others crowd around, waiting nervously, as Martinez slams the business end of the hammer against the padlock at the bottom of the garage door. The lock is stubborn, and the pounding noises echo. Lilly glances over her shoulder, half aware of shuffling sounds coming from the deeper shadows behind her.

The lock finally snaps, and Martinez yanks the door. The thing rolls up with a rusty shriek. The wind and light rush into the warehouse, smelling of tar and burning rubber, making everybody blink. The floor swirls with stray packing straps and litter stirred up by the breeze.

At first, as they take their initial steps outside, nobody sees the pile of wet rubbish and moldy cardboard boxes across the loading dock, next to a garbage Dumpster, which is moving slightly, palpating with something underneath. They're all too busy following Martinez out across the grimy deck with armfuls of supplies.

Gus has the truck revving, the tarp thrown open, the exhaust stack chugging and puffing in the spring winds. They start loading up the back.

In through the gap go the heavy duffel bags. In go the boxes. In go the contents of the pallet, the canned goods, the water jugs, the garden supplies, the tools, and the propane. Nobody even notices the moving cadaver across the loading dock, pushing its way out of the trash pile, then rising to its feet with the creaky, inebriated uncertainty of an overgrown baby. Lilly glimpses movement out of the corner of her eye, and turns toward the biter.

A wiry African American corpse in his late twenties, maybe early thirties, with short cornrows crowning his skull, shuffles clumsily toward them like a drunken mime walking against imaginary wind, clawing at the air. He wears a tattered orange jumpsuit that has a familiar look to Lilly, but she can't place it.

"I got this," Lilly says to no one in particular as she pulls one of her Rugers.

The others notice the commotion and pause in their efforts, drawing their weapons, watching Lilly stand stone-still, steady as a milepost, aiming her front sight at the approaching corpse. A moment passes. Lilly stands as still as a statue. The others stare as Lilly finally, calmly, almost languidly, decides to pull the trigger, again and again, emptying the remaining six rounds in the magazine.

The gun claps and flashes, and the young black corpse does a jitterbug on the dock for a moment, exit wounds spewing atomized blood. The rounds chew through the hard shell of its cranium, shredding its cornrows and sending chunks of its prefrontal lobe and gray cerebrospinal fluid skyward. Lilly finishes and stares emotionlessly.

The biter doubles over and collapses to the dock in a blood-sodden heap.

Standing in a blue haze of her own gun smoke and cordite, Lilly mumbles something to herself. Nobody hears what she says. The others stare at her for a long moment until Austin finally comes over and says, "Good job, Annie Oakley."

Martinez breaks the spell. "Okay . . . let's get a move on, people! Before we draw more of 'em!"

They pile into the back of the truck. Lilly is the last one to climb in and find a spot amid the overloaded cargo bay. She sits on one of the propane tanks, and holds on to a side rail in order to brace herself against the g-forces, as the cab doors slam, and the engine grinds, and the truck suddenly roars away from the loading dock.

Lilly remembers right then—for some reason, the realization popping into her head as the truck pulls away—where she's seen an orange jumpsuit like the one Cornrow was wearing. It's a prison suit.

They get all the way across the lot, out the exit, and halfway down the access road before Barbara Stern breaks the silence. "Not a bad day's work for a bunch of emotional cripples."

The giggling starts with David Stern, then spreads among every passenger, until finally even Lilly is giggling with crazy, giddy relief and satisfaction.

By the time they make it back to the highway, each and every occupant of that dark, malodorous enclosure is buzzing with excitement.

"Can you imagine the look on the DeVries kids' faces when they see all that grape juice?" Barbara Stern looks positively ebullient in her faded denim and wild gray tresses. "I thought they were gonna storm the castle when we ran out of Kool-Aid last week."

"What about that Starbucks instant Via?" David chimes in. "I can't wait to retire those goddamn coffee grounds to the compost pile."

"We got all the food groups, too, didn't we?!" Austin enthuses from his perch on a crate across from Lilly. "Sugar, caffeine, nicotine, and Dolly Madison cupcakes. Kids are gonna be on a sugar buzz for a month."

Lilly smiles at the young man for the first time since they met. Austin returns her gaze with a wink, his long curls tossing around his handsome face from the slipstream currents coming through the flapping tarp.

Lilly glances out through the rear hatch and sees the deserted country road passing in a blur, the afternoon sun strobing pleasantly through the trees receding into the distance behind them. For just an instant, she feels like Woodbury might have a chance after all. With enough people like these folks—people who care about each other—they just might have a shot at building a community.

"You did good today, pretty boy," Lilly says at last to Austin. She looks at the others. "You all did good. In fact, if we can just—"

A faint noise from outside stops her short. At first it sounds merely like the wind buffeting the tarp. But the more Lilly listens to it, the more it sounds like an almost alien noise from another time, another place, a noise that she hasn't heard—a noise *nobody* has heard—since the plague broke out years earlier.

"You hear that?" Lilly looks at the others, all of whom now seem to be listening in awe. The noise rises and falls on the wind. It seems to be coming from the sky, maybe a mile away, vibrating the air like a drum roll. "It sounds like—No. It can't be."

"What the fuck?" Austin pushes his way toward the rear of the chamber and sticks his head out, craning his neck to get a glimpse of the sky. "You're *kidding* me!"

Lilly moves next to him, holding on to the rear hatch and leaning out.

The wind whips her hair and stings her eyes as she peers upward, and sure enough, she catches a fleeting glimpse of it in the western sky.

Just the tail of the craft is visible above the tree line, the rotor spinning wildly, the body of the chopper listing downward. The thing is in trouble. A thin contrail of black smoke flags behind the helicopter like a dark comet as it plunges out of sight.

The cargo truck slows. Martinez and Gus have obviously seen the thing as well.

"Do you think it's—?" Lilly starts to pose the question on everybody's mind when her words are cut off.

The impact of the crash—over half a mile away—rattles the earth.

A mushroom cloud of fire lights up the woods and scrapes the sky.

FIVE

"Here! Right here! Pull off!"

Gus pumps the brakes, the cargo truck groaning as it cobbles off the two-lane. It bumps across a narrow patch of muddy grass along the shoulder, and then rattles to a stop in a cloud of carbon monoxide and dust.

"This is as close as we're gonna get in the truck," Martinez says, leaning forward in the shotgun seat. He cranes his neck to see through the grimy windshield, getting a fleeting glimpse of the column of smoke rising over the trees on the western horizon. It looks to be about a quarter mile away. He reaches for his .357. "Gonna have to hoof it the rest of the way."

"It's a long way off, boss." Gus gazes out his side window, scratching his grizzled cheek. "Looks like it went down in the deep woods."

Martinez thinks about it, chewing the inside of his cheek. In this part of Georgia, many of the roadways cut through shallow, wooded valleys known as hollows. Formed by rivers and surrounded by densely forested hills, these thickets of brushwood, weeds, and muck can be rife with sinkholes, colonies of mosquitoes, and plenty of nooks and crannies in which mudbound biters frequently lurk.

Gus looks at Martinez. "Whaddaya say we try and drive it?"

"Negative." Martinez bites down hard on the word, checking the cylinder on his Magnum. He can hear the truck's rear gate banging down, the others climbing out, their tense voices carrying on the afternoon breeze. "We'll get stuck in this pea soup, sure as shit."

"Whatever you say, boss." Gus rams the shift lever into neutral and cuts the engine. The silence fills with the rush of nature—the jet-engine drone of crickets, the wind in the trees.

"Leave the 12-gauge, take one of the AR-15s, in case it gets hairy, and grab the machete under the seat." Martinez has a black marine raider bowie knife with a fifteen-inch blade strapped to his leg, and now checks it. He does this compulsively, jaw clenched, all business, as he hears the others coming around the side of the truck. He climbs out of the cab.

They all gather at the front of the cab, in the weeds and buzzing clouds of gnats, their faces drawn and pale with tension. The air smells of rot and burning metal. Austin stands there wringing his hands, gazing off at the crash site. The Sterns huddle together, both their brows furrowed with worry. Lilly has her hands on her hips, her Rugers holstered high on her waist. "What are you thinking?" she says to Martinez.

"Dave and Barb, I want you two to stay with the truck, keep watch." Martinez shoves his Magnum behind his belt. "If you get swarmed, just drive 'em off . . . lead 'em away . . . and then circle back and get us. You got that?"

David just nods and nods, looking like a nervous bobblehead doll. "Yes, absolutely."

"Keep the walkie with you, keep the frequency open while we're gone."

Gus hands the two-way to David, who is still nodding and muttering. "Got it, got it."

"There's a box of road flares in the back," Martinez says to Gus. "Go grab a handful. And get the first-aid kit, too, will ya?"

Gus hurries around the back of the truck while Martinez looks at his watch. "We got a good four hours of daylight left. I want to get out there and back before dark, no fucking around."

Lilly has one high-capacity magazine left. She slams it into her Ruger, snapping the slide. "The thing is, what if we find survivors?"

"That's the point," Martinez says, unsnapping the sheath on his leg, positioning the knife hilt for quick access. "Plus the helo might still be in one piece."

Lilly looks at him. "We got no stretcher, no medic, no way to get them back."

"We'll cross that bridge when we get there," Martinez says, adjusting his bandanna, already soaked in sweat, across his forehead.

Gus comes back with an armful of flares, which look like sticks of dynamite.

Martinez gives everybody a flare. "I want everybody to stay together, in tight formation . . . but if for some reason you get separated, light off one of these and we'll find you." He looks at the Sterns. "You run into any trouble back here, you light one off." He glances at the bald man. "Gus, I want you on the right flank with the machete. Keep the noise down. Use the AR-15 as a last resort. I'll take the left flank." He looks at Lilly. "You and Junior take the middle."

Austin gazes up at the sky. The midafternoon clouds have rolled in. The day has turned gray and ashy. The wetland ahead of them crawls with swaying shadows. It's been a wet year and now the ground looks impassable, mired in washouts, deadfalls, and dense groves of white pines standing between them and the crash site.

"There's a creek, runs through the middle of the woods," Martinez is saying, taking a deep breath and drawing his Magnum. "We'll follow it as far as we can, and then navigate by the smoke. Everybody got that?"

They all nod, saying nothing, swallowing back the mounting apprehension that passes between them like a virus.

Martinez nods. "Let's boogie."

It's tough going for a while, the unforgiving mud sucking at the soles of their boots, making wet smacking noises in the primeval silence of the woods. They follow the serpentine bends of the brackish stream, and the deeper they venture into the hollow, the more the trees swallow the daylight.

"You okay, Huckleberry?" Lilly whispers to Austin, who walks alongside her, his Glock gripped tightly in both of his sweaty hands.

"I'm fantastic," he lies. His long curls are pulled back from his glistening face with a leather tie. He chews on his lip nervously as he churns through the mud.

"You don't have to hold your gun like that," she says with a smirk.

"Like what?"

"Like you're some kind of Delta Force commando. Just keep it handy."

"Will do."

"If you get one in the cross hairs, just take your time. They're slow, so make your shots count. You don't have to do the gunslinger routine."

Austin shoots her a glance. "Just want to be ready . . . in case I need to come to your rescue."

Lilly gives him an eye roll. "Yeah, great, I feel totally safe now."

She peers into the trees ahead of them and sees the faint haze of smoke building in the woods. The air, hectic with bugs, smells of burned circuitry and scorched metal. The wreckage is still a few hundred yards off in the distant pines. The faint crackle of fire can be heard, barely audible above the wind rustling in the treetops.

Off to the right, maybe twenty yards ahead of Lilly, Martinez has taken the lead, weaving through the undergrowth, slicing through foliage with his bowie knife. On a parallel path to the left, Gus trudges along, his hound-dog eyes surveying the shadows for biters, his machete on his shoulder. The sky is barely visible above him, blocked by skeins of tree limbs and vines.

Lilly starts to say something else when a figure appears in front of Gus.

Lilly halts, her gun coming up fast, her breath seizing up in her throat. She sees Gus raise the machete. The large male walker, clad in tattered overalls, has its back turned to him, teetering on dead legs, its head cocked toward the crash site like a dog hearing an ultrasonic whistle. Gus sneaks up behind it.

The machete comes down fast, the blade making a crunching noise as it embeds itself in the gristly dura of the walker's cranium. Fluids gush, making watery sluicing noises in the silence of the woods, as the walker collapses. Lilly hardly has a chance to breathe again when another noise draws her attention to the right.

Fifteen feet away, Martinez lashes out at another stray walker—a spindly female with gray hair matted like spider webs—probably a former farmer's wife skulking around the brush. His knife impales the back of her head above the neck cords, putting her down with the speed of a silent embolism. She never saw it coming.

Letting out an involuntary sigh of relief, lowering her pistol, Lilly realizes that the walkers are currently mesmerized by the sights and sounds of the crash.

Martinez pauses to glance over his shoulder at the others. "Everybody good?" he says in a low voice, almost a stage whisper.

Nods from everyone. And then they're moving again, slowly but steadily forward, into the denser trees and fog-bound shadows. Martinez motions for them to hurry up. The ground is spongy and soggy beneath their feet, slowing them down. The shadows close in, the odors of scorched metal and burning fuel engulfing them, the crackling noises rising.

Lilly feels nauseous, her skin prickling with nerves. She senses Austin's eyes on her. "Do you think maybe you could stop staring at me?"

"It's not my fault you're so hot," he says with that same nervous smirk.

She shakes her head in dismay. "Can you just try and focus?"

"I am totally focused, believe me," he says, still gripping his gun with that fake cop-show grip as they continue on.

Less than a hundred yards from the crash site, they come to a washout—a bug-infested, swampy clearing blocking their path—the bog crisscrossed by enormous deadfall logs. With silent hand motions, Martinez directs them to use the logs as bridges. Gus goes first, crabbing across the largest deadfall. Martinez follows. Lilly goes next, and Austin brings up the rear. As he reaches the other side, Austin feels a tugging sensation on his jeans. The others have already crossed, and are now trudging toward the clearing. Austin pauses. At first he thinks he's caught on a piece of bark, but then he looks down.

Decomposing hands rise out of the marsh, clawing at his pants leg.

He lets out a cry and fumbles with his gun as dead fingers clutch at him, pulling him downward. Rising out of the mire, the slimy top half of a moldering creature goes for his legs. Filmed in black gunk, its hairless skull unidentifiable as man or woman, its eyes as white and opaque as light bulbs, it snaps its black turtle-like mouth on the creaky hinges of a ruined jaw.

Austin gets off a single muffled gunshot—the silencer spitting sparks—but the bullet misses its mark. The blast grazes the top of the swamp biter's head, and then plunks harmlessly into the swamp.

Fifty feet away, Lilly hears the blast. She spins around, reaching for her guns. But her legs tangle and she slips on the mud. She sprawls to the weeds, the guns flying out of her hands.

Austin tries to get a second shot off but the swamp biter is going for his leg. It rises out of the mire like a slimy black whale, its jaws unhinging and emitting a noxious growl. Austin jerks back involuntarily—a high-pitched cry blurting out of him—and the gun slips out of his hand. He kicks at the creature's mouth, the toe of his boot getting caught in the mouthful of rotting black teeth and putrid drool. The swamp biter clamps down.

Lilly crawls toward her guns. Martinez and Gus, by this point, have both whirled toward the commotion, but it's too late to intercede. The giant dripping biter is about to chew through Austin's Timberland hiking boot, and Austin is fumbling madly for something in his pocket. Finally Austin gets his hand around the road flare.

At the last possible instant—before the swamp biter is able to break the skin of Austin's foot—the young man sparks the flare and rams it into the biter's left eye. The creature rears back suddenly, releasing its hold and tossing its ragged head back in a fountain of sparks.

Austin stares for a moment, mesmerized by the sight of flames *inside* the rotten cavity of the biter's skull. The left eye glows for one horrible instant, shining with the intensity of a caution light. The biter stiffens in the muck. The back of its head suddenly bursts, spewing flames like the nozzle of a welding torch.

The left eye pops like a bulb overloading, spitting hot tissue on Austin . . . and then the creature sinks into the black void.

Austin shudders, wiping his face and watching for a moment, hypnotized by the spectacle of the biter sinking back into oblivion . . . until the only things that remain are bubbles floating on the surface of the swamp and a dull flickering glow under the muck. Eventually Austin manages to tear his gaze away. He finds his gun and catches his breath.

"Nicely done," Lilly says with a grudging softness in her voice as she makes her way across the log bridge. "Here . . . gimme your hand."

She helps Austin to his feet, holding him steady on the slime-slick log. He gets his breath back, swallows the shock, and shoves his gun back in his belt. He looks into her eyes. "That was close." He manages a shaky grin. "That thing could have easily gotten you."

"Yeah . . . thank God you were around," she says, a smile on her lips now despite the beating of her heart.

"LILLY!"

The booming voice of Martinez intrudes on the moment, drawing Lilly's attention back over her shoulder.

Thirty yards away, through a break in the trees, in a pall of acrid, black smoke, Martinez and Gus have found the crash site.

"Come on, pretty boy," Lilly says, gritting her teeth with nervous tension. "We got work to do."

The chopper lies on its side in a dry creek bed, spewing smoke from its breached fuel tank. No victims in sight. Lilly approaches cautiously, coughing, waving the fumes from her face. She sees Martinez approaching the cockpit, crouching down low, holding his hand over his mouth. "Be careful!" Lilly pulls her guns as she hollers at Martinez. "You don't know what's in there!"

Martinez touches the hatch release and burns himself, jerking his hand back. "Son of a *BITCH*!"

Lilly edges closer. The smoke, already clearing, begins to part like a curtain to reveal the soft, scorched ground around the crash site. It dawns on Lilly that the pilot must have aimed for the soft ground of the stream bed, the surrounding leaf-matted earth now torn up by the violence of the crash. The main rotor, detached and lying on the ground twenty feet away, looks as though it's tied in a knot.

"Gus! Austin! Keep your eyes on the periphery!" Martinez indicates the adjacent wall of white pines higher up the bank. "Noise is gonna draw a swarm!"

Gus and Austin whirl toward the woods and raise their muzzles at the darkness behind the trees.

Lilly feels the heat on her face as she approaches the wreckage. The fuselage lies on its right side, the tail fin and rear rotor horribly bent. One skid is torn off as though from the force of a giant can opener. The canopy and hatch windows are cracked and either steamed up from hyperventilating passengers or clouded over from the smoke. Regardless of the causes, though, it's impossible to see inside the cockpit. The soot has covered most of the markings on the bulwark and chassis, but Lilly sees a series of letters along the tail boom. She sees a W and maybe an R . . . and that's about it.

Martinez raises his hand suddenly as the noise of the fire dies down enough for them to hear the muffled cries coming from inside the cockpit. Martinez duckwalks closer.

Lilly moves in with her Rugers up, cocked and ready to rock. "Just be careful!"

Martinez takes a deep breath, and then climbs onto the side of the fuselage. Lilly moves closer, aiming her twin .22s at the hatch. Balancing on the battered steel frame, Martinez pulls his bandanna off and wraps it around the release handle. Lilly hears a high-pitched voice. "—outta here—!"

Martinez yanks.

The door snaps, squeaking open on shrieking hinges, releasing a puff of smoke and the tattered form of a frantic woman. Clad in a torn down jacket and scarf, stippled in blood, she bursts out of the cockpit, coughing and screaming, "—GET ME OUTTA HERE—!!"

Lilly lowers her guns, realizing that the woman has not yet turned. Martinez pulls the victim out of the death trap. The woman writhes in his arms, her bloodless face a mask of agony.

One of her legs is badly burned, the fabric of her jeans blackened to a crisp, glistening with pus and blood. She holds her left arm against her tummy, the fracture at the elbow bulging through the sleeve of her sweater.

"Gimme a hand, Lilly!"

They carry the woman away from the wreckage and lower her to the ground. She looks to be in her late thirties, maybe early forties. Fair skinned, dishwater-blond hair, squirming in pain, her face wet with tears, she babbles hysterically, "You don't understand! We have to—!"

"It's okay, it's all right," Lilly says to her, gently brushing her damp hair from her face. "We can help you, we have a doctor not far from here."

"Mike—! He's still—!" Her eyelids flutter, her body spasming from the pain, her eyes rolling back in her head from the shock. "We can't leave—we have to—have to get him out—we have to—!!"

Lilly touches her cheek, the flesh as clammy and slimy as an oyster. "Try to stay calm."

"—we have to *bury him* . . . it's something I . . . before he—" The woman's head lolls to the side, and she sinks into unconsciousness with the suddenness of a candle flame snuffing out.

Lilly looks up at Martinez.

"The *pilot*," Martinez utters, meeting Lilly's gaze with a hard look.

By now the smoke has cleared and the heat has dwindled, and both Gus and Austin have returned to gaze over their shoulders. Martinez rises to his feet, and he goes back to the wreck. Lilly follows. They climb up onto one of the mangled skids and boost themselves up enough to see into the open hatchway. The odor of charred meat assaults their senses as they gaze inside.

The pilot is dead. In the hazy, sparking enclosure, the man named Mike sits slumped in his scorched leather bomber jacket—

still harnessed to his seat—the entire left side of his body black-ened and disfigured from the in-flight fire. The fingers of one gloved hand have melted and fused to the control stick. And just for an instant, staring into that hellish cockpit, Lilly gets the feeling this guy was a hero. He brought the craft down in the spongy cleavage of the creek, saving the life of his passenger—his wife, his girlfriend?

"Too late to do anything for *this* guy," Martinez murmurs next to her.

"Obviously," she says, lowering herself back to the ground. She glances across the clearing, where Austin now kneels by the unconscious woman, feeling her neck for a pulse. Gus nervously keeps an eye on the woods. Lilly wipes her face. "But we should probably honor her request, right?"

Martinez climbs down and looks around the clearing, the smoke wafting away on the wind. He wipes his eyes. "I don't know."

"Boss!" Gus calls out from the edge of the woods. Troubling sounds from the surrounding forest drift on the wind. "We ought to be thinking about gettin' the hell outta here pretty soon."

"We're coming!" Martinez turns to Lilly. "We'll take the woman back."

"But what about—?"

Martinez lowers his voice. "You know what the Governor's gonna do with this guy, right?"

Lilly's spine tingles with rage. "This doesn't have anything to do with the Governor."

"Lilly—"

"This guy saved this woman's life."

"Listen to me. We're gonna have a hell of a time just getting *her* back through these woods."

Lilly lets out an anguished sigh. "And you don't think the Governor's gonna find out we left the pilot?"

Martinez turns away from her and spits angrily. Wipes his mouth. Thinks it over.

"Boss!" Gus calls out again, sounding exceedingly nervous.

"I said we're coming, goddamnit!" Martinez stares at the scorched ground, thinking and agonizing . . . until the whole issue becomes a foregone conclusion.

SIX

They get back to the truck just as the sun is starting to set, the shadows of the forest lengthening around them. Exhausted from the trip back through the hollow, where they encountered an increasing number of walkers, they enlist the help of David and Barbara in order to drag the bodies—each one tied to a makeshift stretcher of birch logs and willow switches—quickly toward the truck's rear hatch. They lift them one at a time into the crowded cargo bay.

"Be careful with her," Lilly cautions as David and Barbara shove the stretcher bearing the woman between two stacks of food crates. The woman is slowly coming back around, her head lolling back and forth, her eyes fluttering. There's not much room for extra bodies in the truck, and Barbara has to hastily rearrange the boxes and stacks of cartons in order to make space.

"She's hurt pretty bad but she's hanging in there," Lilly adds as she climbs up into the cargo hold. "Wish I could say the same for the pilot."

All heads turn toward the rear hatch as Gus and Martinez lift the dead pilot—his disfigured remains still strapped to the gurney—up and into the back of the truck. David has to make room for the corpse by shoving a stack of canned peaches against one wall, and clearing a narrow strip of corrugated floor between a tower of Hamburger Helper cartons and a half-dozen propane tanks.

David wipes his arthritic hands on his silk jacket as he gazes down at the scorched remains of the pilot. "This presents somewhat of a dilemma."

Lilly glances over her shoulder at the open hatch, as Martinez peers into the shadowy chamber. "We need to bury him, it's a long story."

David stares at the cadaver. "What if he—?"

"Keep an eye on him," Martinez orders. "If he turns on the way back, use a small-caliber round on him. We promised the lady we'd—"

"Not gonna make it!"

The sudden outburst yanks Lilly's attention back to the woman, who writhes on the iron floor, still cocooned in willow branches, her bloodstained head drooping back and forth. Her feverish eyes are wide open, her gaze pinned to the truck's ceiling. Her mutterings come fitfully, as though she's talking in her sleep. "Mike, we're south of there. . . . What about . . . what about the tower?!"

Lilly kneels next to the woman. "It's okay, honey. You're safe now."

Barbara goes to the opposite corner of the hold and quickly rips the protective lid off a gallon of filtered water. She returns to the injured woman with the jug. "Here, sweetheart . . . take a sip."

The woman on the stretcher cringes at a wave of pain that ripples through her, as the water dribbles into her mouth. She coughs and tries to speak. "—Mike—is he—?"

"Shit!"

Austin's voice rings out from the rear as he struggles to climb into the truck. Shooting nervous glances over his shoulder, he sees a pack of walkers lurching out of the woods—about twenty yards away and closing—at least ten of them, all large males, their hungry mouths working busily as they approach. Their milky eyes gleam in the dusky light. Austin climbs on board with his gun still gripped in his sweaty hand.

"GET THE FUCK OUTTA HERE!"

The slamming of the cab doors makes everybody jump. Gears grind. The chassis shudders and vibrates beneath them. Lilly holds on to the crates as the truck heaves into reverse in a whirl-wind of fumes and dust.

Through the flapping rear tarp, Lilly sees the walkers looming.

The truck barrels directly into the dead, knocking them over like bowling pins, making wet thuds beneath the massive wheels. The truck bumps over them as the engine whines noisily, and the tires spin for a moment in the grease of rotten organs.

The wheels gain purchase on the pavement, Gus slams it into drive, and the truck rumbles out of there, fishtailing down the two-lane in the direction they had come. Lilly looks back down at the woman with the dishwater hair. "Just hang in there, sweetie, you're gonna be okay . . . gonna get you to a doctor."

Barbara tips more water across the woman's chapped, burned lips.

Lilly kneels closer. "My name's Lilly, and this is Barbara. Can you tell me your name?"

The woman utters something inaudible, her voice drowned out by the roar of the truck.

Lilly leans closer. "Say it again, honey. Tell me your name."

"Chrisss . . . Chris-*tina*," the woman manages through clenched teeth.

"Christina, don't worry . . . everything's gonna be okay . . . you're gonna make it." Lilly strokes the woman's sweat-damp brow. Shivering, twitching on the stretcher, the woman takes shallow, quick breaths. Her eyes close to half mast, her lips moving, forming a silent, pained litany that nobody can hear. Lilly smooths her matted hair. "Everything's gonna be okay," Lilly keeps muttering, more to herself than to the victim.

The truck rumbles down the two-lane, the rear flap snapping in the wind.

Lilly glances out the back and sees the tall pines outside, passing in a blur. The setting sun behind the treetops causes a strobe-like effect that is almost hypnotic. Lilly wonders for a brief moment if everything will *indeed* be okay. Maybe Woodbury has stabilized now. Maybe the Governor's Machiavellian methods will actually keep them safe, keep a lid on the place. She wants to believe in Woodbury. Maybe that's the key . . . simply *believing*. Maybe that alone will get them through. . . .

Maybe, maybe, maybe, maybe . . .

"W-where am I?" The voice is hoarse, choked, unsteady.

Dr. Stevens stands over the bed in his shopworn lab coat and wire-rimmed glasses, gazing down at the woman from the chopper. "Gonna be a little groggy for a while," he says to her. "We gave you a couple happy pills."

The woman named Christina lies in a supine position on a makeshift gurney in the cinder block–lined catacombs beneath the racetrack. Clad in a cast-off terrycloth robe, her right arm wrapped in an improvised cast of kindling and medical tape, she turns her pale, ashen face away from the harsh halogen light shining down on her.

"Hold this, Alice, just for a second." Stevens hands the plastic vial of IV fluids to the young nurse. Also in a tattered lab coat, her hair pulled back in a ponytail, Alice forces a smile as she holds the vial aloft, its line connected to a stick in the injured woman's arm.

Again Christina manages to croak, "W-where am I?"

Stevens goes to an adjacent sink, washes his hands, and towels off. "I could level with you and say the Ninth Circle of Hell but I'll refrain from the editorial comments for the moment." He turns back to her and says with a warm but slightly cynical smile, "You're in the sprawling metropolis of Woodbury, Georgia . . . population *who-the-hell-knows*. My name is Dr. Stevens and this is Alice, and it's a quarter after seven, and I understand you were fished out of the wreckage of a helicopter this afternoon . . . ?"

She manages a nod, and then flinches at a twinge in her midsection.

"That's gonna be a little tender for a while," Stevens says, wiping his hands on the towel. "You had third-degree burns over twenty percent of your body. Good news is, I don't think you'll need any skin grafts . . . just a little edema we're treating intravenously. Lucky for you, we had three liters of glucose left. Which you're sucking down like a drunken sailor. You managed to fracture your arm in two places. We'll watch that as well. They said your name is Christina?"

She nods.

Stevens clicks a penlight, reaches down, and checks her eyes. "How's your short-term memory, Christina?"

She inhales an excruciating breath, which whistles softly in her throat. "Memory's fine. . . . My pilot . . . Mike is his name . . . *was* his name. . . . Did they—?"

Stevens puts his penlight back into his pocket and gets serious. "I'm sorry to say your friend died in the crash."

Christina manages a nod. "I'm aware of that . . . but I just wondered . . . his body . . . Did they bring him back?"

"As a matter of fact, they did."

She swallows thickly, licks her dry lips. "That's good . . . because I promised him a Christian burial."

Stevens looks at the floor. "That's very admirable . . . a Christian burial." Stevens and Alice exchange a glance. Stevens looks back at the patient and smiles. "One step at a time . . . okay? For now, let's just concentrate on getting you up and running."

"What's the matter? Did I say something wrong?"

Stevens ponders the injured woman. "It's nothing, don't worry about it."

"Is there a problem with me wanting to give my pilot a proper burial?"

Stevens sighs. "Look . . . I'll be honest with you. I don't think that's gonna happen."

Christina lets out a grunt as she struggles to a sitting position. Alice helps her sit up, gently keeping her arm elevated. Christina looks at Stevens. "What the hell is the problem?"

Stevens looks at Alice, then back at the patient. "The Governor is the problem."

"Who?"

"Guy who runs this place." Stevens takes off his glasses, pulls out a handkerchief, and cleans the lenses carefully as she speaks. "Fancies himself a civil servant, I guess. Hence the name."

Christina furrows her brow, confused. "Is this guy—?" She searches for the words. "Is he—?"

"Is he what?"

She shrugs. "Is he—what would you call it? 'Elected'? Is he an elected official?"

The doctor shoots another loaded glance at Alice. "Um . . . wow . . . that's an interesting question."

Alice grumbles, "He's elected, all right . . . by a single vote . . . *his own*."

The doctor rubs his eyes. "It's a little more complicated than that." He measures his words. "You're new here. This man . . . he's the alpha dog here in our little kennel. He leads by default. Keeps order by doing the dirty work." A thin smile crosses Stevens's narrow features. The smile drips with disdain. "Only problem is, the man has developed a taste for it."

Christina stares at the doctor. "I don't know what that means."

"Look." Stevens puts his glasses back on and wearily runs his fingers through his hair. "Whatever happens to your friend's remains . . . take my advice. Grieve on your own, pay tribute silently."

"I don't understand."

Stevens looks at Alice, his smile fading. He looks into Christina's eyes. "You're gonna be okay. A week or so . . . when your arm's healed up . . . you might think about leaving this place."

"But I don't—"

"And one other thing." Stevens fixes her with his gaze. His voice drops an octave, gets very serious. "This man. The Governor. He is not to be trusted. You understand? He is capable of *anything*. So just steer clear of him . . . and bide your time until you can get out of here. Do you understand what I'm saying?"

She doesn't answer, just stares at him, soaking it in.

Darkness closes in around the town. Some of the windows begin to glow with lantern light, others already pulsing with the unpredictable current of generators. At night, Woodbury has the surreal, retrofitted feel of the twenty-first century transported to the nineteenth—an atmosphere that has become de rigueur among most post-plague settlements. At one corner, torch flames bathe a boarded, desecrated McDonald's, the yellow-orange light reflecting off the ruins of its crumbling golden arches.

Martinez's men, posted on cherry pickers at key junctures of the barricade, now begin to deal with an increasing number of moving shadows on the edges of the adjacent woods. Walker traffic has picked up slightly since of the return of the reconnaissance party, and now .50 caliber placements on the north and west sides crackle with intermittent gunfire. It gives the little town— which now basks in the purple, hazy twilight of dusk—a warzone feel.

Trundling past a portico of storefronts, carrying a peach crate brimming with provisions, Lilly Caul heads for her building. She hears the spit of automatic weaponry behind her, echoing across the windswept street. She pauses and glances over her shoulder at the sound of a voice rising over the gunfire.

"LILLY, WAIT UP!"

In the strobelike volleys of tracer bullets arcing across the sky, the silhouette of a young man in leather and flowing dark curls lopes toward Lilly. Austin has a duffel bag heavy with supplies over his shoulder. He lives half a block west of Lilly's place. He comes up with a big, expectant grin on his face. "Let me help you with that."

"It's okay, Austin, I got it," she says as he tries to take the crate from her. For an awkward moment, they play push-pull with the crate. Finally Lilly gives up. "All right, all right . . . *take it.*"

Now Austin happily walks alongside her with the crate in his arms. "That was quite an adrenaline rush today, was it not?"

"Easy, Austin . . . pace yourself."

They walk toward Lilly's building. In the distance, an armed man paces along a row of semitrailers at the end of the street. Austin gives Lilly that same provocative little grin he's been plying her with for weeks. "Guess we tasted the camaraderie of the battlefield together, huh? Kinda bonded out there, didn't we?"

"Austin, can you *please* give it a rest."

"I'm wearing you down, though, aren't I?"

Lilly shakes her head and lets out a little laugh despite her nerves. "You *are* relentless, I'll give you that."

"What are you doing tonight?"

"Are you asking me out?"

"There's a fight in the arena. Why don't you let me take you to it, I'll bring those Twizzlers I found today."

Lilly's smile fades. "Not a big fan."

"Of what? Twizzlers?"

"Very funny. Those fights are barbaric. I'd rather eat broken glass."

Austin shrugs. "If you say so." His eyes glint with an idea. "How about this: Instead of a date, why don't you give me some more pointers sometime?"

"Pointers on what?"

"On dealing with the dead." All at once he gets a solemn expression on his face. "I'll be honest with ya. Since all this shit started up, I've kinda hidden out with big groups . . . never really had to fend for myself. I've got a lot to learn. I'm not like you."

She gives him a glance as they walk. "What do you mean by that?"

"You're a badass, Lilly . . . you got that cold, calculating, Clint Eastwood thing going on."

They reach the parkway in front of Lilly's apartment building, now draped in shadow, the dead kudzu vines on the redbrick exterior looking like a cancerous growth in the waning light.

Lilly pauses, turns to Austin, and says, "Thanks for the help, Austin. I'll take it from here." She takes the crate and looks at him. "One thing, though." She licks her lips and feels a twinge of emotion pinching her insides. "I wasn't always like this. You should have seen me back at the beginning. Scared of my own shadow. But somebody helped me when I needed it. And they didn't have to. Believe me. But they did, they helped me."

Austin doesn't say anything, just nods his head and waits for her to finish her thought, because it looks as though something is eating at her. Something important.

"I'll show you some things," she says at last. "And by the way . . . this is the only way we're going to survive. By helping each other."

Austin smiles, and for the first time since Lilly has known him, it's a warm, sincere, guileless smile. "I appreciate it, Lilly. I'm sorry I've been such a dick."

"You haven't been a dick," she says, and then, without warning, she leans over the crate and gives him a platonic little kiss on the cheek. "You're just young."

She turns and goes inside, gently shutting the door in his face.

Austin stands there for quite some time, staring at that wide oak entrance door, rubbing his cheek as though it were touched with holy water.

"Doc?" Three hard, sharp knocks shatter the stillness of the makeshift infirmary . . . followed by the unmistakable throaty voice, with its faint rural Georgia accent, just outside the door: "The new patient taking any visitors?"

Across the gray, cinder block–lined room, Dr. Stevens and Alice glance at each other. They stand at a stainless steel basin, sterilizing instruments in a pail of scalding water, the steam drifting up across their taut expressions. "Hold on a second!" Stevens calls out, wiping his hands and going over to the door.

Before opening the door, Stevens glances across the infirmary at the patient sitting up on the side of her gurney, her spindly, bandaged legs dangling. Christina, still in her robe, sips filtered water from a plastic cup, a woolen blanket pulled up across her midsection. Her swollen face—still beautiful, even with her matted wheat-straw hair pulled back into a knotted scrunchy—registers the tension.

In that instant before the door opens, something unspoken passes between doctor and patient. Stevens nods, and then opens the door.

"I understand we got a brave little lady in our midst!" the visitor booms as he sweeps into the room like a force of nature. The Governor's gaunt, coiled body is now clad in weekend warrior garb—a hunting vest, black turtleneck, and camo pants tucked into black combat boots—making him look like a degenerate third-world dictator. His shoulder-length onyx hair shines and bounces as he saunters into the room, his handlebar mustache curled around a smirk. "Came to pay my respects."

Gabe and Bruce enter on the Governor's heels, the two men as dour and alert as secret service agents.

"There she is," Philip Blake says to the girl sitting on the gurney. He walks over to the bed, grabs a nearby metal folding chair, and slams it down backwards next to the bed. "How ya doing, little lady?"

Christina puts her water down, and then chastely pulls the blanket up over the top of her threadbare décolletage. "Doing all right, I guess. Thanks to these folks."

The Governor plops down on the chair in front of her, resting his wiry arms on the seat back. His stare is the jovial gaze of an overzealous salesman. "Doc Stevens and Alice here are the best . . . they surely are. Don't know what we'd do without them."

Stevens speaks up from across the room. "Christina, say hello to Philip Blake. Also known as the Governor." The doctor lets out a sigh and looks away, as though disgusted by this whole display of fake conviviality. "Philip, this is Christina."

"*Christina*," the Governor purrs, as though trying the name on for size. "Now isn't that just the prettiest name ever?"

A sudden and powerful tremor of apprehension trickles down the small of Christina's back. Something about this man's eyes—as deep-set and dark as a puma's—sets her immediately on edge.

The Governor doesn't take his glittering dark gaze off her as he speaks to the others. "You folks mind if the lady and I speak in private?"

Christina wants to say something, wants to object, but the force of this man's personality is like a roaring river flowing through the room. Without a word, the others glance at each other, and then, sheepishly, one by one, they file out of the infirmary. The last one out is Gabe, who pauses in doorway. "I'll be right outside, boss," he says. And then . . .

Click.

SEVEN

"So, Christina . . . welcome to Woodbury." At first, the Governor keeps his high-voltage smile trained on the injured woman. "Can I ask where you're from?"

Christina takes a deep breath, looking down at her lap. For some inchoate reason, she feels compelled to keep the TV station she worked at a secret. Instead she simply says, "Suburb of Atlanta, got hit pretty bad."

"I'm from a little shithole town outside Savannah, name of Waynesboro." His grin widens. "Nothing fancy like them rich sections of Hot-Lanta."

She shrugs. "I sure as heck ain't rich."

"Them places are all gone to hell now, ain't they? Biters won *that* war." He aims that grin at her. "Unless you know something I don't."

She stares at him, says nothing.

The Governor's smile fades. "Can I ask how you ended up in that chopper?"

For a brief instant she hesitates. "The pilot was . . . a friend. Name's Mike." She swallows back her reticence. "Problem is, I promised him a Christian burial." She feels the heat of the Governor's stare like a furnace. "You think I could possibly see to that?"

The thin man scoots his chair closer to the bed. "I think we ought to be able to accommodate you in that department . . . that is . . . if you play ball."

"If I what?"

The Governor shrugs. "Just answer a few questions. That's all." He pulls a pack of Juicy Fruit gum from his vest pocket, peels off a piece, and pops it into his mouth. He offers her a piece. She declines. He puts the gum away and scoots the chair closer. "You see, Christina . . . the thing is . . . I have a responsibility to my people. There's a certain . . . *due diligence* I gotta tend to."

She looks at him. "I'll tell you anything you want to know."

"Were you and the pilot alone? Or were there other people with you before you took off?"

Again she swallows hard, girding herself. "We were holed up with a few people."

"Where?"

She shrugs. "You know . . . here and there."

The Governor smiles and shakes his head. "Now, see, Christina . . . that just won't do." He shoves the seat back against the gurney—close enough now for her to smell his scent: cigarettes and chewing gum and something unidentifiable like spoiled meat—and he speaks softly now. "In a court of law, a good counselor might see his way to making an objection on the grounds that the witness is withholding information."

He's about to cross a boundary, a voice drones in Christina's head, *he's not to be trusted, he's capable of anything.* In barely a whisper, she says, "I wasn't aware I was on trial here."

The Governor's lean, deeply lined face transforms, any trace of mirth going out of it. "You don't have to be scared of me."

She looks at him. "I'm not scared of you."

"The truth of the matter is, I don't want to force anybody to do anything they don't want to do . . . nobody has to get hurt." With the casual gesture of a man shooting his cuffs, he puts his gnarled hand on the edge of the bed, between her thighs, provocatively—not touching her, just resting it between her bandaged legs. His gaze doesn't waver. It stays locked on to her. "It's just that . . . I will do whatever it takes to make sure this community survives. You understand?"

She looks down at his hand, at the dirt under his nails. "Yes."

"Why don't you go ahead and start talking, sweetheart, and I'll listen."

Christina lets out an anguished breath, her posture changing. She stares into her lap. "I worked at Channel 9, WROM, the Fox affiliate out of North Atlanta. . . . I was a segment producer . . . bake sales and lost pets and such. Worked in that big tower on Peachtree, the one with the helipad on the roof." Her breathing gets labored, the pain pressing down on her as she talks. "When the Turn happened, about twenty of us got trapped at the station. . . . We lived off the food in the cafeteria on the fourth floor for a while . . . then we started taking the traffic copter out on supply runs." She runs out of breath for a moment.

The Governor stares. "They got any of them supplies left up there?"

Christina shakes her head. "Nothing . . . no food . . . no power . . . nothing. When we ran out of food . . . people started turning on *each other*." She closes her eyes and tries to block out the memories that come flooding back like flash frames from a snuff film: the blood-spattered steam tables and all the monitors filled with snow and the severed head in the festering walk-in freezer and the screams at night. "Mike protected me, bless his heart. . . . He was the traffic pilot . . . we worked together for years . . . and finally he and I . . . we managed to sneak up to the roof and steal away in Mike's traffic copter. We thought we were home free . . . but we didn't realize . . . there was somebody in our group who was dead set on stopping anybody *else* from leaving. He sabotaged the helicopter's engine. We knew it immediately. Barely made it out of the city . . . got maybe fifty miles or so . . . before we started hearing . . . before we saw the . . ." She shakes her head forlornly, and then looks up. "Anyway . . . you know the rest." She tries to hide the fact that she's trembling. Her voice sharpens, turns rueful. "I don't know what you want from me."

"You've been through a lot." The Governor pats her bandaged thigh, his demeanor changing suddenly. He gives her a smile, pushes himself away from the bed, and rises to his feet. "I'm sorry you had to go through that. These are tough times . . . but you're safe here."

"Safe?" She can't turn off her simmering anger. Her eyes water with rage. The hard-bitten side of her comes out now, the veteran segment producer who doesn't take shit from anybody. "Are you serious?"

"I'm totally serious, sweetheart. We're building something good here, something solid. And we're always looking for good people to join us."

"I don't think so." She glowers at him. "I think I'll take my chances out there with the biters."

"Now calm down, honey. I know you've been through the mill. But that's no reason to pass up something good. We're building a community here."

"Give me a break!" She practically spits the words at him. "I know all about you."

"All right, that's enough." He sounds like a teacher trying to calm an unruly student. "Let's dial it back a little."

"Maybe you can fool some of these hayseeds with your little Benevolent Leader routine—"

He lunges at her and slaps her—a backhand across her bruised face—hard enough to whiplash her head against the wall.

She gasps and blinks, and swallows the pain. She rubs her face and finds enough breath to speak very softly and evenly. "I've worked with men like you my entire career. You call yourself a governor? Really? You're just a schoolyard bully who's found a playground to rule. The doctor told me all about you."

Standing over her, the Governor nods and smiles coldly. His face hardens. His eyes narrow, the halogen light reflecting in his dark irises like two silver pinpricks. "I tried," he murmurs, more to himself than to her. "God knows I tried."

He lunges at her again, this time going for her neck. She stiffens on the bed as he chokes her. She looks into his eyes. She calms down all of a sudden as he strangles her. Her body starts to spasm involuntarily against the gurney, making the casters squeak, but she feels no pain anymore. The blood drains from her face. She wants to die.

The Governor softly whispers, "There we go . . . there . . . *there* . . . gonna be all right . . ."

Her eyes roll back, showing the whites, as she turns livid in his grip. Her legs kick and twitch, knocking over the IV stand. The steel apparatus clatters to the floor, spilling glucose.

In the silence that follows the woman grows stone-still, her eyes frozen in an empty pale stare. Another moment passes, and then the Governor lets go.

Philip Blake steps back from the gurney on which the woman from Atlanta now lies dead, her arms and legs akimbo, dangling over the side of the bed. He catches his breath, inhaling and exhaling deeply, getting himself together.

In some distant compartment of his brain, a faint voice objects and pushes back, but he stuffs it back down into that dark fractured place in his mind. He mutters to himself, his voice barely audible to his own ears, as though an argument is under way, "Had to be done . . . I had no choice in the matter . . . no choice. . . ."

"BOSS?!"

The muffled sound of Gabe's voice on the other side of the door brings him back. "Just a second," he calls out, the forceful tone of his voice returning. "Just gimme a second here."

He swallows hard and goes over to the sink. He runs water, splashes his face, washes his hands, and dries himself on a damp towel. And just as he's about to turn away, he catches a glimpse of his own reflection in the surface of the stainless steel cabinet over the sink. His face, shimmering back at him in the liquid silver surface of the cabinet, looks almost ghostly, translucent, unborn. He turns away. "C'mon in, Gabe!"

The door clicks, and the stocky, balding man peers inside the room. "Everything okay?"

"Gonna need a hand with something," the Governor says, indicating the dead woman. "This has to be done just right. Don't talk, just listen."

In a residential building next to the racetrack, on the second floor, in the dusty stillness, Dr. Stevens slouches drowsily with his lab coat unbuttoned, a *Bon Appétit* magazine tented over his poochy, patrician belly, a half-empty bottle of contraband Pinot Noir on the crate next to him, when a knock at his door makes him jerk in his armchair. He gropes for his eyeglasses.

"Doc!" The muffled voice outside his door gets him up and moving.

Woozy from the wine and lack of sleep, he trundles across the nominal living room of his Spartan apartment. A warren of cardboard boxes and stacks of found reading material, dimly lit by kerosene lanterns, his place is an end-of-the-world refuge for a lifelong intellectual. For a while, Stevens followed sporadic dispatches on the plague coming out of the CDC and Washington— often arriving with survivor groups, published on quickie print-on-demand circulars—but now the data sits collecting dust on his windowsill, all but forgotten in the doctor's radioactive grief for his lost family.

"Need to have a little chat," the man in the hallway says when Stevens opens the door.

The Governor stands outside, in the darkness of the corridor, with Gabe and Bruce hovering on his flanks, assault rifles slung over their shoulders. The Governor's dark, hirsute face is aglow with fake cheer. "Don't bother with the cookies and milk, we won't be staying long."

Stevens shrugs and leads the three men into the living room. Still woozy, the doctor motions at a ratty sofa stacked with newspapers. "If you can find a place to sit in this pigsty, you're welcome to take a load off."

"We'll stand," the Governor says flatly, looking around the hovel. Gabe and Bruce move around behind Stevens, predators circling for the kill.

"So . . . to what do I owe this unexpected—?" the doctor starts to say when the barrel of an APC pistol swings up and kisses the back of his skull. He realizes Gabe is pressing the muzzle of the semiautomatic against his neck cords, the mechanism cocked and ready to fire.

"You're a student of history, Doc." The Governor circles, jackal-like. "I'm sure you remember, back in the Cold War days, when the Ruskies were still swinging their nuclear dicks at us . . . they had an expression. Mutually assured destruction . . . M-A-D, they called it."

Stevens's heart races, his mouth drying. "I'm aware of the expression."

"That's what we got going on here." The Governor comes around in front of him. "I go down, and you go down with me. And vice versa. You following me?"

Stevens swallows. "In all honesty, I have no inkling as to what you're talking about."

"This gal Christina, she got the impression that I was a bad guy." The Governor keeps circling. "You don't have any idea where she would have gotten such an impression, do ya?"

Stevens starts to say, "Look, I don't—"

"Shut the fuck up!" The Governor draws a black 9 mm pistol,

thumbs the hammer, and sticks the muzzle under the doctor's chin. "You got blood on your hands, Doc. This girl's demise is on *you.*"

"Demise?" Stevens's head is upturned now, from the pressure of the gun's barrel. "What did you do?"

"I did my duty."

"What did you do to her?"

The Governor hisses at him through clenched teeth. "I removed her from the equation. She was a security risk. You know why?"

"What does that—?"

"You know why she was a security risk, Doc?" He increases the pressure on his chin. "She was a security risk because of *you.*"

"I don't know what you're talking about."

"You're a smart man, Doc. I think you know exactly what I'm talking about." He releases the pressure, pulls the gun back, and continues circling. "Gabe, stand down. Let him be, now."

Gabe pulls his weapon away, stands back. The doctor lets out a thin breath, his hands shaking. He looks at the Governor. "What do you want, Philip?"

"I WANT YOUR LOYALTY, GODDAMNIT!!"

The sudden roar of the Governor's booming voice seems to change the air pressure in the room. The other three men stand deathly still. The doctor stares at the floor, fists clenched, heart thumping.

The Governor continues pacing around the doctor. "You know what happens when you damage my image in this town? People get nervous. And when they get nervous, they get careless."

The doctor keeps gazing at the floor. "Philip, I don't know what this woman told you—"

"Lives hang in the balance here, Doc, and you're fucking with that balance."

"What do you want me to say?"

"I don't want you to say anything, I want you to listen for once. I want you to shut that smartass trap of yours, and listen and think about something."

The doctor emits a faint sigh of exasperation, but says nothing.

"I want you to consider what happened to this gal before you poison anyone else against me." The Governor comes closer to him. "I want you to focus your big brain on that. Can you do that for me?"

"Whatever you want, Philip."

"And I want you to consider something else. I want you to consider how lucky you are . . . you got skills that keep you around."

The doctor looks up at him. "Meaning what?"

The Governor bores his gaze into him. "Lemme put it this way. You better fucking pray we don't run across another doctor. You follow me?"

The doctor looks down. "I follow you, Philip. You don't have to threaten me."

Now the Governor cocks his head at him and smiles. "Doc . . . c'mon . . . it's me." The old Fuller Brush salesman charm is back. "Why would I threaten my old sawbones?" He pats the doctor on the back. "We're just a couple of neighbors flapping our jaws around the pickle barrel." Philip looks at his watch. "In fact, we would love nothing more than to play a game of checkers with you, but we got—"

Out of nowhere, a sound outside cuts off his words and gets everybody's attention.

Faint at first, carrying on the wind, the unmistakable crackle of .50 caliber gunfire comes from the east. The duration and fury of it—more than one gun placement barks for several moments— speaks to a serious firefight.

"Hold on!" The Governor raises his hand and cocks his head toward the window. It sounds as though it's coming from the northeast corner of the barricade, but at this distance, it's hard to tell for sure. "Something major's going down," the Governor says to Gabe.

Both Gabe and Bruce swing their Bushmaster machine guns around in front of them, safeties going off.

"C'mon!" The Governor charges out of the room, Gabe and Bruce on his heels.

They burst out of Stevens's building with machine guns at the ready, the Governor in the lead, his 9mm in hand, locked and cocked.

The wind skitters trash around their feet as they head east. The echoes of automatic gunfire have already faded on the breeze, but they can see a pair of tungsten searchlights—about three hundred yards away—the twin beams bouncing up across the silhouettes of rooftops.

"BOB!" The Governor sees the old medic huddled against a storefront half a block away. Shrouded in a ratty blanket, the drunkard crouches, shivering, his eyes popping wide toward the commotion. He looks as though the gunfire awakened him only moments ago, his expression bloodless and agitated, a man awakened from one nightmare by another. The Governor hurries up to him. "You see anything, buddy? We under attack? What's going on?"

The medic sputters for a moment, hacking and wheezing. "Don't know for sure . . . heard a guy . . . he was coming from the wall just a second ago . . ." He doubles over then with a coughing attack.

"What did he say, Bob?" The Governor touches the old man's shoulder, gives him a little shake.

"He said . . . it's a new arrival . . . something like that . . . new people."

The Governor lets out a breath of relief. "You're sure now, Bob?"

The old man nods. "Said something about new folks coming in with a pack of walkers right on their tail. They got 'em all, though—the *walkers*, that is."

The Governor pats the old man. "That's a relief, Bob. You stay put while we check it out."

"Yes, sir, I'll do that."

The Governor turns to his men, speaking under his breath now. "Until we get a handle on this situation, you boys keep them guns handy."

"Will do, boss," Gabe says, lowering the Bushmaster's muzzle, but keeping the weapon cradled in his beefy arms. With his gloved hand, he releases the trigger pad, but keeps his index finger against the stock. Bruce does the same, sniffing nervously.

The Governor glances at his reflection in the hardware store window. He smooths his mustache, brushes a lock of raven-black hair from his eyes, and mutters, "C'mon, boys, let's go roll out the welcome wagon."

At first, standing in a halo of magnesium light and cloud of cordite, Martinez doesn't hear the heavy footsteps coming toward him from a dark stretch of adjacent street. He's too distracted by the mess that has tumbled into town in the newcomers' wake.

"I'm taking them to the big man," Martinez says to Gus, who stands near a gap in the wall, holding an armful of confiscated weapons—a couple of riot batons, an ax, a pair of .45 caliber pistols, and some kind of fancy Japanese sword still in its ornate scabbard. The air smells of flesh-rot and hot steel, and the night sky has clouded over.

Behind Gus, in a haze of gun smoke, ragged bodies are visible on the ground outside the barricade, and scattered across the pavement inside the gap. The freshly vanquished corpses steam in the night chill, their glistening black spoor spattered across the pavers.

"If I hear about a biter getting so much as twenty feet close to the wall," Martinez barks, making eye contact with every one of the twelve men who stand sheepishly around Gus, "*you're* going to hear about it! Clean house!"

Then Martinez turns to the newcomers. "You guys can follow me."

The three strangers pause for a moment, leery and hesitant against the wall—two men and a woman—squinting in the tungsten radiance, their backs against the barricade like prisoners caught in mid-escape. Disarmed and disoriented, filthy from their hard travels, the men wear riot gear, the woman clad in a hooded garment that at first glance appears almost displaced in time, like a cloak from a monastery or some secret order.

Martinez takes a step closer to the trio and starts to say something else, when the sound of a familiar voice rings out from behind him.

"I can take it from here, Martinez!"

Martinez whirls to see the Governor walking up, with Gabe and Bruce on his heels.

As he approaches, the Governor plays the role of town host to the hilt, looking all hail-fellow-well-met, except for the clenching and unclenching of his fists. "I'd like to escort our guests myself."

Martinez gives a nod, steps back, and says nothing. The Governor pauses, gazing out at the gap left by the missing semi-trailer.

"I need you at the wall," the Governor explains under his breath to Martinez, motioning at all the carnage on the ground, "cleaning off all the biters they no doubt drug with them."

Martinez keeps nodding. "Yes, sir, Governor. I didn't know you'd be coming out to get them when we gave word of their arrival. They're all yours."

The Governor turns to the strangers—a big smile here. "Follow me, folks. I'll give you the nickel tour."

EIGHT

Austin gets to the arena early that night—around eight forty-five—and sits alone, down front, behind the rusted cyclone-fence barrier, on the end of the second row, thinking about Lilly. He wonders if he should have pushed harder to get her to come along with him tonight. He thinks about that look she gave him earlier that evening—the softness that crossed her hazel eyes right before she kissed him—and he feels a strange mixture of excitement and panic burning in his gut.

The great xenon arc lamps boom to life around the stadium, illuminating the dirt strip and littered infield, and the stands slowly fill up around Austin with noisy townspeople hungry for blood and catharsis. The air has the snap of a chill in it and reeks of fuel oil and walker rot, and Austin feels weirdly *removed* from it all.

Clad in a hoodie, jeans, and motorcycle boots, his long hair pulled back in a leather stay, he fidgets on the cold hard seat, his muscles sore from the afternoon's adventures in the hinterlands. He can't get comfortable. He gazes out across the infield at the far side of the arena and sees the dark portals filling with clusters of upright corpses, each leashed to a handler by thick chains. The handlers start leading the biters out into the jarring light of the infield, the silver follow-spots making the dead faces look almost Kabuki-like, painted, like morbid clowns.

The crowd simmers with noise and catcalls and clapping. The phlegmy growling and moaning of the walkers as they take their places on the gravel warning track blends with the rising voices of the spectators to create an unearthly din. Austin stares at the spectacle. He can't get Lilly out of his head. The roar that's building all around him begins to fade . . . and fade . . . and fade away . . . until all he can hear in his head is Lilly's voice softly making a promise.

I'll show you some things . . . the only way we're going to survive . . . helping each other.

Something pokes Austin in the ribs, and yanks him back to reality.

He jerks around and realizes an old man has taken a seat right next to him.

Sporting a nicotine-yellowed beard, an ancient face as wrinkled as wadded parchment, and a tattered black overcoat and wide-brimmed hat, he's a feisty old Hasidic Jew who somehow managed to survive the streets of Atlanta after the Turn. His name is Saul, and he shows Austin his stained, rotting teeth as he says with a smile, "Gonna be a hot time in the old town tonight . . . am I right?"

"Yeah, absolutely." Austin feels dizzy, light-headed. "Can't wait."

Austin turns back to the gathering of dead on the track's periphery, and the sight of it makes him feel sick to his stomach. One of the biters, an obese male in bile-spattered painter's overalls, sprouts a knot of small intestines from a sucking wound in his porcine belly. Another one is missing the side of her face, her upper teeth gleaming in the spotlights as she moans and tugs on her chain. Austin is quickly losing his enthusiasm for the fights. Lilly has a point. He looks down at the sticky tread beneath the bench, the cigarette butts and puddles of soft drinks and stale beer. He closes his eyes and thinks of Lilly's sweet face, the spray of freckles across the bridge of her nose, the slender curve of her neck.

"Excuse me," he says, standing up and pushing himself past the old man.

"Better hurry back," the geezer mumbles, blinking fitfully. "Show's gonna start lickety-split!"

Austin is already halfway down the aisle. He doesn't look back.

On his way across town, moving past the shadows of storefronts and the dark, boarded buildings of the main drag, Austin sees a half-dozen people coming toward him on the opposite side of the street.

Pulling his hoodie tighter, thrusting his hands in his pockets, he keeps moving, his head down. Avoiding eye contact with the oncoming group, he recognizes the Governor, who walks out in front of three strangers like a tour guide, his chest all puffed up with pride. Bruce and Gabe bring up the rear with assault rifles cradled and ready.

"—Guard station about a mile away—completely abandoned," the Governor is saying to the strangers. Austin has never seen these people before. The Governor is treating them like VIPs. "All kinda supplies left inside," the Governor is saying. "Been making good use of it. Night-vision goggles, sniper rifles, ammo, you seen it in action. This place wouldn't be shit without it."

As Austin passes on the opposite sidewalk, he gets a better glimpse of the newcomers.

The two men and one woman look battle-scarred, somber, and maybe even a little nervous. Of the two men—each of whom is clad in riot gear—the older one looks tougher, meaner, more cunning. Sandy-haired, with a grizzle of a beard, the older man walks alongside the Governor, and Austin hears him say, "You sound lucky. Where is it you're taking us? We're walking toward the light. What is that? A baseball game?"

Before they vanish around the corner, Austin glances over his shoulder and gets a better look at the other two strangers. The younger man wears a riot helmet and looks maybe Asian, his age hard to tell at this distance and in this light.

The woman is far more interesting to look at. Her lean, sculpted face barely visible within the shadow of her hooded garment, she looks to Austin to be in her mid-thirties, African American, and exotically beautiful.

Just for an instant, Austin has a bad feeling about these people.

"Well, stranger," he hears the Governor saying, as they pass out of view, "it looks like we're not the only ones lucky around here. You showed up on the perfect night. There's a fight tonight. . . ."

The wind and the shadows drown the rest of the conversation as the group rounds the corner. Austin lets out a sigh, shakes off the inexplicable feeling of dread, and continues on toward Lilly's place.

A minute later, he finds himself standing in front of Lilly's building. The wind has picked up, and litter swirls across the threshold. Austin pauses, lowers his hood, brushes a strand of curly hair from his eyes, and silently rehearses what he wants to say.

He goes up to her door and takes a deep breath.

Lilly sits by her window in a cast-off armchair, a candle flickering on a side table next to her, a paperback cookbook open to the chapter on great Southern side dishes, when the sound of knocking interrupts her reverie.

She had been thinking about Josh Hamilton, and all the great meals he would have prepared had he survived, and the mixture of sorrow and regret drove away Lilly's hunger for something better than canned meat and instant rice. She had also been thinking a lot that night about the Governor.

Lately, Lilly's fear of the man has been morphing into something else. She can't get the memory out of her head of the Governor sentencing Josh's killer—the town butcher—to a horrible death at the hands of hungry walkers. With a combination of shame and satisfaction, Lilly keeps reliving the act of vengeance in her darkest thoughts. The man got what he deserved. And perhaps—just perhaps—the Governor is the only redress they have to these kinds of injustices. An eye for an eye.

"Who the hell . . . ?" she grumbles, levering herself out of her chair.

She crosses the room on bare feet, her ripped bell-bottom jeans dragging on the filthy hardwood. She wears an olive green thermal underwear top deftly ripped at the neck in a perfect V, a sports bra underneath, rawhide necklaces and beads around her slender neck. Her flaxen locks are pulled back in a loose Brigitte Bardot parfait on the top of her head. Her funky sense of fashion—first developed in the thrift shops and Salvation Army stores of Marietta—has died hard in the post-plague world. In a way, her sense of style is her armor, her defense mechanism.

She opens the door and looks out at Austin standing in the dark.

"Sorry to keep bothering you," he says sheepishly, one arm holding the other as though he's about to break apart at the seams. He has his hoodie drawn tight around his narrow face, and for the briefest instant he looks like a different person to Lilly. His eyes have lost the arrogant swagger that perpetually gleams there. His expression has softened, and the real person underneath the hard shell has emerged. He levels his gaze at her. "Are you in the middle of something?"

She proffers a smile. "Yeah, you caught me on the phone with my stockbroker, moving my millions around all my off-shore hedge funds."

"Should I come back?"

Lilly sighs. "It's called a joke, Austin. Remember humor?"

He nods sadly. "Oh . . . right." He manages a smile. "I'm a little slow tonight."

"What can I do for you?"

"Okay . . . um." He looks around the dark street. Practically the entire town has relocated to the arena for the night's festivities. Now the wind scrapes trash along the deserted sidewalks and rustles in the defunct power lines, making an eerie humming noise. Only a few of Martinez's men remain at the corners of the barricades, patrolling with their AR-15s and binoculars. Every now and then a searchlight sweeps its silver beam across the neighboring woods. "I was wondering, um, you know, if you're not too busy," he stammers, avoiding eye contact with her, "if you might be willing to, like, do a little training tonight?"

She looks askance at him. "Training?"

He clears his throat awkwardly, looks down. "What I mean is, you said you might consider showing me some things . . . giving me some pointers on how to . . . you know . . . deal with the biters, protect myself."

She looks at him, and she takes a deep breath. Then she smiles. "Give me a second—I'll get my guns."

They go down by the train station on the eastern edge of town, as far away from the lights and noise of the arena as they can get. By the time they get there, Lilly has turned the collar up on her denim jacket to ward off the gathering chill. The air smells of methane and swamp gas—a mélange of rot—and the odor braces them in the moonlit shadows of the train yard. Lilly runs Austin through a few scenarios, quizzes him, challenges him. Austin has his 9mm Glock with him, as well as a buck knife sheathed on his right thigh, tied with rawhide.

"C'mon, keep moving," she says to him at one point, as he slowly inches his way along the threshold of the woods, his pistol at his side, gripped in his right hand, his finger outside the trigger pad. They've been at it for almost an hour now and Austin is getting restless. The forest pulses and drones with night noises—crickets, rustling branches—and the constant threat of shadows moving behind the trees. Lilly walks alongside him with the quiet authority of a drill instructor. "You always want to keep moving, but not too fast, and not too slow . . . just keep your eyes open."

"Lemme guess—like *this*, right?" he says, a trace of exasperation in his voice. His gun has one of Lilly's silencers attached to the muzzle. His hoodie is pulled tight around his face. A high chain-link fence runs along the woods, once serving as security for the railroad depot. A cinder-strewn trail runs along a row of derelict railroad tracks overgrown with prairie grass.

"I told you to pull your hood down," she says. "You're cutting off your peripheral vision."

He does so, and keeps moving along the tree line. "How's this?"

"Better. You always want to know your surroundings. That's the key. It's more important than what weapon you're using, or how you're holding your gun or your ax or whatever. Always be aware of what's on either side of you. And what's behind you. So you can make a fast getaway if necessary."

"I get it."

"And never ever-ever-*ever* let yourself get surrounded. They're slow but they can horde in on you if there are enough of them."

"You said that already."

"The point is, you always know which way to run if you have to. Remember, you're always going to be faster than they are . . . but that doesn't mean you can't get penned in."

Austin nods and gazes intermittently over his shoulder, keeping track of the darkness on all sides of the trail. He turns and slowly backs along the trail for a moment, searching the shadows.

Lilly watches him. "Put your gun away for a second," she says.

"Grab your knife." She watches him switch weapons. "Okay, now let's say you're out of ammo, you're isolated, maybe lost."

He gives her a sidelong glance. "Lilly, we've been through this part . . . like twice already."

"That's good, you can count."

"C'mon—"

"And we're going to go through it again, a third time, so answer the question. How do you hold your knife?"

He sighs, backing along the trees, his boots crunching in the cinders. "You hold it blade-down, a tight grip on the hilt. . . . I'm not stupid, Lilly."

"I never said you were stupid. Tell me why you hold your knife like that."

He keeps backing along the edge of the woods, moving absently now, shaking his head. "You hold it like that because you got one chance to bring it down hard on their skull, and you want to do it decisively."

Lilly notices a stray timber—a piece of creosote-soaked railroad tie—lying beside the trail, about twenty feet away. She silently moves toward it. "Go on," she says. With one quick, discreet movement, she kicks the timber across Austin's path. "Why do you do it decisively?"

He lets out another weary sigh, blithely backing along. "You do it decisively because you got one chance to destroy the brain." He keeps backing slowly toward the timber, gripping the knife, unaware of the obstruction lying across his path. "I'm not an idiot, Lilly."

She grins. "Oh, no, you're a regular ninja, the way you were clearing the woods for us today at the crash site. You got it all going on."

"I'm not afraid, Lilly, I've told you a million times, I've been around—"

He trips on the railroad tie. "Ouch!—FUCK!" he blurts when he hits the ground, raising a puff of cinder dust.

At first Lilly lets out a blurt of laughter as Austin sits there for a second, looking defeated, embarrassed, humiliated. In the darkness, his eyes shimmer with emotion and his curls dangle in his face. He looks like a whipped dog. Lilly's laughter dies, and guilt twinges in her gut. "I'm sorry, sorry," she murmurs, kneeling by him. "I didn't mean to—" She strokes his shoulder. "I'm sorry, I'm being an asshole."

"It's okay," he says softly, taking deep breaths, looking down. "I deserve it."

"No. No." She sits down next to him. "You don't deserve any of this."

He looks at her. "Don't worry about it. You're just trying to help me and I appreciate it."

"I don't know *what* I'm doing half the time." She rubs her face. "All I know is . . . we gotta be ready. We gotta be . . . I hate to say it . . . but we gotta be as fucking bloodthirsty as the biters." She looks at him. "It's the only way we're gonna get through this."

His gaze locks on to hers. The ambient drone deepens around them, the roar of night sounds rising. In the distance, barely audible, come the hyena howls of the dirt track spectators cheering for blood.

At last Austin says, "You're starting to sound like the Governor."

Lilly gazes into the distance and says nothing, just listens to the sounds drifting on the breeze.

Austin licks his lips and looks at her. "Lilly, I've been thinking . . . what if there's no other side to get through to? What if this is it? What if this is all there is for us?"

Lilly thinks about it. "It doesn't matter. As long as we have each other . . . and we're willing to do what it takes . . . we'll survive."

The words hang in the night air for a moment. Almost imperceptibly they have come closer together, Lilly's hand lingering on his shoulder, his hand finding the small of her back.

Lilly realizes—all at once—that she might have originally been thinking about the whole community sticking together but now she's thinking only about Austin and her. She finds herself leaning in closer to him, and he responds by leaning toward her. She senses something unraveling, a letting go, and their lips coming together, and the kiss about to happen, when suddenly Lilly draws back. "What's this? Jesus, what's this?"

She feels something wet down around his waist, and she looks down.

The bottom hem of his sweatshirt is soaked in blood. Some of it drips in runnels onto the leafy ground, as black and shiny as axle oil. The knife blade sticks out of a tear in his denims where it sliced through the flesh of his hip in the fall. Austin puts his hand over it. "*Shit*," he utters through gritted teeth, the blood seeping through his fingers. "I thought I felt something bite me."

"C'mon!" Lilly springs to her feet and gives him a hand, carefully hoisting him to his feet. "We gotta get you to Dr. Stevens."

Her full name was Christina Meredith Haben, and she grew up in Kirkwood, Georgia, and she went away to college in the 1980s to study telecommunications at Oberlin. She had a child out of wedlock that she carried to term and then gave up for adoption on the day after 9/11. She had suffered through a series of romantic misadventures in her life, never found Mr. Right, never married, and always considered herself wed to her job as the senior segment producer at one of the biggest stations in the South. She had won three Emmys, a Clio, and a couple of Cable Ace awards—all of which made her justifiably proud—and she never felt her superiors respected her or provided her with the remuneration that she deserved.

But at the present moment—on this filthy tile floor, in the glare of fluorescent lights—all of Christina Haben's regrets, fears, frustrations, hopes, and desires are long gone, vanquished by death, her remains lying scattered across the gore-spattered parquet, while seventeen captive walkers tear into her organs and tissues.

The watery, orgiastic eating noises bounce around the cinderblock walls, as the dead feast on mostly unidentifiable body parts that used to comprise Christina Haben. Blood and spinal fluid and bile mingle in the corners of the room like multicolored cordials, sluicing through the seams in the tile, splashing the walls in blooms of deep scarlet, and drenching the frenzied biters. Selected for their physical integrity, earmarked for the gladiatorial arena, most of these creatures appear to be former adult males, some of them now crouching apelike in the bright light, gnawing on gristly nodules that used to belong to Christina Haben's lower skeleton.

Across the room, a pair of rectangular portal windows are embedded in a garage door that encloses the room. Within the frame of the window on the left, a gaunt, weathered, mustachioed face peers in at the action.

Standing in the silent corridor outside the enclosure, gazing intently through the window glass, the Governor registers little emotion on his face other than stern satisfaction with what he is seeing. His left ear is bandaged from a recent encounter with the newcomers, and the pain braces him. It makes him clench his fists. It courses down his marrow like electricity, girding him, crystallizing his mission. All his doubt, all his second-guessing—in fact, all his remaining humanity—are being pushed aside by the rage and the vengeance and the voice deep within him that serves as a compass. He knows now the only way to keep this tinderbox from going up in flames. He knows what he must do now in order to—

The shuffling of footsteps from the opposite end of the corridor interrupts his thoughts.

Lilly has her arm around Austin as she reaches the bottom of the stairs, turns a corner, and hurries down the main corridor that cuts through the foul-smelling, cinder-block catacombs of garages and service bays beneath the arena.

At first she doesn't see the dark figure standing alone at the far end of the corridor, gazing through the portal window. She's too preoccupied with Austin's injury, and the effort required just to keep pressure on the wound with her right hand as she shuffles along toward the infirmary.

"Look what the cat dragged in," the figure says as Lilly and Austin approach.

"Oh . . . hey," Lilly says awkwardly as she shuffles up with Austin dripping a few blood droplets on the floor, nothing life-threatening, but enough to be worrisome. "Gotta get this one to the doctor."

"Hope the other guy looks worse," the Governor jokes as Lilly and Austin pause outside the battered garage door.

Austin manages a smirk, his long, damp curls hanging in his face. "It's nothing . . . just a flesh wound . . . fell on my knife like an idiot." He holds his side. "Bleeding's basically stopped, totally okay now."

Very faintly the muffled noises of the feeding frenzy can be heard through the sealed glass. It sounds like an immense stomach growling. Lilly gets a glimpse through the nearest window of the gruesome orgy going on in the pen, and she glances at Austin, who sees it too. They say nothing. The sight of it barely registers to Lilly. Once upon a time she would have been repulsed. She glances back at the Governor. "They're getting their vitamins and minerals, I see."

"Nothing is wasted around here," the Governor says with a shrug, nodding toward the window. "Poor gal from the helicopter up and died on us . . . internal injuries from the crash, I guess . . . poor thing." He turns toward the glass and looks in. "She and the pilot are serving a larger purpose now."

Lilly sees the bandaged ear. She shoots another glance at Austin, who also stares at the Governor's blood-spotted bandage and the mangled ear underneath.

"It's none of my business," Austin says finally, pointing at the ear. "But are *you* okay? Looks like you got a nasty wound yourself."

"Them new people, came in tonight," the Governor murmurs, not taking his gaze off the window. "Turned out to be more of a liability than I first thought."

"Yeah, I saw you with them earlier." Austin perks up. "You were kinda taking them on a tour of the place, right? What happened?"

The Governor turns and looks directly at Lilly as though *she* asked the question. "I try to extend every courtesy to people, show them hospitality. We're all in the same boat these days, am I right?"

Lilly gives him a nod. "Absolutely, yeah. So what was *their* problem?"

"Turns out they were a scouting party from another settlement somewhere nearby, and their intentions were not exactly neighborly."

"What did they do?"

The Governor stares at her. "My guess is, they were going to try and raid us."

"*Raid* us?"

"It's happening all over the place now. Scouts slip in, secure a place, they take everything. Food. Water. The shirt off your back."

"So what happened?"

"Got into a major tussle with them. I wasn't gonna let them fuck with us. Not in a million years. One of them—the colored girl—tried to chew my ear off."

Lilly shares another tense glance with Austin. She looks at the Governor. "Jesus . . . what is going on? These people are fucking *savages*."

"We're all savages, Lilly-girl. We just gotta be the biggest savages on the block." He takes a deep breath. "Got into it pretty bad with the main guy. Fella fought back hard. Ended up cutting his hand off."

Lilly can't move. She feels contrary emotions flowing through her, pinching her insides, triggering sparks of trauma in the back of her mind—memories of a bullet destroying the back of Josh Hamilton's head. "*Jesus Christ*," she utters, almost to herself.

The Governor takes another deep breath, then lets out an exasperated sigh. "Stevens is keeping him alive. Maybe we'll learn something from him. Maybe not. We're safe now, though. And that's what counts."

Lilly nods and starts to say something when the Governor cuts her off.

"I am not going to let *anyone* fuck with our town," he says, making eye contact with both of them. A single pearl of blood tracks down his neck from the bandaged ear. He wipes it away and sighs again. "You people are my number-one priority, and that's all there is to it."

Lilly swallows hard. For the first time since she came to this place, she feels something other than contempt for this man . . . if not trust, then maybe a scintilla of sympathy. "Anyway," she says, "I better get Austin to the infirmary."

"Go on," the Governor says with a weary smile. "Get Gorgeous George here a Band-Aid."

Lilly puts her arm around Austin and helps the young man shuffle down the corridor. But before they turn the far corner, Lilly pauses and looks back at Philip. "Hey, Governor," she says softly. "Thank you."

On their way through the maze of corridors leading to the infirmary, they run into Bruce. The big African American is coming in the opposite direction, striding along with purpose, his jackboots echoing, his .45 bouncing on his big muscular thigh, his face burning with urgency. He glances up when he sees Lilly and Austin. "Hey, guys," he says in his tense baritone. "You two seen the Governor around here?"

Lilly tells him where the man is, and then adds, "Must be a full moon tonight, huh?"

Bruce looks at her. His expression taut, his eyes narrowing, he looks as though he's wondering just exactly how much she knows. "Whaddaya mean?"

She shrugs. "It just seems like things are getting crazier by the minute."

"How do you mean?"

"I don't know—these assholes trying to raid us—people acting crazy and stuff."

He looks relieved. "Yeah . . . right . . . it's some crazy shit. I gotta go."

He brushes past them and hurries on down the hall toward the walker pens.

Lilly furrows her brow, watching him.

Something isn't adding up.

NINE

When they get to the infirmary, Lilly and Austin find Dr. Stevens preoccupied, hunched over the partially nude form of an unconscious adult male sprawled on a gurney in the corner. The man—thirtyish, fit, sandy-haired, a grizzle of a beard—has a towel thrown across his privates, and a blood-sodden bandage on his right stump of a wrist. The doctor is carefully removing battered, blood-stippled body armor from the man's shoulders.

"Doc? Got another patient for ya," Lilly says as she crosses the room with Austin shuffling alongside her. The unconscious man on the gurney is unknown to Lilly, but Austin seems to recognize the sandy-haired man immediately and gives Lilly a poke in the ribs.

Austin whispers, "It's *him* . . . the dude the Governor tangled with."

"What now?" the doctor says, glancing up from the gurney and looking at them over the tops of his wire-rimmed glasses. He sees Austin's fingers stained in blood, pressing against his ribs. "Put him over there, I'll be right with you." The doctor glances over his shoulder. "Alice, give us a hand with Austin, will you?"

The nurse comes out of an adjacent storage room with an armful of cotton bandages, medical tape, and gauze. Dressed in her lab coat, hair pulled back from her youthful face, she looks frazzled. She makes eye contact with Lilly but says nothing as she hurries across the room.

Lilly helps Austin over to an examination table in the opposite corner.

"Who's the patient, Doc?" Lilly asks, playing dumb, gently helping Austin hop onto the edge of the table. Austin cringes slightly at a twinge of pain but seems more fascinated by the man lying out cold on the gurney across the room. Alice comes over and begins to gingerly unzip Austin's sweatshirt, inspecting the wound.

Across the room, the doctor carefully pulls a threadbare hospital smock over the grizzled man's lolling head, guiding his limp arms into sleeves. "I think I heard somebody say his name is Rick, but I'm not positive about that."

Lilly walks over to the gurney and gazes distastefully down at the unconscious man. "What I heard is that he attacked the Governor."

The doctor doesn't look at her, he simply purses his lips skeptically as he gently ties the back of the gown. "And where, pray tell, did you hear this?"

"From the man himself."

The doctor smiles ruefully. "That's what I thought." He shoots her a glance. "You think he's giving you the straight scoop, do you?"

"What do you mean?" Lilly comes closer. She looks down at the man on the gurney. In the blank-faced stupor of sleep, his mouth slightly parted and emitting shallow breaths, the sandy-haired man could be anybody. Butcher, baker, candlestick maker . . . serial killer, saint . . . *anybody.* "Why would the Governor lie about this? What good would it do?"

The doctor finishes tying off the back of the smock, and then gently pulls a sheet over the patient. "You seem to have forgotten, your fearless leader is a congenital liar." Stevens says this in a casual tone, as though imparting the time and temperature. He stands and faces Lilly. "It's old news, Lilly. Look up the word 'sociopath' and see if you don't find his picture."

"Look . . . I know he's no Mother Teresa . . . but what if he's exactly what we need now?"

The doctor looks at her. "What we need? Really? He's what we *need*?" Stevens shakes his head, turns away from her, and goes over to the pulse-ox monitor on a table next to the gurney. The machine is off, its screen blank. Hooked to a twelve-volt car battery, it looks as though it's fallen off the back of a truck. Stevens fiddles with it for a moment, readjusts the terminals. "You know what we *really* need? We need a monitor down here that actually works."

"We have to stick together," Lilly persists. "These people are a threat."

The doctor whirls angrily toward her. "When did you drink the Kool-Aid, Lilly? You once told me it's the *Governor* who's the biggest threat to our safety. You remember? What happened to the freedom fighter?"

Lilly narrows her eyes at him. The room goes still, Alice and Austin feeling the tension, their silence fueling the awkward edge to the atmosphere. Lilly says, "He could have killed us back then and he didn't. I just want to survive. What is this thing you have for him?"

"This *thing* I have is lying right here," the doctor says, indicating the unconscious man. "I believe the Governor attacked *him*."

"What are you talking about?"

The doctor nods. "Without provocation, I'm talking about. The Governor mutilated this man."

"That's ridiculous."

The doctor ponders her. His tone of voice changes, lowers, goes cold. "What happened to you?"

"Like I said, Doc, I'm just trying to survive."

"Use your head, Lilly. Why would these people traipse in here with bad intentions? They're just groping around like the rest of us."

He looks down at the man on the gurney. The man's eyes jerk slightly under his lids, a desperate fever dream unfolding. His breathing gets a little frenzied for a moment, then calms again.

The silence stretches. At last, Austin speaks up from the other side of the room. "Doc, there were two others—a younger guy and a woman with him. Do you know where they are? Where they went?"

Stevens just shakes his head, looking at the floor now. His voice comes out in barely a whisper. "I don't know." Then he looks up at Lilly. "But I'll tell you this much . . . I wouldn't want to be them right now."

A muffled voice can be heard coming from behind a sealed garage door at the end of a lonely corridor in the arena's subbasement. Hoarse with exhaustion, stretched thin with nervous tension, the voice is feminine, low, and indecipherable to the two men standing outside the door.

"She's been at it ever since I put her in there," Bruce says to the Governor, who stands facing the door with arms folded judiciously across his chest. "Talking to herself like that."

"Interesting," the Governor comments, his senses sharpened by the latent violence in the air. He can feel the rumble of generators in his bones. He can detect the odors of decay and plaster rotting.

"These people are fucking crazy," Bruce adds, shaking his glistening bald head, his hand instinctively resting on the grip of the .45 holstered on his hip.

"Yeah . . . crazy like foxes," the Governor murmurs. His ear throbs. His skin tingles with anticipation. *Control.* The refrain bubbles up from the voice that lives in the lowest compartment of his brain: *Women are meant to be controlled . . . managed . . . broken.*

For one fleeting instant, it feels to Philip Blake as though part of him is outside his body, watching all this transpire, fascinated by the voice within him that is second nature now, a second skin: *You have to find out what these people know, where they come from—what they have—and most importantly how dangerous they are.*

"That lady in there is tough as shit," Bruce says. "She ain't gonna give anything up."

"I know how to break her," the Governor mutters. "Leave it to me."

He breathes deeply, inhaling slowly, preparing himself. He senses danger here. These people could very easily hurt him—they could tear apart his community—and so he must call on that part of him that knows how to hurt *others*, knows how to break people, knows how to control women. He doesn't even blink.

He simply turns to Bruce and says, "Open it."

The garage door rolls up on rusty, shrieking casters, banging against the top rail. At the rear of the enclosure, the woman in the darkness jerks against her ropes with a start, her long dreadlocks matted to her face.

"I'm sorry," the Governor says to her. "Don't let me interrupt."

In the slice of light coming from the corridor, the woman's left eye shimmers through a gap in her braids, just that one eye, balefully taking in the visitors standing like giants in the doorway, silhouetted by the bare bulbs in cages along the hallway ceiling behind them.

The Governor takes a step closer. Bruce comes in behind him. "You seemed to be having a nice, spirited conversation with—I'm sorry, who exactly was it you were talking to? Actually—never mind—I don't even care. Let's get this under way."

The woman on the floor brings to mind an exotic animal leashed inside a pen—dark and lithe and supple, like a panther, even in her ratty work clothes—her slender neck strapped and roped to the back wall. Each arm is tied to an opposite corner of the chamber, and her espresso-colored skin gleams with perspiration, her Medusa braids shiny and flowing off her shoulders and back. She glares through her hair at the wiry man, who approaches her with menacing calm.

"Bruce, do me a favor." The Governor speaks with the absent, businesslike tone of a workman approaching a faulty pipe or a pothole to be filled. "Take her pants off and tie one leg to that wall over there."

Bruce moves in and does what he's told. The woman tenses as her pants are yanked down. Bruce does this with the brisk certainty of someone ripping a Band-Aid off a sore. The big man steps back, and then pulls a coil of rope off his belt. He starts hog-tying one leg.

"And tie her other leg to that wall over there," the Governor instructs.

The woman doesn't take her gaze off the Governor. She glowers through that hair, eyes so filled with hate they could spot-weld steel.

The Governor comes closer to her. He starts to unbuckle his belt. "Don't struggle too much just yet, girl." He undoes his belt and unsnaps his camo pants. "You're going to want to save your energy."

The girl on the floor glares with the intensity of a black hole swallowing all matter. Every particle in the room, every molecule, every atom, is being drawn toward the black void of her eyes. The Governor comes closer. He feeds off her hate like a lightning rod.

"After you're done there, Bruce . . . leave us to it," the Governor says, his gaze clamped down on the woman. "We need the privacy." He smiles at her. "And shut the door on the way out." His smile widens. "Tell me something, girl. How long do you think it would take for me to ruin your life—shatter your sense of security—really fuck you up?"

No answer comes from the woman, only that ancient, hunched-back gaze of an animal bristling right before a fight to the death.

"I think half an hour could probably do it." That smile. That heavy-lidded, serpentine stare. He stands only inches away from her. "But really, I plan on doing this every day as often as I can. . . ." His pants are down around his ankles now. Bruce moves off toward the door as the Governor steps out of his trousers. His spine tingles.

The outer door comes down as Bruce exits. The reverberation of the bang makes the woman jerk again, just slightly.

The Governor's voice fills the vacuum of space as the underwear comes off. "This is going to be fun."

Above ground. In the night air. In the stillness of the dark town. Late. Two figures walk side by side along the ramshackle storefronts.

"I can't wrap my head around all this shit," Austin Ballard is saying with his hands in his pockets as he strolls along the forlorn promenade. He shudders in the chill. His hood is drawn up and over his curls, the lingering dread of what he has just seen showing on his face in brief flashes as the intermittent light spills across their path.

"The feeding room?" Lilly ambles alongside him with her denim coat buttoned up to her neck. She holds herself, her arms around her midsection in some unconscious gesture of self-preservation.

"Yeah . . . that and the dude with his hand chopped off. What the fuck is going on, Lilly?"

She starts to answer when the distant pop of large-caliber gunfire echoes. The noise makes both of them jump. Martinez and his boys are still out there, burning the midnight oil, cleaning up any stray biters drawn to the wall by the earlier commotion of the racetrack arena.

"Business as usual," Lilly says, not really believing it. "You'll get used to it."

"Sometimes it seems like the biters are the least of our problems." Austin shivers. "You think these people really are planning a raid?"

"Who knows?"

"How many more of them do you think there are?"

She shrugs. She can't shake the woozy feeling in her gut that something dangerous and inexorable has already started. Like a foreboding black glacier moving undetectably beneath their feet, the course of events seems to be slipping now toward some undefined horizon. And for the first time since she stumbled upon this ragtag little community . . . Lilly Caul feels a bone-deep fear that she can't even identify. "I don't know," she says at last, "but I feel like we can kiss any restful night's sleep good-bye for a while."

"To be honest, I haven't slept that great since the Turn broke out." A twinge of pain from his injury makes him flinch, and he holds his side as he walks. "Matter of fact, I haven't slept the night through since the beginning."

"Now that you mention it, I haven't either."

They walk a little farther in silence . . . until Austin says, "Can I ask you something?"

"Go ahead."

"Are you really on board with the Governor now?"

Lilly has been asking herself the same thing. Was it a case of Stockholm syndrome—that weird psychological phenomenon where hostages start to feel empathy and positive feelings toward their captors? Or was she projecting all her rage and pent-up emotions through the man as though he were some kind of attack dog hard-wired to her id? All she knew was that she was scared. "I know he's a psycho," she says finally, measuring her words. "Believe me . . . if circumstances were different . . . I would cross the street and walk on the other side if I saw him coming toward me."

Austin looks unsatisfied, anxious, tongue-tied. "So you're saying . . . it's like . . . the whole . . . when-the-going-gets-tough thing? Or something like that?"

She looks at him. "What I'm saying is this. Knowing what's out there, we could be in serious danger again. Maybe the worst danger we've been in since the town was established." She thinks about it. "I guess I see the Governor as . . . I don't know . . . like fighting fire with fire?" Then she adds, a little softer, a little less sure of herself, "As long as he's on our side."

Another distant crackling volley of gunfire makes both of them twitch.

They come to the end of the main drag, where two streets intersect in the darkness with a petrified railroad crossing. In the dark of night, the broken-down street sign and shoulder-high weeds look like the end of the world. Lilly pauses, preparing to go her separate way to her apartment building to the north.

"Okay, well, anyway . . ." Austin looks as though he doesn't know what to do with his hands. "Here's to another sleepless night."

She gives him a weary grin. "Tell you what. Why don't you come over to my place and you can bore me some more with your tales of surfing off the coast of Panama City Beach. Hell, maybe you'll be boring enough to put me to sleep."

For a moment, Austin Ballard looks like a thorn has just been removed from his paw.

They settle down for the night in Lilly's makeshift living room amid the cardboard boxes and carpet remnants and useless things left behind by nameless former residents. Lilly makes them some instant coffee on a chafing dish, and they sit in the lantern light and just talk. They talk about their childhoods—how they share similar innocuous suburban backgrounds full of cul-de-sacs and Scout troops and weenie roasts—and then they have that patented post-Turn discussion of what they'll do if and when the cure comes and the Troubles go away. Austin says he'll probably look to move somewhere warm and find a good woman and settle down and build surfboards or something. Lilly tells him about her dreams of being a clothing designer, of going to New York—as though New York still exists—and making a name for herself. Lilly finds herself growing more and more fond of this shaggy, good-natured young man. She marvels that he is such a decent, gentle person underneath the swagger. She wonders if the playboy routine wasn't some kind of messed-up defense mechanism. Or maybe he's just dealing with the same thing every other survivor is dealing with right now—the thing nobody can put a name to but feels like some kind of virulent stress disorder. Regardless of her epiphanies about Austin, however, Lilly is glad for the company that night, and they talk into the wee hours.

At one point, very late that night, after a long moment of awkward silence, Lilly looks around her dark apartment, thinking, trying to remember where she put her little stash of hooch. "You know what," she says at last. "If memory serves, I think I have half a bottle of Southern Comfort hidden away for emergencies."

Austin gives her a loaded glance. "You sure you want to part with it?"

She shrugs, getting up off the couch and padding across the room to a stack of crates. "No time like the present," she mutters, rifling through the extra blankets, bottled water, ammunition, Band-Aids, and disinfectant. "Hello, gorgeous," she says finally, locating the beautifully etched bottle of tea-colored liquid.

She comes back and thumbs off the cap. "Here's to a good night's sleep," she toasts, and then knocks back a healthy swig, wiping her lips.

She sits down on the sofa next to him and hands the bottle over. Austin, who cringes again from the pain in his side, takes a pull off the bottle and then grimaces from the burn in his throat as well as the stitch in his rib cage. "Jesus, I'm such a goddamn pussy."

"What are you talking about? You're not a pussy. Young guy your age, going on runs . . . kicking ass outside the safe zone." She takes the bottle and slugs down another gulp. "You're gonna be fine."

He gives her a look. " 'Young guy'? What are you, a senior citizen? I'm almost twenty-three years old, Lilly." He grins. "Gimme that thing." He takes the bottle and swallows another gulp, shuddering at the burn. He coughs, and holds his side. "Fuck!"

She stifles a giggle. "You all right? You need some water? No?" She takes the bottle from him and takes another sip. "Truth is, I'm old enough to be your . . . *older sister*." She belches. Then she giggles, covering her mouth. "Jesus Christ, excuse me."

He laughs. The pain surges up his rib cage again and he flinches.

They drink and talk for a while, until Austin starts coughing again, holding his side.

"You okay?" She reaches over and moves a lock of his curly hair out of his eyes. "You want some Tylenol?"

"I'm fine!" he snaps at her. Then he lets out a pained sigh. "I'm sorry . . . thank you for the offer, but I'm good." He reaches up and touches her hand. "I'm sorry I'm being so . . . cranky. I feel like an idiot . . . like a fucking invalid. How could I be so fucking clumsy?"

She looks at him. "Would you shut up? You're not clumsy, and you're not an invalid."

He looks at her. "Thanks." He touches her hand. "I appreciate it."

For a moment, Lilly feels the darkness around her shifting and spinning. She feels a loosening in her midsection, a warmth flowing down through her from her tummy all the way to her toes. She wants to kiss him. She might as well face it. She wants to kiss him a lot. She wants to prove to him he's not a pussy . . . he's a good, strong, virile, decent man. But something holds her back. She's not good at this. She's no prude—she's had plenty of men—but she can't bring herself to do it. Instead she just looks at him, and the look on her face apparently sends a signal to him that something interesting is going on. His smile fades. He touches her face. She licks her lips, pondering the situation, wanting so badly to grab him and suck his face.

At last, breaking the tension, he says, "You gonna hog that bottle the rest of the night?"

She grins and hands it over, and he downs a huge series of gulps, polishing off a major portion of the remaining booze. This time, he doesn't cringe. He doesn't flinch. He just looks at her and says, "I think I should warn you about something." His big brown eyes fill with embarrassment, regret, and maybe even a little shame. "I don't have a condom."

It starts with drunken laughter. Lilly roars with belly-deep guffaws—she hasn't laughed this hard since the outbreak of the plague—and she doubles over with chortling, honking laughter until her sides ache and her eyes begin to glaze over with tears. Austin can't help joining in, and he laughs and laughs, until he realizes Lilly has grabbed him by the front of his hoodie, and she says something about not giving a flying fuck about condoms, and before they even know what's happening, she has yanked his face toward hers, and their lips have locked onto each other.

The liquor-fueled passion erupts. They wrap themselves around each other, and they start making out so vigorously they knock over the bottle and the lamp next to the couch and the stack of books that Lilly was meaning to read at some point. Austin slips off the edge of the sofa and slams onto the floor, and Lilly tackles him, sticking her tongue into his mouth. She tastes the sweet liquor on his breath and spicy musk of his scent and she burrows between his legs.

They bathe in the heat flowing off each other—the latent desire repressed for so many months—and they go at it for many minutes there on the floor. She feels Austin caressing the curve of her breasts under her top and the softness of her hips and the sweet spot between her legs, and she moistens and begins breathing hard and fast, flushed with excitement. At last she realizes that he's cringing from the pain in his side again, and she sees the bandage where his hoodie has been wrenched up toward his chest, and she pulls back. The sight of it breaks her heart—she feels responsible for it—and now she wants so badly to make it all better.

"C'mere," she says, taking his hand and lifting him back onto the couch. "Watch me," she whispers to him as he flops down on the sofa, out of breath. "Just watch."

She takes off her clothes, one piece at a time, not taking her eyes off him. He already has his hands on his belt, unbuckling it. She slips out of her top, gazing at him with twinkling eyes. She takes her time. She folds each article of clothing as it comes off— her jeans, her bra, her panties—transfixing him, holding him rapt, until she is standing completely nude in the slice of moonlight in front of him, her hair in her face now, her head spinning, tipsy from booze and desire. Goose bumps rash down her arms.

She goes to him without another word. Not taking her eyes off him, she sits on him. He lets out a breathy, lusty sigh as she guides him into her. The feeling is extraordinary. She sees artifacts of light and sparks in her vision as she rhythmically rocks up and down. He arches his back and thrusts up into her. He is no longer injured. He is no longer just a young dude trying to be cool.

Austin comes first, his orgasm shaking both of them. She shudders then, the tingling sensation starting at the tips of her toes, and then coursing up through her until it converges on her solar plexus and explodes. The orgasm rocks her, and nearly knocks her off him, but she holds on to his long, lustrous, curly hair, landing in a heap of sweaty satisfaction in his arms. They collapse onto each other, holding each other, letting the calm return like a tide rolling back in.

For the longest time, they lie there in each other's arms, listening to a silence broken only by the soft syncopated symphony of their breathing. Lilly pulls a blanket over herself and comes down hard to reality. A stabbing pain starts at her temples and travels down the bridge of her nose. What has she done? As the buzz fades, a vague sense of regret knots itself in her gut, and she gazes out the window. Finally, she starts to say, "Austin, listen—"

"No." He strokes her shoulder, and then begins to pull on his pants. "You don't have to say it."

"Say what?"

He shrugs. "I don't know . . . something about this being just one of those things . . . and we shouldn't make too much of it . . . and it's just the alcohol or whatever."

She smiles sadly. "I wasn't going to say that."

He looks at her and grins. "I just want to do the right thing by you, Lilly . . . I don't want to pressure you or anything."

She kisses him on the forehead.

And then they start cleaning up their mess—picking up the spilled contents of the side table, propping lamps back in place, stacking books, and putting clothes back on. Neither of them has much more to say, although both are dying to talk about it.

Sometime later, near dawn, Austin says, "You know . . . something's been bothering me about that feeding room down there in those garages underneath the track."

She looks at him, flopping back down on the couch, exhausted. "What's that?"

He swallows air. "I don't mean to be gross but it's bothering me."

"What."

He looks at her. "Okay . . . so . . . the Governor supposedly fed the dead pilot and the girl from the helicopter to those walkers. Right?"

Lilly nods, not wanting to think about it. "Yeah. I guess so. Alas."

He chews his lip. "Again, I don't mean to be disgusting but I just can't shake this feeling there was something missing."

"And that would be?"

He looks at her. "The heads. There were no heads. Where were the fucking heads?"

TEN

Bruce Allan Cooper stands outside the garage door in the sub-basement beneath the arena, a single tungsten bulb in a cage above him providing the only illumination flickering in the narrow corridor. He puts the sounds coming from behind the door out of his mind—how the hell does a man go at this for so long? The angry shrieks from the black girl have now deteriorated into garbled, choked, sobbing sounds.

Bruce has his big arms—as thick as stovepipes—crossed against his broad chest, and his mind keeps wandering to those pre-plague days when he ran the gas station with his dad. He would lose track of time back then as well—buried in a 427 Camaro with overhead shafts and hemispherical combustion chambers. Now he's lost track of time again. He thinks about his old girlfriend, Shauna, and how long they used to go at it—a memory that makes him happy in a vaguely melancholy way. But *this*. This is different.

He's been standing there so long his legs are starting to cramp, and he keeps shifting his weight from one leg to the other. He weighs over two hundred and fifty pounds and has the hard muscle of a stevedore, but this is ridiculous. He can only stand for so long.

For the last twenty minutes or so, Bruce has heard the low

mutterings of the Governor's voice egging on the woman, taunting her, needling at her. God only knows what he's doing to her now.

Silence crashes down.

Bruce puts his ear to the door: What the *fuck* is he doing to her?

In the dark holding cell, the Governor stands over the limp figure of the woman, buckling his pants, zipping up. The tethers on the woman's bleeding wrists are the only things holding her ravaged body off the floor. Her labored breathing fills the silence, her dreadlocks hanging across her battered face. Tears, snot, and blood mingle and drip off her swollen lips.

Catching his breath, the Governor feels good and spent and flushed with exertion as he gazes down at her. His hands are sore, his knuckles skinned from working her over, repeatedly catching his fists on her teeth. He got pretty good at strangling her to the point of putting her under, but always bringing her back at the last moment with a well-timed slap or gut-punch. He stayed away from her mouth as much as possible but lavished her other orifices with a great deal of attention. The engine inside him kept him going strong, kept him sharp and hard.

"Okay . . . I'll admit it," he says calmly to her. "I got a little carried away."

She huffs and sniffs and holds on to consciousness by a slender thread. She can't lift her head, but it's obvious she wants to do so. She really wants to say something to him. The floor beneath her is puddled with fluids and blood, her long braids dangling in the mess. Her spandex shirt is riddled with gouges, torn open at her breasts. Her nude lower half—still splayed apart by the rope tethers—shimmers with sweat and shows the darker welts and abrasions of the Governor's handiwork on her caramel-colored flesh.

The Governor stares at her. "But I don't regret a *thing*. I enjoyed every *minute* of it. What about you?" He waits to see if she says anything. She pants and heaves and lets out a garbled combination of cough, sob, and moan. He smiles. "No? I wouldn't think so."

He walks over to the door and bangs on it. Then he smoothes his long hair back. "We're through here!" he calls out to Bruce. "Let me out!"

The door squeals up on ancient rollers, letting in the harsh light of the corridor.

Bruce stands there as silent and stoic as a cigar store Indian. The Governor doesn't even make eye contact with the man. Turning back to the woman on the floor, the Governor cocks his head and studies her a moment. She's a tough one, no doubt about that. Bruce was right. There is no way in hell this bitch is going to talk. But now—*now*—the Governor notices something about her that gives him an unexpected shiver of pleasure. He has to look closely to see it—with all that hair hanging down, masking her features—but the noise it makes is very distinct. He notices it then and grins.

She's crying.

The Governor revels in it. "You go ahead and cry it out, honey. Just get it all out. You earned it. You don't have anything to be ashamed of. Cry your little head off." He turns to leave.

And then he pauses when he hears something else. He turns back to her, and cocks his head again. For the briefest instant, he thinks he hears her say something. He listens closely, and it comes out of her between huffs of agony.

"I'm—not—crying for *me*," she says to the floor, her head lolling heavily with pain. She has to suck in shallow breaths of air in order to get the words out. "I'm—crying—for you."

He stares at her.

She lifts her head enough to make eye contact through the curtain of wet braids. Her tawny brown face covered with mucus and blood, the tears tracking down her swollen cheeks, she stabs her gaze into him. And all the pain and despair and anguish and loss and hopelessness of this brutal plague world is displayed there for a moment, just for an instant—on her sculpted, desecrated face—until all of it is cauterized away in the space of a breath by the woman's pure white-hot hatred . . . and what is left is a mask of feral kill-instinct. "I think about all the things I'm going to do to you," she says very evenly, almost calmly, "and it makes me cry. It scares me."

The Governor smiles. "That's cute. Get some rest—as much as you can, at least. A guy's going to be in here later to clean you up, maybe give you some bandages. Maybe have a little fun himself. But mostly he'll be getting you ready for when I come back." He winks at her. "Just want to give you something to look forward to." He turns and gives her a wave over his shoulder. "Later."

He walks out.

The rolling door comes down with a metallic thud.

The sun comes up while the Governor is walking back to his place.

The air smells clean—rich earth and clover—the dark mood of the catacombs washing away in the golden light and breeze of a Georgia spring morning. The Governor sheds his hard demeanor along the way, and steps into the skin of the benevolent town leader. He sees a few early risers, and gives them neighborly waves, bidding them a good morning with the jovial smile of a town constable.

He walks along with a bounce in his step now, the master of his little fiefdom, thoughts of breaking women and controlling outsiders evaporating, stuffed back down into the lower compartments of his brain. The sounds of truck engines and nails going into new timber already fill the air—Martinez and his crew fortifying the new sections of the barricade.

Approaching his building, the Governor runs into a woman and her two children, the little boys scampering across the street.

The Governor chuckles at the kids, stepping out of their way. "Morning," he says to the mother with a nod.

Preoccupied with her brood, the woman—a matronly gal from Augusta—shouts at the boys, "Kids, please! I told you to stop running!" She turns to Philip and gives him a demure little smile. "Morning, Governor."

The man walks on, and he sees Bob hunched on the sidewalk near his steps.

"Bob, please," he says as he walks over to the ragged wreck of a human being hunkered down under an awning next to the Governor's entrance. "Get some food. I hate to see you wasting away like this. We got rid of the barter system, they'll just *give* you something."

Bob gurgles and lets out a belch. "Fine . . . okay . . . if it'll get 'Mother Hen' off my back."

"Thanks, Bob," the Governor says, heading for his foyer. "I worry about you."

Bob mumbles something that sounds like "Whatever . . ."

The Governor goes inside his building. A fly—a huge bluebottle—buzzes over the staircase. The hallways are as silent as empty crypts.

Inside his apartment, he finds his dead baby girl crouching on the floor of the living room, staring emptily down at the stained carpet, making little noises that sound almost like snores. The stench wafts around her. The Governor goes to her, filled with affection. "I know, I know," he says to her lovingly. "Sorry I was out so late . . . or early, depending on how you look at it."

She roars suddenly—a screechy growl that comes out of her like the squeal of a tortured cat—and she springs to her feet and lunges at him.

He slaps her—hard—backhanding her, sending her slamming against the wall. "Behave yourself, goddamnit!"

She staggers and gazes up at him through milk-glass eyes. An expression like fear flutters across her livid blue face, twitches at her lipless rictus of a mouth, and makes her look oddly sheepish and docile. The sight of it makes the Governor deflate.

"I'm sorry, honey." He wonders if she's hungry. "What's got you so riled lately?" He notices her bucket has overturned. "No food, huh?"

He goes over and picks up the bucket, shoving a severed foot back into it. "You need to be more careful. If you knock your bucket over, it'll roll outta your reach. I raised you better than this."

He looks inside the bucket. The contents have decomposed severely. The severed foot looks so bloated and livid it resembles a balloon. Furry with mold, radiating an indescribable stench that literally leeches tears from the eyes, the body parts stew in a thick, viscous substance with which pathologists are all too familiar: the yellow, bilelike goo that is essentially the signal that advanced decomposition has started—that all the maggots and blowflies have departed and left behind a mass of drying proteins.

"You don't want *that,* do you?" the Governor asks the dead girl, plucking the swollen, blackened foot distastefully from the bin. He holds it with thumb and index finger, forming a pincerlike tong, and tosses it to the creature. "Here . . . go ahead."

She gobbles the morsel on her hands and knees, her back arched with simian fervor. She seems to stiffen suddenly at the taste of it. *"PFUH!"* she grunts as she spits out the chewed particles.

The Governor just sadly shakes his head as he turns away and heads for the dining room, chastising her over his shoulder. *"See* . . . you knocked your bucket over and now your food has spoiled. That's what you get." He lowers his voice, adding under his breath, "Even *fresh,* I don't see how you eat that stuff . . . really."

He collapses into his Barcalounger, the chair creaking as it reclines. Eyelids heavy, joints aching, his genitals sore from all the exertion, he lies back and thinks about the time he actually tasted Penny's food.

It was late one night about three months ago, and the Governor was drunk, and trying to get the dead child to calm down. It happened almost spontaneously. He simply grabbed a piece of tissue—part of a human finger; he can't even remember its original owner—and popped it in his mouth. Contrary to all the jokes, it did not taste even *remotely* like chicken. It had a bitter, metallic, gamey taste—coppery like blood but with a mouth-feel similar to extremely tough, extremely granular stew meat—and he had immediately spit it out.

There is an axiom among gourmets that the food that is closest in genetic makeup to its consumer is the most delicious, the most succulent, the most satisfying. Hence the existence of exotic dishes among Eastern cultures such as trepanned chimpanzee brains and various sweetbreads. But Philip Blake knows this belief to be a lie—humans taste like shit. Perhaps if served raw with seasoning—human tartare, let's say—the tissue and organs might be tolerable, but the Governor has yet to be in the mood to experiment.

"I'd get you some more food, honey," he softly calls out now to the tiny cadaver in the other room, his body relaxing as he drifts off in his recliner to the soothing sounds of bubbles percolating in the shadows across the dining room. The soft hissing noises of aquariums are omnipresent in the apartment, like white noise, or static from a defunct television station. "But Daddy's tired today, needs some shut-eye . . . so you'll have to wait, honey . . . until I wake up."

He falls fast asleep to the drone of burbling water tanks and has no idea how long he's been out when the sound of knocking penetrates his slumber, and makes him sit up with a jerk.

At first he thinks it's Penny making noise in the other room but then he hears it again, harder this time, coming from the back door. "This better be good," he mumbles as he trudges across the apartment.

He opens the back door. "What?"

"Here's what you asked for," Gabe says, standing outside the storm door, holding a blood-speckled metal container. The thick-necked man looks grim and jumpy, uncertain of the prevailing mood, glancing over his shoulder. The ammo box he's holding, procured from the Guard station, has been serving them well as a makeshift bio-container. He looks at the Governor. "The two from the helicopter." He blinks. "Oh . . . and I put something else in there." Another blink. "Didn't know if you'd want to keep it. You can just get rid of it if you don't want it."

"Thanks," the Governor mumbles, taking the container from him. The metal is warm, and sticky from the blood. "Make sure I get some sleep, okay? Don't let anyone else up here."

"Okay, boss."

Gabe turns and descends the stairs quickly, happy to be rid of the package.

The Governor shuts the door, turns, and heads back to his dining room.

Penny lurches at him as he passes, stretching her chain, snuffling at him, reaching her spindly little dead arms for the goodies. She can smell the mortified flesh. Her eyes are big silver coins, locked onto the box.

"No!" the Governor scolds her. "This ain't for you, honey."

She snarls and sputters.

He pauses. "Well . . . okay . . . hold on." Thinking it over, he pries open the top and reaches into the container. Wet, fleshy objects are enclosed inside large Ziplocs. One of the objects—a severed human hand curled like a fleshy white crab frozen in death—brings a smirk to the Governor's lips. "I suppose you can have *this*." He pulls out the hand once belonging to the intruder named Rick, and tosses it to the girl. "That should keep you quiet long enough for me to doze off."

The dead child goes to town on the dripping appendage, making lusty slurping noises, cartilage crackling like chicken bones in her black little teeth. The Governor walks away, carrying the container around the corner and into the dining room.

In the dimly lit chamber, the Governor pulls the other two objects from their bags.

"You guys have got guests," he says to somebody in the shadows, kneeling down and pulling a severed female head from the plastic. The dripping cranium belongs to the woman named Christina. The expression fixed on its face—now as doughy, puffy, and soft as unbaked bread—is one of unadulterated horror. "New neighbors, actually."

He opens the top of an empty aquarium, which is pushed against the far wall, and drops the news producer's head into the fluid.

"You can keep each other company," he says softly, almost tenderly, as he drops the second cranium, the one belonging to the pilot, into the murky water of an adjacent aquarium. He lets out a sigh. The housefly buzzes somewhere nearby, invisible, incessant. "Gotta get off my feet now."

He returns to his chair and plops down with a weary, satisfied groan.

Twenty-six aquariums bubble softly across the room, each one containing at least two—some of them as many as three or four—reanimated human heads. The filters pop and gurgle, the top-lights humming softly. Each apparatus is connected to a master power strip, its anaconda-thick cord running across the baseboard and up the corner of the wall to a generator on the building's roof.

Encapsulated in their green vials of water, rows of livid, discolored faces twitch as though invisible puppet strings are tugging at them. Eyelids as thin and veined as ancient dried leaves blink at random intervals, the cataract-filmed eyeballs fixed on passing reflections and shadows refracted by the water. Mouths gape open and snap shut intermittently, like a perpetual Whac-A-Mole game spanning the length of the glass panels. The Governor has collected the heads over the course of twelve months with the care of a museum curator. The selection process is instinctive, the effect of all these dead faces quite mysterious.

He leans back in his chair, the springs squeaking as the footrest levitates. He lounges there, the heaviness of exhaustion pressing down on him as he stares at the totality of faces. He barely notices the new visage—the head of a woman once known for brilliant segment producing at WROM Fox Atlanta—now gasping and spewing bubbles from her insensate mouth. The Governor sees only the whole, the totality of all the heads—the larger impression of all these random victims.

The screams of that skinny black gal in the underground vault are still reverberating in the back of his mind. The part of him that is repulsed by such behavior still whines and objects in a deeper partition of his brain. *How could you do that to another human being?* He stares at the heads. *How could* anybody *do that to another person?* He gapes harder at those pale, bloated visages.

The nauseating horror of all those helpless faces—gasping for a deliverance that will never come—is so bleak, so grim, so perfectly timely, that it once again, somehow, penetrates Philip Blake's rumination and cleanses him. Somehow, it seals his wounded psyche with the caustic nature of reality. It inoculates him from doubt, from hesitation, from mercy, from empathy. This, after all, could be how we all end up: heads floating in tanks for eternity. Who's to say? This is the logical extreme, a constant reminder of what is waiting if one is weak for one millisecond. The heads represent the old Philip Blake. The weak one, the milquetoast . . . the eternal complainer. *How could you do this horrible thing? How could anyone do such a thing?* He stares. The heads gird him, empower him, energize him.

His voice drops a full octave and comes out in barely a murmur, "Fifty-seven channels and nothing on."

How?—

Could?—

You?—

He ignores the voice inside him and gets sleepy staring at those moving mouths, bubbling and twitching and screaming their silent watery screams.—*How?*— He sinks into the darkness of sleep. Staring. Absorbing. He begins to dream—the nightmare world seeping into the real world—and he is running through a dark forest. He tries to scream but his voice won't make a sound. He opens his mouth and lets out a silent cry. No sound comes out of him—only bubbles, which spew up into the darkness and vanish. The woods close in on him. He stands still, fists clenched, white-hot rage flowing out of him, pouring out of his mouth. Burn it all down. Burn it all. Destroy it. Destroy everything. Now. Now! *NOW!*

The Governor jerks awake sometime later. He can't tell at first if it's day or night. His legs have fallen asleep, and his neck aches from lolling at an odd angle on the armchair's headrest.

He gets up and goes into the bathroom and gets himself together. Standing at the mirror, he can hear the low snoring groans of his little girl chained to the wall in the other room. The windup alarm clock on the commode tells him it's almost noon.

He feels refreshed. Strong. He has a busy day ahead of him. He uses pumice soap to wash away the black lady's blood from under his fingernails. He cleans up, changes into fresh clothes, and has a quick breakfast—powdered milk for his Post Toasties, instant coffee heated on a Sterno can—and he gives Penny another fresh morsel from the steel container.

"Daddy's gotta go to work," he says cheerfully to the tiny corpse as he heads for the door. He grabs his gun and the walkie-talkie charging by the door. "I love you, honey. Stay outta trouble while I'm gone."

On his way out of the building, he gets Bruce on the two-way. "Meet me at the track," he says into the mouthpiece, "at the top of the service entrance." He thumbs the walkie off without waiting for an answer.

Ten minutes later, the Governor stands at the apex of a greasy staircase, which leads down into the cavernous, dark, underground maze. The sky over the racetrack looks threatening, the day turning dark and blustery.

"Hey, boss," the big bald man says as he lopes up from the parking lot.

"Where the hell have you been?"

"I came right over, I'm sorry."

The Governor glances over his shoulder, a few passersby catching his eye. He lowers his voice. "What's the situation with the woman?"

"Still talking to herself. Bitch is bug-fuck crazy, you ask me."

"Is she cleaned up?"

"Yeah, pretty much. Albert paid her a visit, looked her over, gave her some food . . . which she didn't touch. I guess she had some water, that's about it."

"She still awake?"

"Yep. Far as I can tell. I looked in on her about an hour ago."

"What was her . . . demeanor?"

"Her what?"

The Governor sighs. "Demeanor, Bruce. Her mood. What the fuck was she doing?"

Bruce shrugs. "I don't know, just staring at the floor, talking to the voices in her head." He licks his lips. "Can I ask you a question?"

"What?"

"Is she telling you anything? Giving you any information?"

The Governor runs his fingers through his long hair. "I'm not asking her anything . . . so there's nothing for her to tell me, is there?"

Bruce furrows his brow, looks at him. "You're not asking her anything?"

"That's right."

"Mind if I ask why?"

The Governor glances off into the distance at the plumes of exhaust puffing out of a bulldozer moving earth against the barricade, the workmen securing the last sections, the buzz of engines and hammers filling the air. "That's coming," he says, thinking about it. "Speaking of that . . . I want you to do something for me. Where's the young one being kept?"

"The Asian kid? He's on B-level, in the warehouse room next to the infirmary."

"I want you to move him to the stall right next to the woman's."

Bruce's brow furrows deeper, the folds and creases spreading up across his bald head. "Okay, but . . . you want him to hear what's going on in that room?"

The Governor gives him a cold smile. "You ain't so dumb, Brucey. I want that kid to hear everything I do to that bitch tonight. Then one of them'll talk. Trust me."

Bruce starts to say something else when the Governor turns and walks away without another word.

In the dusty stillness of her apartment, Lilly and Austin each manage to grab a few hours of restless sleep that morning, and when they finally awaken around one o'clock, the convivial atmosphere of the previous night has transformed into a series of awkward negotiations.

"Oh . . . sorry," Austin says when he pushes the door to the bathroom open and finds Lilly on the toilet in her Georgia Tech T-shirt with her panties around her ankles. Austin turns away immediately.

"No problem," she says. "Can you just give me a minute or two? Then it's all yours."

"Absolutely," he says, thrusting his hands in his pockets and pacing the hallway. Earlier that morning, he had dozed off on the floor of the living room, covered in a packing blanket from the truck, while Lilly slept in the bedroom on her broken-down futon. From the hallway, Austin calls to her, "You got time to give me another lesson today?"

"You're really a glutton for punishment," she says inside the bathroom, flushing the toilet and getting herself together at the mirror. She comes out and gives him a good-natured punch in the arm. "Whaddaya say we give that side a chance to heal up first?"

"What are you doing tonight?"

"Tonight?"

"I could make you dinner," he says, his eyes bright and guileless.

"Oh . . . um . . . wow." Lilly wants so badly to say the right thing. She doesn't want to lose Austin as a friend. Contrary emotions roil through her as she searches for the right words. She feels at once closer to him and strangely alienated from him. The fact is she can't ignore her feelings for the scruffy young man. He is good-hearted, ballsy, loyal, and—she might as well admit it to herself—an amazing lover. But what does she really know about him? What does *anybody* really know about *anybody* in this fucked-up new society? Is Austin one of those old-school men who think sex seals the deal? And for that matter, why can't Lilly just surrender to her tender feelings for him? What's wrong with her? The answer is elusive—fear, self-preservation, guilt, self-loathing—she can't quite put her finger on it. But she knows one thing for sure: She's not ready for a relationship. Not yet. And she can tell by the look in the young man's eyes right now, he's already halfway there. Lilly finally says, "Let me . . . think about it."

He looks crestfallen. "Lilly, it's just dinner . . . I'm not asking you to pick out furniture."

"I know . . . I just . . . I need to think about it."

"Did I do something wrong?"

"No. Not at all. It's just . . ." She pauses. "It's just that . . ."

He gives her a grin. "Please don't say 'it's not you, it's me.'"

She laughs. "Okay, I'm sorry. All I'm saying is . . . just give me some time."

He gives her a little bow. "You got it, m'lady . . . I will give you time and space." He goes out into the living room and gathers his gun, his coat, and his knapsack, and she follows him to the front door.

They go outside.

"Looks like a storm brewing," Austin says, glancing up at the dark cloud cover.

"That it does," she says, squinting up at the gray light, her headache returning.

He starts to descend the steps when Lilly reaches out and gently tugs on his arm. "Austin, wait." She searches for the proper words. "I'm sorry . . . I'm being ridiculous. I just want to take it slow. What happened last night . . ."

He takes her by the arms, looks deep into her eyes, and says, "What happened last night was beautiful. And I don't want to fuck it up." His face softens. He touches her hair, and plants a platonic little smack on the side of her face. He does this without guile, without premeditation. He simply kisses her temple with great tenderness. "You want to know the truth of the matter?" He looks into her eyes. "You're totally worth the wait."

And with that, he shuffles down the steps and plods off into the gathering storm.

The rain comes in waves that afternoon. Martinez has to suspend the last of the construction on the northeast corner of the rampart, and he and his crew relocate under the awnings along the derelict train station, where they stand around, smoking, watching the weather, and keeping an eye on the woods to the north.

Walker sightings have increased over the last few weeks out there in the thickets and swamps behind the palisades of white pines. Now the curtains of rain unfurl from the heavens, strafing the forest and washing out the meadows. The sky unleashes volleys of thunder, while veins of lightning crackle off the horizon. It's an angry storm, biblical in its volume and fury, and it makes Martinez nervous. He smokes his filterless cigarette with a vengeance—he rolls his own—sucking it down to the nub as he gazes at the storm. The last thing he needs right now is drama.

But that very moment it comes around the corner in the form of Lilly Caul. She hurries across the adjacent lot with her jean jacket held high over her head to ward off the rain. She approaches with an anxious expression on her face, hustling under the temporary shelter, out of breath, shaking the moisture from her jacket. "Jesus Christ, that came on quick," she pants at Martinez.

"Afternoon, Lilly," he says, stubbing out his cigarette on the pavement.

She catches her breath, looking around. "How's it going?"

"It's going."

"What's happening with the interlopers?"

"The who?"

"The strangers," she says, wiping her face. "The ones . . . came in the other night?"

"What about them?" Martinez gives her a shrug, glancing nervously over his shoulder at his men. "I don't have anything to do with that."

"Aren't they being questioned?" She looks at him. "What's wrong?"

He gives her a strange look. "You weren't even supposed to know about that."

"About what?"

Martinez grabs her, leads her away from the men, over to the far edge of the awning. The rain has settled into a steady downpour, and now the jet-engine hum of the storm masks their conversation. "Look," Martinez says to her, measuring his words, "this has nothing to do with us, and I would advise you to stay out of it."

"What the hell's the matter? I just asked a simple question."

"The Governor wants to keep it on the down-low, he doesn't want people to worry about it."

She sighs. "I'm not worried about it, I was just curious if he found anything out."

"I don't know, and I don't want to know."

"What the hell is the matter with you?"

Anger flares in Martinez's gut, traveling up his spine and drying his mouth. He wants to strangle this busybody. He grabs her by the shoulders. "Listen to me. I got enough problems, I have to deal with this shit, too!? Stay out of it. Just leave it alone!"

Lilly pulls away. "Whoa, Kemosabe! Back off." She rubs her shoulder. "I don't know who pissed in your cereal this morning but you can take it out on somebody else."

Martinez takes deep breaths, looking at her. "Okay, look. I'm sorry. But we're on a need-to-know basis here. The Governor knows what he's doing. If there's something we need to know, he'll tell us."

Lilly waves him off, turns, and walks away in the rain, mumbling, "Whatever."

Martinez watches her vanish in the mist. "He knows what he's doing," he says again, softly, under his breath, as though trying to convince himself.

ELEVEN

The rains continue, an unremitting deluge over south central Georgia for nearly three straight days. It's not until midweek that the weather moves on, leaving flash floods and downed power lines in its wake all the way to the Eastern seaboard. The land around Woodbury is left drenched and bound up in mud holes and washouts, the fallow fields to the south so sodden and inundated that the men on the wall notice clusters of walkers driven out of the woods, wallowing in the flooded areas like giant glistening leeches climbing on top of each other. It's like shooting fish in a fishbowl for the .50 caliber gunners on the northeast and southeast corners of the barricade. But other than these noisy, gruesome little displays of what the Governor has started calling "waste management," the town of Woodbury remains almost eerily calm that week. In fact, it's not until the *end* of that week that Lilly notices something amiss.

Up until then, she keeps a low profile, spending most of her days inside, honoring Martinez's directive to keep any news of hostile strangers in their midst to herself. She passes the time reading, watching the rain, thinking, and lying awake at night agonizing over what to do about Austin. On Thursday, he shows up at her door with a bottle of wine that he nicked from the old storage room at the courthouse, along with a bouquet of Russian sage he picked down by the post office, and she is so touched by the gesture that she lets him in but insists that he avoid the subject of their relationship or any mention of that night they went over the line. He seems happy to just spend time with her. They polish off the entire bottle of wine playing Pictionary—at one point, Austin makes her laugh so hard she does a spit-take when he reveals that his drawing, which appears to be a fried egg, is his brain on drugs—and he doesn't leave until the gray light of dawn is playing at the seams of the boarded windows. The next day, Lilly has to admit to herself that she likes this guy— regardless of the awkward circumstances—and maybe, just maybe, she would be open to the possibilities.

Then Sunday morning comes. Exactly one week after the fateful night, Lilly awakens with a start sometime before dawn. Something amorphous and unformed in the back of her mind has been bothering her, and for some reason—be it something she dreamed, or something that percolated down through her subconscious over the course of that week—it strikes her full force right then, *that morning*, like a ball peen hammer right between the eyes.

She jumps out of bed and hurries across the room, tearing open a three-ring binder lying on a makeshift desk of two cinder blocks and a plywood panel. Frantically she rifles through the pages.

"Oh no . . . no, no, no," she utters under her breath as she searches through her calendar. For almost a year, she has been religiously keeping track of the date. For many different reasons. She wants to know when the holidays fall, she wants to know when the seasons turn, and most of all, she simply wants to keep in touch with the old order, with civilized life, with normalcy. She wants to stay connected with the passage of time—although there are many in this dark era who have given up, who don't know their Arbor Day from their Yom Kippur.

She looks at the date and slams the calendar shut with a gasp.

"Oh shit . . . fuck . . . shit," she mutters to herself, backing away from the desk and whirling around as though the floor is about to drop away from under her feet. She paces a nervous circle in the dark bedroom for a moment, her thoughts swimming and crashing into each other. It *can't* be the twenty-third. It can't be. She's imagining this whole thing. She's just paranoid. But how can she be sure? How can anybody be sure of *anything* in this fucked-up Plague World? There must be something she can do to set her mind at ease—to prove to herself she's just being paranoid. All at once, she freezes and gets an idea.

"Okay!"

She snaps her fingers, and then rushes over to the old battered metal armoire in the corner where she keeps her coats and guns and ammo. She grabs her denim waistcoat, her twin Ruger .22s, the silencers, and a pair of twenty-five-round banana clips. She puts on her coat and then screws on the silencer attachments and shoves the guns behind her belt. She stows the clips in her pockets, takes a deep breath, raises her collar, and heads out the door.

Her breath shows in the predawn air as she emerges from her building. The town is still asleep, and the sun is just peeking out from behind the east woods—sending angelic rays of light across low-lying motes of fog—as Lilly crosses the street and pads quickly down the narrow sidewalk toward the old, derelict post office.

Just beyond the post office—on the other side of the south wall, outside the safe zone—stands a ransacked drugstore. Lilly needs to get into that store, just for a second, in order to find out if she's crazy or not. There's only one problem.

It's outside the wall, and with the passing of the rainstorm, walker activity has picked up out there.

In the dimly lit subbasement beneath the racetrack arena, Bruce hears the telltale banging on the inside of the last garage door on the left.

He braces himself for what he's about to see, leans down, unsnaps the lock, grasps the release, and yanks the door up on its congealed rollers. The door shrieks. The opening reveals a dark cement enclosure once used to store greasy chassis and spare parts—now a place of degradation and pain—and the Governor standing in the gloom, breathless from all the hard work.

"That's entertainment," he mutters, his face shiny with sweat, the dark wet spots under his armpits and the blood on his hands worse than they were after the last session two days ago. He worked on the woman all night—the third round of torture this week—and now the fatigue and the toll it's taking on the man show in his sunken gaze.

For a brief instant, Bruce glimpses the ragged figure on the floor behind the Governor. Her torso hangs inches above the floor, the ropes barely keeping her aloft, her braids dangling, fluids dripping off her swollen face. Her narrow shoulders heave rhythmically, lungs gasping for air, her nude lower half crumpled like a broken doll. She is barely alive—at least at first glance—although on closer inspection, one might note a furnace burning behind her hemorrhaged eyes, a nuclear reactor of rage keeping her awake, keeping her clinging to a thin hope of vengeance.

"Close it," the Governor says, grabbing a towel draped over Bruce's shoulder.

Bruce obliges, slamming the rolling door to the deck with a metallic clang.

The Governor towels off his face. "She ain't ever gonna talk. How many times we been at it now—three, four—I lost count." He tosses the towel. "What about the kid? He break yet?"

Bruce shakes his head. "Gabe says he's been hearing everything through the wall, says he's been blubbering like a baby, day in and day out, and hasn't let up since you started in on her."

The Governor sniffs, stretching his overworked neck muscles, cracking his bloody knuckles. "But he didn't give anything up, did he?"

Bruce shrugs. "According to Gabe, he just bawled and bawled and that's about it. Wouldn't talk."

"That tears it." The Governor takes deep breaths, thinking, turning things over in his mind. "These people are tighter than I thought, tough fucking nuts to crack."

Bruce considers it. "Can I make a suggestion?"

"What's that?"

Bruce shrugs again. "In the joint, they break people in solitary."

The Governor looks at him. "So?"

"So what I'm thinking, we just keep 'em locked up, separated, you know, like solitary fucking confinement. Might be the easiest way to do it."

"This ain't no prison, Bruce, I got a town to—" The Governor blinks, cocking his head at a sudden revelation. "Wait a minute."

Bruce looks at him. "What is it, boss?"

"Wait . . . hold on a second."

"What?"

The Governor stares at the big black man. "Didn't Gabe say those riot suits they came dressed in was the kind of shit they use in prisons?"

Bruce silently nods, looking around the corridor, thinking about it.

The Governor starts toward the stairs, muttering as he goes. "Now that I think of it, that Rick dude was wearing a prison jumpsuit under his gear."

Bruce hurries after him. "Where you going, boss?"

The Governor is already climbing the steps, calling over his shoulder. "Clean that bitch up . . . and then get Gabe . . . and meet me at the infirmary. I think I got a better way to do this!"

Lilly pauses next to the wall, heart racing, the sun now fully risen, the early morning rays of light hammering down on the back of her neck. Fifty yards away, one of Martinez's men—his husky form silhouetted against the dawning sky—strolls along a makeshift catwalk.

Lilly waits until the guard passes behind a vent stack, and then makes her move.

She quickly scuttles up and over the wall, landing hard on a parkway of gravel on the other side. The impact of her boots on the rocks makes a loud crunch, and she crouches down for a moment—her pulse quickening—waiting to see whether or not the guard notices her.

After a moment of breathless silence, she silently duck walks across the gravel road and slips behind a burned-out building. She checks her gun, jacking the slide. She keeps it at her side as she moves on, plodding down a side road strewn with wreckage and heaps of decomposing, headless walkers. The stench is extraordinary.

The cold wind blows the smell around her like a net as she passes the post office—staying low, creeping silently past old torn posters of happy postmen handing colorful packages to children, and graffiti-splashed placards of smiling retirees collecting stamps. She hears shuffling noises behind her—leaves on wind, maybe—and doesn't look back.

She keeps heading south.

The bombed-out remains of Gold Star Sundries and Drugs sits at the end of the road, a tiny box of crumbling red brick with a bullet-riddled, boarded front window. The old R/X sign—a big mortar and pestle—hangs by frayed cables, twisting in the breeze. She hurries up to the entrance. The door is jammed shut, and she has to plow through it with one shoulder.

She bursts into the store's dark interior, the glass from the broken door raining down on the floor. Her heart thrums in her chest as she surveys the disaster area that once offered cough medicine, denture creams, and cotton balls to farm wives and sniffling locals.

The aisles have been completely ransacked—the shelves scoured clean, only a few empty cartons and puddles of unidentified fluids lying here and there. She weaves through the detritus and heads toward the pharmacy counter in the shadowy rear aisles.

A noise gets her attention to her immediate right—a hiss of air, a bottle overturning—and her gun immediately goes up. She sees a blur of yellow fur. She lets up on the hammer when she realizes it's a feral cat—the ragged creature darting between fallen displays of mouthwash and teeth whitener with a mouse in its jaws.

Lilly lets out a thin breath of relief, turns back toward the pharmacy counter . . . and she suddenly screams.

The old pharmacist lumbers out of the shadows next to her with reaching arms and blackened, gnarled hands curling into claws—his gigantic rotting mouth working like a wood chipper. His long, jowly face is the consistency of bread pudding, filmed in mildew the color of old rust, his milk-pod eyes as huge as hard-boiled eggs. He wears a white coat desecrated by blood and bile.

Lilly jerks backward, raising the gun and knocking over a display of dog food.

She falls on her ass, cans clattering to the floor all around her, the air knocked out of her lungs, and she starts firing. The clap of silenced gunfire sparks and flares and reverberates through the tight space, half the rounds going high, shattering fluorescent tubes. But half the slugs go into the balding head of the pharmacist.

Cranial bones shatter and fly, blood and tissue spattering the empty shelves. The giant biter falls like an old oak, landing directly on Lilly. She screams and writhes beneath the reeking dead weight of the corpse, the stench unbearable. Finally she rolls free.

For several frenzied, silent moments, she crouches there on the floor next to the fallen biter. She swallows back the repulsion, the urge to flee this hideous dark store, the voice in the back of her head telling her she's crazy, she's insane to be risking her life for this ridiculous little bit of personal reconnaissance.

She drives the thoughts away and manages to get her bearings back.

The pharmacy counter lies in darkness twenty feet away. Lilly cautiously negotiates the rear aisle, her eyes adjusting slowly to the gloom. She sees the counter, swamped with sticky, drying fluids, wadded documents, and mold so thick it looks like a coat of fur over everything.

She squeezes through the pass gate, and starts rifling through the meager contents of the pharmacy shelves. Nothing but useless drugs and tinctures remain unscathed by the looters—acne medicines, hemorrhoid treatments, and cryptically named medicines nobody bothered to identify—all the valuable central nervous system drugs and opiates and painkillers long gone. But she doesn't care.

She's not looking to get high or knock herself out or block pain.

After a seemingly endless, agonizing search, she finally finds what she's looking for on the floor under the computer terminal, in a pile of discarded boxes and plastic pill vials. There's only one box left, and it looks as though someone stepped on it at some point. Smashed flat, its top broken open, the container still holds its contents in a sealed, intact blister pack.

Lilly stuffs it into her pocket, rises to her feet, and gets the hell out of there.

Fifteen minutes later, she has returned to her apartment with the kit.

Five minutes after that, she waits to see if her life is about to change.

———

"He was a good man," a muffled voice is saying on the other side of the closed infirmary door—unmistakable in its sardonic tone, its faint accent, its weary sarcasm—clearly the voice of the estimable Dr. Stevens. *"Emphasis on was."*

The Governor stands outside the door to the infirmary with Gabe and Bruce. The three men pause before going in, listening to the low murmuring on the other side of the door with great interest.

"We found this town pretty early on," the doctor's voice continues. *"The National Guard station, the narrow alleys—we decided we could defend this place. So we staked our claim."* There's a brief beat of silence, the faint sound of water running. *"Started out he was tough,"* the voice goes on, *"but he got the job done."*

The Governor balls his fists as he listens, the anger stiffening his spine, mixing with the sheer adrenaline of discovery.

"Philip emerged as the leader of our group very quickly," the voice is saying. *"He did what had to be done, what needed to be done to keep people safe. But after a while—"*

The rage jolts up the Governor's spinal cord, tingles in his fingers, fills his mouth with bitter, flinty bile. He leans toward the door to listen more closely.

"—it was clear to some of us that he was doing this more out of enjoyment than the need to protect us. It was clear he was little more than an evil bastard. I can't even talk about his daughter."

The Governor has heard enough. He reaches for the doorknob but something stops him.

On the other side of the door, a deeper, huskier voice with a thicker working-class Kentucky accent is speaking: *"Why do you allow it to go on? The fights? Feeding the zombies?"*

The doctor's voice: *"What do you think he'd do to anyone who opposed him? I hate the son of a bitch but I can't do anything. Whatever else he does . . . he keeps these people safe. That's enough for most people."*

The Governor swallows back the urge to break the door down with a battering ram and kill them all.

The doctor: *"As long as there's a wall between them and the biters they're not too concerned with who's with them on their side of the wall."*

Philip Blake kicks the door in, the lock-bolt snapping off and flying across the room, skipping across the tile floor like a spent shell casing. The door bangs against the adjacent wall, making everybody in the room jump.

"Well said, Doctor," the Governor says as he calmly saunters into the infirmary, followed closely by his associates. "Well said."

If it's possible for an entire room to bristle with static electricity, that's exactly what happens in that ensuing instant in which the eyes of everyone—Stevens, the stranger sitting on the bed, Alice over by the sink—snap toward the thin man strolling into the infirmary with hands on his hips like he owns the place. The coolly amused expression on the Governor's face is belied by the sullen, baleful expressions on the faces of Bruce and Gabe, who enter like attack dogs on the heels of their master.

"What do *you* want?" the doctor finally manages in a taut tone.

"You said to come in today, Doc," the Governor replies with the casual congeniality of just another patient arriving for a checkup. "You wanted to change my bandage?" He points helpfully at his wounded ear. "Remember?" The Governor then shoots a glance at the intruder, now frozen in a sitting position on the bed across the room. "Bruce, point a gun at Lefty over there."

The big black man calmly draws a silver-plated .45 and trains it on the man named Rick.

"Sit down, Philip," the doctor says. "I'll make it quick." His voice dips into a lower register, dripping with contempt. "I'm sure you have more important things to do."

The Governor flops down on an examination gurney flooded with halogen light.

The man named Rick cannot take his eyes off the Governor,

and the Governor returns his gaze—two natural predators in the wild, backs arched, sizing each other up—and the Governor smiles. "You're looking well, stranger. Healing up nicely?" He waits for the stranger to reply but the man does not say a word.

"Well," the Governor mutters to himself, as Stevens moves in and bends down to take a closer look at the bandaged ear, "as nice as you can."

At last, the sandy-haired man across the room manages a retort: "So . . . when do you start torturing me?"

"You? Never." The Governor's eyes positively twinkle with derision. "I pegged you from the start, you're not going to say shit. You've got family back wherever you're from. You're not about to sell them out."

Stevens carefully folds back the bandage and shines a penlight on the mangled ear.

"No, I was going to torture the others in front of you," the Governor explains. "I didn't think you'd crack but I was pretty sure one of them would." Now he winks. "But plans changed."

The man on the bed glances at the muzzle of Bruce's long-barrel Magnum, and then says, "To what?"

"You're going into the arena," the Governor tells him cheerfully. "I want to at least get some entertainment out of you." He looks away with a faint grin. "I'm currently planning on raping the dogshit out of that bitch who took off my ear until she finds a way to kill herself."

The room—almost as a whole organism—absorbs this in thunderstruck silence. The strange tableau stretches, the only sound being Stevens tearing a piece off a roll of medical tape, and the rustle of gauze.

"And the young Asian boy with the overacting tear ducts?" the Governor adds, his smile spreading practically from ear to injured ear. "I let him go."

A moment of stunned silence. The man named Rick, taken aback, stares at him. "You let him *go*? Why?"

By this point, Stevens has finished examining and replacing the old bandage on the Governor's ear.

The doctor steps back as the Governor lets out a satisfied breath, slaps his thighs jovially, and rises off the table. "Why?" He grins at the stranger. "Because he sang like a parakeet. Told me exactly what I needed to hear."

The Governor nods at his men, and then heads for the door with a smile. "I know everything I need to know about your prison," he murmurs on the way out. "And if he's stupid enough to go there, he'll lead us right to it."

The three men slip out of the room, slamming the broken door behind them.

In their slipstream, the infirmary festers in horrible silence.

At first light that next day, the .50 caliber gunner on the northeast corner of the barricade starts shooting at a cluster of walkers skulking around the edge of the woods, sending fountains of brain matter and dead tissue up into the crisp morning air.

The noise wakes up the town. The bark of high-caliber clapping reaches a narrow alley behind the apartment blocks at the end of Main Street, echoing down the passageway, penetrating the inebriated slumber of a filthy, tattered figure huddling under a fire escape platform.

Bob stirs, coughs, and tries to figure out where he is and what year it is and what the fuck his name is. Rainwater still rings off the gutters and downspouts all around him. His pants are wet. Floundering in his alcohol-fueled stupor, soaked to the bone from the rain, he rubs his grizzled face and notices tears on his sunken, deeply lined cheeks.

Was he dreaming of Megan again? Was he having another nightmare where he can't reach her as she hangs by the neck from her suicide perch? He can't even remember. He feels like crawling into the garbage Dumpster next to him and dying but instead he struggles to his feet and staggers down the alley toward daylight.

He decides to have his breakfast—the last few fingers of cheap whiskey in the pint bottle in his jacket pocket—on the sidewalk, against the brick facade of the Governor's building, Bob's lucky spot, his home away from home. He collapses against the wall, digs in his pocket with greasy blackened fingers, and pulls out his "medicine."

He takes a healthy swig, finishing up the last of the bottle, and then sinks against the wall. He can't cry anymore. His grief and despair have burned out his tear ducts. Instead, he just lets out a phlegm-clogged sigh of noxious breath and lies back and dozes for an indeterminate amount of time before hearing the voice.

"Bob!"

He blinks and blinks, and through his rheumy eyes he sees the blurry figure of a young woman approaching from across the street. At first, he can't even remember her name, but the look on her face as she draws near—frustration, anxiety, even a trace of anger—reaches down into some inner chamber of Bob's soul and kindles memories.

"Howdy, Lilly," he says, lifting the empty bottle to his lips. Good to the last drop. He wipes his mouth and tries to focus on her. "Top of the morning."

She comes over, kneels, and gently snatches the bottle away from him. "Bob, what are you doing? Trying to kill yourself in slow motion?"

He breathes in, and then exhales a sigh so foul and flammable it could light a barbecue. "I've been . . . weighing my options."

"Don't say that." She looks into his eyes. "It's not funny."

"Ain't trying to be funny."

"Okay . . . whatever." She wipes her mouth, glances over her shoulder, nervously scanning the street. "You haven't seen Austin, have you?"

"Who?"

She looks at him. "Austin Ballard? You know. Young guy, kinda scruffy."

"The kid with the hair?"

"That's him."

Bob lets out another chorus of hacking, wheezing coughs. He doubles over for a moment, trying to cough it out. He blinks it back. "No, ma'am. Ain't seen that rascal in days." Finally he gets his coughing under control and then fixes his yellow eyes on her. "You're sweet on him, ain't ya?"

Lilly gazes out at the far reaches of the town, chewing a finger-nail. "Huh?"

Bob manages a cockeyed grin. "You two an item?"

She just shakes her head, letting out a weary chuckle. "An item? I wouldn't say that. Not exactly."

Bob keeps looking at her. "Saw you two heading into your place together last week." Another crooked grin. "I may be a juicer but I ain't blind. The way you two was walking, talking to each other."

She rubs her eyes. "Bob, it's complicated . . . but right now I have to find him." She looks at him. "Think hard. When was the last time you saw him?"

"Lilly, I ain't too good with particulars. My memory ain't ex-actly—"

She grabs him, shakes him. "Bob, wake up! This is important! I have to find Austin—it's *super* important! Do you understand?" She gives him a little slap. "Now concentrate, try to get those booze-addled brain cells working and *THINK*!"

Bob shudders in her grip, his droopy eyes wide and wet. His liver-colored lips tremble, and he tries to form the words but the tears are coming. "I-I don't—It's been—I ain't real clear on—"

"Bob, I'm sorry." All the anger, urgency, and frustration drain out of her face, and she releases her hold on him, and her expres-sion softens. "I'm so sorry." She puts an arm around him. "I'm a little—I'm not—I'm dealing with a bit of a—"

"It's okay, darlin'," he says and hangs his head. "I ain't been myself lately, ain't exactly on top of the world right now."

She looks at him. "You're still hurting, aren't you? Hurting bad."

He sighs again. He feels almost normal when he's around this woman.

For a moment, he considers telling her about his Megan dreams. He considers telling her about the enormous black hole in his heart that is sucking every last ounce of his life into it. He considers explaining to Lilly how he was never really that good at grief. He lost dozens of close friends in the Middle East. As an army medic, he saw so much death and heartache that he thought it would rip his insides out. But none of it even compared to losing Megan the way he lost her. He considers all this over the course of an agonizing instant and then looks up at Lilly and simply murmurs, "Yeah, honey, I'm still hurting."

They sit there in the overcast morning light for a long while, saying nothing, both of them drowning in their thoughts, both of them ruminating over dark and uncertain futures, when finally Lilly looks at him. "Bob, is there anything I can get you?"

He lifts his empty bottle, and taps it. "Got another one of these stashed back at the fire escape. That's all I need."

She sighs.

Another long moment of silence passes. Bob feels himself drifting again, his eyelids getting heavy. He looks up at her. "You seem a little outta sorts, darlin'," he says. "Is there anything I can get *you*?"

Yeah, she thinks to herself, the weight of the world pressing down on her. *How about a gun and two bullets so Austin and I can finish each other off?*

TWELVE

Martinez paces along the catwalk that crowns a semitrailer parked along the north corner of the wall when he hears somebody calling out to him.

"Hey, Martinez!" the voice cuts through the wind and distant thunder scraping the sky to the east. Martinez looks down and sees Rudy, the bearded former tuck-pointer from Savannah, coming across the construction site. Rudy is built like a redwood and keeps his dark hair pomaded back in a Dracula widow's peak.

"What do you want?" Martinez calls down. Dressed in his trademark sleeveless shirt, bandanna, and fingerless racing gloves, the lantern-jawed Martinez carries a Kalashnikov with a banana clip and a sawed-off stock. From the rusty steel roof of the Kenworth, he can see for over a mile in any direction, and he can easily pick off half a dozen undead in one controlled burst if necessary. Nobody fucks with Martinez—neither man nor biter—and this unexpected visitor is already getting on his nerves. "My shift ain't over for another couple hours."

Squinting up into the sun, Rudy delivers a stoic shrug. "Well, I'm here to relieve you so I guess you're getting an early break. Boss man wants to see you."

"Shit," Martinez mutters under his breath, in no mood to go to the principal's office this morning. He starts climbing down the side of the cab, grumbling softly, "What the hell does he want?"

Martinez hops off the running board.

Rudy gives him a look. "Like he's gonna tell *me*."

"Stay alert up there," Martinez orders, gazing out through the narrow gap in front of the truck, surveying the flooded fields to the north. The farmland is deserted but Martinez has a bad feeling about what lies out there behind the distant, dark pillars of pine. "It's been quiet so far today . . . but that usually never lasts."

Rudy gives him a nod and starts climbing up the side of the cab.

Martinez strides away as Rudy's voice trails after him. "You going to watch the fight today?"

"Let's see what the Governor wants to see me about first," Martinez mumbles, passing out of Rudy's earshot. "One fucking thing at a time."

It takes Martinez precisely eleven minutes to cross town on foot, pausing a couple of times to kick the asses of workmen loitering in the nooks and crannies of merchant's row, some of them already passing flasks at two o'clock in the afternoon. By the time Martinez reaches the Governor's building, the sun has broken through the clouds and turned the day as humid as a steam room.

Sweat breaks out on the big Latino as he slips around back and climbs the wooden decking to the Governor's back door. He knocks hard on the jamb.

"Get your ass in here," the Governor greets him, pushing open the storm door.

Martinez feels the flesh on his neck crawling as he enters the sour atmosphere of the kitchen. The place smells of grease and black mold, and something putrid underneath. A pine-scented car deodorizer hangs over the sink. "What's going on, boss?" Martinez says, putting his assault rifle down, leaning it against a lower cabinet.

"Got a job for you," the Governor says, running water into a drinking glass. This apartment is one of the few left in Woodbury with working plumbing, although the tap often spews brown, rusty well water. The Governor guzzles the water. He wears a shopworn wifebeater over his sinewy upper body, his camo pants tucked into his combat boots. The bandage on his ear has turned orange from the blood and Betadine. "You want a glass of water?"

"Sure." Martinez leans against the counter, crossing his muscular arms across his chest to quell the beating of his heart. He already doesn't like where this is going. In the past, people sent on the Governor's "special assignments" have ended up in pieces. "Thanks."

The Governor fills another glass and hands it over. "I want you to go see this Rick character, and I want you to let slip how disgruntled you are with the way things are going around here."

"Pardon?"

The Governor looks the man in the eyes. "You're fed up, you understand?"

"Not really."

The Governor rolls his eyes. "Try to keep up with me, Martinez. I want you to get to know this prick. Gain his confidence. Tell him how dissatisfied you are with the way the town's being run. I want to take advantage of what's going on in that fucking infirmary."

"What's going on in the infirmary?"

"This prick is wooing Stevens and his little cocker spaniel of a nurse. These strangers seem like decent people to them, they seem nice—but don't you fucking believe it. They bit my fucking ear off!"

"Right."

"They fucking attacked me, Martinez. They want our town, they want our resources . . . and they'll do anything to fucking get them. Trust me on this. They will do anything. And I will do anything to prevent that from happening."

Martinez drinks his water, nodding, thinking it over. "I get it, boss."

The Governor goes over to the back window and peers out at the muggy afternoon. The sky is the color of spoiled milk. No birds are evident anywhere. No birds, no planes, nothing but endless gray sky. "I want you to go in deep," he says in a low, somber voice. He turns and looks at Martinez. "I want you to try and get them to take you back to this prison they live in."

"They live in a prison?" This is news to Martinez. "Did one of them talk?"

The Governor gazes back outside. Very softly, in a low voice, he tells him about the prison coveralls on the men, under their riot gear, and the logic of it—the perfect logic. "We got a few jailbirds in town," he says finally. "I asked around. There are three or four state prisons within a day's drive, one in Rutledge, one down by Albany, one over in Leesburg. It would be a hell of a lot better if we could pinpoint the location without a bunch of road trips." He turns and looks at Martinez. "You follow me?"

Martinez nods. "I'll do what I can, boss."

The Governor looks away. A beat of silence passes, and the Governor says, "Clock's ticking, Martinez. Get to work."

"One question?"

"What is it?"

Martinez measures his words. "Let's say we find this place . . ."

"Yeah?"

Martinez shrugs. "Then what?"

The Governor doesn't answer. He just continues staring out at the empty sky, his expression as mean and desolate as the plague-ridden landscape.

———

The dominoes begin falling that afternoon, the seemingly random sequence of events unfolding with the dark implications of atomic nuclei colliding.

At 2:53 P.M. eastern standard time, one of the Governor's best fighters, a lanky former truck driver from Augusta named Harold Abernathy, pays an unexpected visit to the infirmary. He asks the doctor to get him ready for that day's fight. He wants his bandages removed so he looks badass for the crowd. With the stranger named Rick looking on, Stevens reluctantly begins working on Abernathy, unwinding gauze and removing the man's myriad bandages from earlier bouts, when all at once a fourth man bursts into the room, his baritone voice booming, "Where is that fucker?! WHERE IS HE?!" Eugene Cooney—a toothless, tank-shaped man with a shaved head—goes straight for Harold, snarling and spitting something about Harold not pulling his punches out there and now Eugene has lost his last viable front teeth and it's all Harold's fault. Harold tries to apologize for getting "a little carried away" out there with the crowd and all but according to the crazed bald man "sorry ain't gonna cover it" and before anybody can intercede, Eugene pulls a nasty-looking buck knife and goes for Harold's throat. In the chaos, the blade slices through Harold Abernathy's neck and severs his carotid artery and sends gouts of blood flinging across the tile walls in a gruesome display. Before Stevens has a chance to even react, or even begin to stanch the bleeding, Eugene Cooney has turned on his heels and made his exit with the casual satisfaction of a slaughterhouse worker bleeding a pig. "Fucker," he comments over his shoulder before lumbering out of the room.

News of the attack—and Harold's subsequent death from massive blood loss—wends its way across town over the course of that next hour. Word passes from man to man on the wall until it reaches the Governor at exactly 3:55 P.M. EST. The Governor hears about it on his back deck, peering out through his storm door and listening to Bruce calmly recount the incident. The Governor absorbs the report stoically, thinking it over, and finally tells Bruce not to make a big deal out of it. He should not alarm the townspeople. Instead, he should spread the word that Harold Abernathy succumbed to internal injuries sustained in the fights because Harold was a trooper and gave his all and was almost kind of a hero, and also because these fights are the real thing, and people should remember that. Bruce wants to know who will replace Harold in that day's match, which is scheduled to begin in a little over an hour. The Governor says he has an idea.

At 4:11 P.M. that afternoon, the Governor leaves his apartment with Bruce at his side, and proceeds across town to the racetrack, which is already beginning to fill up with early birds eager for the day's festivities to begin. By 4:23 P.M., the two men have descended two flights of stairs and passed through thousands of feet of narrow cinder-block corridor to the last stall on the left side of the lowest sublevel. Along the way, the Governor explains his idea, and tells Bruce what he needs. At last, they reach the makeshift holding tank. Bruce unlatches the rolling door, and the Governor gives a nod. The shriek of ancient casters pierces the silence as Bruce yanks the door up.

Inside the dark, squalid chamber of greasy cement and mold, the slender brown-skinned figure tied to the far wall lifts her head with every last scintilla of her strength, her dreadlocks dangling across her ravaged face. Hate as incandescent as fire kindles again in the pits of her almond eyes, the laser-hot stare peering through strands of hair, as the Governor takes a step toward her. The door bangs shut behind him. Neither one of them moves. The silence presses in on them.

The Governor takes another step closer and gets within twelve inches of her, and he starts to say something when she lunges at him. Despite her weakened condition, she comes close to biting him—so close that the Governor rears back with a start—the faint clacking of her teeth, and the creaking of the ropes holding tight filling the silence.

"Right, you're gonna bite me and *then what*?" the Governor says to her.

Nothing but a faint hiss of air comes out of her mouth, her lips peeled away from her teeth in a grimace of pure, unadulterated hatred.

"How do you think you could get out of here?" he says, leaning toward her so their faces are centimeters apart. The Governor drinks in her rage. He can smell her—a musky odor of sweat and cloves and blood—and he savors it. "You really should just stop struggling. Things would be so much easier on you. Besides, last time you almost broke your wrists. We don't want *that*, do we?"

She locks her serpentine gaze on him, the bloodlust in her eyes almost feral.

"So, for your sake," he says, relaxing a bit, stepping back and taking her measure, "I'd appreciate it if you'd just give it a rest . . . but enough about *that*." He gives the moment a dramatic pause. "We've got a bit of a problem. Well, *you've* got a *huge* problem, and depending on your definition, I've got plenty of 'problems' . . . but what I mean is, I've got a *new* problem, and I need your help."

Her face holds its cobra stillness, its laser focus on the Governor's dark eyes.

"I've got a fight scheduled today in the arena—a big one." He takes on the flat tone of a dispatcher ordering a taxi. "A lot of people are supposed to be coming . . . and I just lost a fighter. I need a replacement—and I want it to be you."

Something glints now behind the woman's veiled expression, something new in her shiny eyes. She says nothing but cocks her head at him, almost involuntarily, as she absorbs his every word.

"Before you start spouting out the 'I-would-never-do-anything-for-you' and 'who-the-fuck-do-you-think-you-are-to-ask-me-anything' . . . I want you to consider one thing." He gives her a hard look. "I am in the position to make your life easier." For a fleeting instant, a grin crosses his features. "Hell, a bullet is in the position to make *your* life easier . . . but still, I can help you."

She stares at him. Waiting. Dark eyes blazing.

The Governor smiles at her. "I just don't want you to lose sight of that." He glances over his shoulder at the door. "Bruce!"

The rolling door jerks, and a gloved hand appears under the edge.

Bruce yanks the door up, letting in the cold, naked light of the corridor.

The big man holds an object that catches the light, the steel edge gleaming with an almost liquid radiance.

The woman on the floor fixes her gaze on the object in the black man's hand.

The scabbard is missing, but the glorious sword—exposed in the dim light—calls out to the woman like a homing beacon. The style originally created for samurai in the fifteenth century, hand-forged today by only a handful of master swordsmiths, the katana sword is pure steel poetry. With its long blade as gracefully curved as a swan's neck, and its handle grip wound with hand-beaded snakeskin, the weapon is both a work of art and a precision instrument of death.

The sight of the thing simultaneously stiffens the dark woman's spine and sends gooseflesh down her arms and legs. And all at once, all of her rage, all of the searing agony between her legs, all of the white noise in her mind goes away . . . replaced by the innate need to get her hands around that perfectly balanced grip. The presence of the thing so transports her, so mesmerizes her, that she barely hears the voice of the monster continuing to jabber at her.

"I would like to give *this* to you," he is saying. "I'm sure you'd like to have it." His voice fades as the weapon grows more and more radiant to the woman—the shimmering crescent of steel a sliver of new moon eclipsing everything else in the cell, in the world, in the universe.

"You're going to be fighting a man," the monster explains, his voice fading into nothingness. "And to the crowd, well, you're going to need to appear to have the *advantage*. People don't like watching guys beat the shit out of girls." A pause here. "I know . . . I don't get it either. I guess if you're coming at him with a sword, it'll be okay for him to clip you a good one with a base-ball bat."

In the woman's traumatized brain, the sword seems to almost be softly humming now, vibrating, gleaming so brightly in the gloomy enclosure it appears as though it has caught fire.

"In return, you get a full week of rest," the monster is saying. "And food, and maybe even a chair or a bed, I'll have to look into it." The monster's shadow looms over her now. "To be honest, our little relationship has been pretty exhausting. I need a break." He looks at her with an obscene grin on his face. "This is okay be-cause, well, I'm still totally pissed off about the ear. But I feel like I've gotten at least a little payback already." A pause. "And well, the fella you're fighting tonight could kill you."

In the woman's imagination, rays of celestial light seem to be flaring off the sword's chiseled tip.

"And I don't want you to kill this guy," the monster continues. "That's the little secret we don't really tell people. Our little arena fights are more than a little staged. The danger with the biters is there—sure—but you're really not supposed to hurt your oppo-nent *too* much."

The tinsel of light reflecting off the weapon seems to be reach-ing out to the woman on the floor now, the voice in her head promising her, whispering to her . . . *be patient, just wait, patience.*

"You don't have to decide now," the Governor says at last, giv-ing Bruce a nod. They head for the door, the Governor muttering, "You got twenty minutes."

Lilly looks for Austin in every corner of the town that day. She gets worried at one point—after talking to the Sterns—that he might have lit out on his own to go find a mythical marijuana farm not far from Woodbury.

Austin had talked about the place off and on, usually adopting the wistful tone of someone describing Xanadu, claiming he had heard rumors that some government medical program was farming weed for Pfizer in preparation for the legalization laws to roll out. Lilly was fixing to go after him—the infamous farm apparently lay just east of Barnesville, a short car ride from Woodbury, or a long day's hike on foot—when, late that afternoon, she started noticing signs that he might very well be right under her nose.

Gus mentions to her at one point that the young man was seen around noon that day skulking through the wild thickets next to the railroad yard, searching for something, which made no sense to Lilly whatsoever. But since when did Austin Ballard's movements make sense?

Later that day, after her sad encounter with Bob, Lilly was on her way home when she ran into Lydia Blackman, an aging dowager from Savannah who had gladly taken on the role of town gossip. According to Lydia, Austin was seen only an hour or so earlier, rummaging around the trash heap behind the storage warehouse on Main Street, rifling through buckets and oil drums. A few passersby made snarky comments about the young man "turning into a hobo" and "the next thing you know, he'll be pushing a shopping cart down Woodbury road looking for tin cans."

Nonplussed by it all, nearing the end of her tether, her skin crawling with nervous tension, Lilly decides the best way to find somebody is to stay put. So she trudges over to Austin's apartment building on the east side of town, near the rows of semitrucks, and plants herself on the porch. Which is exactly where she now sits, Indian style, her elbows resting on her legs, her head in her hands.

The sun has dipped below the gigantic, saucer-shaped arena to the west, and the breeze has cooled, and now Lilly watches the last of the townspeople file past Austin's place on their way to the big show. The fights are scheduled to start in a half hour, and Lilly doesn't want to be anywhere near this place at that point, but she *is* determined to find the long-haired young man and drop her bombshell.

Less than five minutes later, Lilly is just about to give up when she sees a familiar figure emerging like a curly-maned avatar in hoodie and ripped jeans from the nimbus of sun rays slanting down across the mouth of the adjacent alley. He carries his knapsack slung over his shoulder, the unidentified contents bulging inside it. He looks solemn, maybe even a little lonely, until he turns the corner and heads for his building and sees Lilly on the stoop. "Oh my God," he says, walking up to her, his eyes brightening suddenly like a little boy discovering an Easter basket under his bed. "I've been looking all over for you."

Lilly stands, thrusts her hands in her pockets, and gives him a terse shrug. "Really . . . that's funny. I've been looking for *you*."

"Sweet," he says and kisses her on the cheek, carefully dropping his knapsack on the entryway steps. "I got something for you."

"Yeah? I got something for you, too," she says, her expression blank.

Austin digs in the knapsack. "I was waiting for you over at your place but you never showed up." He pulls out a lovely bouquet of purple aster surrounded by ivory-white baby's breath, collected in a big rusty can with the Clabber Girl baking powder insignia faded on the side. All of which explains his strange behavior that day, rooting around the weeds and the trash piles. "Barbara said this white stuff is called Doll's Eyes . . . isn't that creepy and cool?!"

"Thank you," Lilly says, taking the gift from him without emotion and setting it down on the step. "That's very sweet of you."

"What's the matter?"

She looks at him. "So, what are your plans?"

"Huh?"

"You heard me." Lilly puts her hands on her hips as if she's about to fire him from a job. "For the *future,* I'm talking about."

He cocks his head at her with a puzzled frown. "I don't know . . . I guess I'm going to keep practicing with the Glock, get better at zapping the biters . . . maybe try to score another generator so I can get some tunes in my place?"

"That's not what I'm talking about and you know it." She chews her lip for a moment. "I'm talking about when and if we get outta this mess. What are your plans? For the rest of your life?"

His head cocks even farther, a more profound confusion crossing his features. "You mean like . . . a job and shit?"

"I mean like a career. I mean like growing up. What are your plans? You gonna be a professional beach bum? Rock star? Drug dealer . . . *what*?"

He stares at her. "What's going on?"

"Answer the question."

Austin puts his hands in his pockets. "Okay, first of all, I don't know if there's even gonna *be* a future to make plans for. Second of all, I have, like, no idea what I'm gonna do." He studies her morose expression. He can tell this is no joke. "I got a degree and shit."

"From where?"

He sighs, his voice losing some of its verve. "ATC."

"ATC . . . what's that?"

His voice goes even lower. "Atlanta Technical College."

"Really?" She gives him a look. "What's that, Austin? Some fucking Internet Web site where you pay nineteen ninety-five for a paper diploma and they send you coupons for an oil change and a résumé service?"

Austin swallows hard. "It's a real school." He looks down. "There's a campus out by the airport." His voice drops an octave. "I was studying to be a paralegal."

"That's just perfect."

He looks at her. "What the hell, Lilly? Where are you going with this?"

She turns away from him for a moment and gazes out across the empty street. The noise of the crowd revving up for the fights a block and a half away echoes across the sky. She slowly shakes her head. "Truck pulls and strip clubs," she mutters to herself.

Austin stares at the back of her head, listening intently, getting more and more worried. "What was that?"

She turns and looks at him. "It's a man's world, pretty boy." Her face is a mask of pain. Her eyes have already started to well up. "You guys think everything is just a quick pop, and then it's 'sayonara.' Well, it's not. It's not, Austin. Actions have consequences. The simplest choices can get your ass killed."

"Lilly—"

"It's true more than ever right now." She holds herself as though she's freezing. She gazes off again. "This world of shit we're in, it isn't very forgiving. You get yourself in a jam, and you're dead . . . or worse."

He reaches out and gently strokes her shoulder. "Lilly, whatever it is . . . we can deal with it. Together. Isn't that what you told me? Gotta stick together? Tell me what's going on. What happened?"

She pulls away from him and starts down the steps. "I don't know what I was thinking," she says in a voice crackling with disdain.

"Wait!" he calls to her. "Lilly, I can fix it . . . whatever it is."

She pauses at the bottom of the steps. She turns and looks at him. "Is that right? You can fix it?" She reaches into her pocket and pulls out a small plastic instrument. It looks like a digital thermometer. "Fix this!" She tosses it to him.

He catches it and looks down at it. "What the hell is this?" Upon closer scrutiny, he sees the little window on the digital test vial and the words stamped next to it:

not pregnant: |

pregnant: ||

The display shows two vertical lines, indicating a positive test result.

PART 2

Showtime

For then shall be great tribulation, such as was not since
the beginning of the world to this time, nor ever shall be.
—Matthew 24:21

THIRTEEN

The huge tungsten spotlight on the north end of the track snaps on with a pistol-shot sound, sparking like a giant match tip igniting, the silver beam hitting the infield of the arena formerly known as the Woodbury Veterans Speedway. The advent of the artificial light gooses the crowd of more than fifty spectators strewn across the bench seats on the west side of the field. Whoops and hollers and catcalls from all ages and dispositions tumble up into the dusky, yellow sky and mingle with the smell of wood smoke and gasoline on the chill air. The shadows are lengthening.

"Quite the turnout, eh?" The Governor surveys the meager yet boisterous crowd as he leads Gabe and Bruce up the press stairs to the crow's nest, where local reporters and NASCAR scouts once passed bottles of Jack and chewed Red Man as they watched the controlled chaos down in the dust.

Gabe and Bruce follow the Governor toward the glass-encased box seats, giving him a "yes-sir," and a "you-got-that-right" . . . and just as they are about to seal themselves inside their little clubhouse, a voice rings out from below.

"Hey, boss!" It's a grizzled, former peanut farmer in a CAT hat, sitting in the back row, glancing over his shoulder as the Governor passes. "Better be a good one today!"

The Governor gives him the kind of look one gives a child who's about to ride a roller coaster for the first time. "Don't worry, pal. It will be. I promise."

Underneath the arena, minutes before the evening's festivities get under way, the door to the infirmary unexpectedly swings open, and a tall, handsome man with a bandanna tied around the crown of his head walks in with an expectant look on his face. "Doc? Dr. Stevens?"

Across the room, Rick Grimes, the ill-fated stranger, shuffles along the back wall, which is lined in second-hand medical gear. Hardly noticing the visitor, he moves almost robotically, his mind a million miles away. He holds his mutilated arm like a dead baby, the missing hand now apparent in a bulbous, stained bandage in the shape of a giant peg.

"Hey, man!" Martinez pauses inside the door, hands on his hips. "Have you seen—?" He stops himself. "Oh, hey—you're— What was your name?"

The injured man slowly whirls, the bloody stump catching the light. His voice comes out of him in a heavy, hoarse, stringy garble. "Rick."

"Oh my God." Martinez stares, taken aback by the grisly sight of the severed wrist. "What happened to—? Jesus, what happened to you?"

Rick looks down. "An accident."

"What?! *How?!*" Martinez comes over to him, places a hand on his shoulder. Rick pulls away. Martinez musters up as much outrage and sympathy as he can. It's a fairly decent performance. "Did someone *do* this to you?"

The man named Rick lunges at him, grabs his shirt with the one good hand. "Shut up! Shut the fuck up!" The man's blue eyes flare with rage as hot as cinders. "You handed me to that *psycho*! You fucking did this!"

"Whoa—hey!" Martinez rears back, mortified, playing dumb. "STOP IT!"

The sound of Dr. Stevens's voice is like a splash of cold water on the two men. The doctor steps into the fray, holding each man at bay with an open palm. "Stop it, stop it right fucking *now*!" He sears his gaze into each of them. Then he puts an arm around Martinez. "Come on, Martinez. You need to leave."

Rick deflates, staring at the floor, holding his stump, as Martinez walks away.

"What's *with* that guy?" Martinez asks the doctor under his breath as he passes out of earshot on the other side of the room, satisfied with the ruse. The seeds have been planted. "Is he okay?"

The doctor pauses in the doorway, speaking softly, confidentially. "Don't worry about him. What did you want? You were looking for me?"

Martinez rubs his eyes. "Our fine Governor asked me to talk to you—said you didn't seem too happy here. He knows we're pals. He wanted me to just—" Martinez pauses here, genuinely at a loss. He does feel a certain fondness for the cynical, wisecracking Stevens. Secretly, deep down, Martinez admires the man—an educated man, a man of substance.

For the briefest instant, Martinez glances over his shoulder at the man across the room. The stranger named Rick leans against the wall, holding his bandaged wrist, a faraway look on his face. He seems to be staring into the void, looking into the abyss, struggling to understand the cold reality of his situation. But at the same time, at least in Martinez's eyes, the man somehow looks as solid as a rock, ready to kill if necessary. The jut of his whiskered chin, the crow's-feet crimping the edges of his eyes from years of either laughter or bemusement or suspicion, or maybe all three—all of it seems to comprise a man of a different *kind* of substance. Maybe not advanced degrees and private practices, but definitely a man to be reckoned with.

"I don't know," Martinez mutters at last, turning back to the doctor. "I guess he wanted me to just . . . make sure you weren't going to cause any trouble or something." Another pause. "He just wants to make sure you're happy."

Now it's the doctor's turn to gaze back across the room and ponder things.

Finally Stevens aims one of those patented smirks at Martinez and says, "*Does* he now?"

The arena comes alive with a fanfare of thunderous heavy metal thrash-music and a fusillade of hyena yelps from the stands—and on cue, the crusty, scabrous, subliterate tank known as Eugene Cooney emerges from the shadows of the north vestibule like some thrift shop Spartacus. He wears secondhand football pads over his iron-girder shoulders, and carries a bloodstained bat wound with reams of tape.

The crowd eggs him on as he passes the gauntlet of walking dead chained to the gateposts on the edge of the infield. The creatures reach for him—rotting mouths working, blackened teeth gnashing, delicate stringers of black bile looping through motes of dusty light. Eugene gives them a middle-finger salute. The crowd loves the man, and roars their approval as Eugene takes his place out in the center of the infield, brandishing the bat with a kind of pumped-up majesty that would shame a marine color guard. The stench of ripe body organs and stewing offal mingles with the breeze.

Eugene twirls his bat and waits. The spectators wait. The entire arena seems to go quiet in a strange tableau as everybody awaits the challenger.

Way up in the press box, standing behind the Governor, looking on, Gabe wonders aloud, raising his voice enough to be heard, "You sure about this, boss?"

The Governor doesn't even look at him. "The chance to see this bitch take a beating without me breaking a sweat? Yeah—I think it's a good move."

A noise down on the field wrenches their attention to the pool of light around the south portal.

The Governor smiles. "This is going to be good."

She enters the showground from the darkness of the vestibule with a brusque, almost curt rhythm to her stride. Head down, shoulders square under her monastic cloak, dreadlocks flagging in the wind, she moves quickly and decisively despite her wounds and exhaustion, as though she's about to simply grab a stray rabbit by the nape of the neck. Her long, curved saber, gripped firmly in her right hand, points downward at a forty-five-degree angle.

It happens so quickly, so casually, so authoritatively, that the exotic nature of this person—the strange officiousness of her demeanor—seems to momentarily hold the audience rapt, as though the entire gathering has inhaled and held its collective breath. The moving corpses reach for this woman as she passes—this odd specimen with the fancy sword—almost like supplicants, surrounding her, converging on her as she approaches Eugene with no expression, no pleasure, no emotion.

Eugene cocks the bat, and he growls some inane threat at her and then lashes out.

The man's movements might as well be in slow motion as the woman simply and swiftly delivers a perfectly placed kick to the big brute's genitals. The blow lands in the soft spot between his legs and elicits an almost girlish squeal from the behemoth, doubling him over as though he's suddenly intoxicated with agony. The spectators howl.

The next part transpires with the swift and certain arc of a chef's knife.

The woman in the cloak simply does a quick turn, a sort of low pirouette, the sword gripped in both hands now—a movement so natural, so practiced, so precise, so inevitable, as to be almost innate—and then brings the sword down on the big man's neck. The hand-forged blade, tooled by artisans in the tradition of ancestors down through millennia, severs Eugene Cooney's head with barely a whisper.

At first, up in the bleachers, the sight of steel flashing, a glimmer of tungsten on the blade—and the entire cranium of this giant man being lopped off with the ease of a band saw cutting through Brie—is so surreal that the crowd reacts awkwardly: a coughing sound among many, a chorus of nervous laughter . . . and then a tsunami of silence.

The sudden hush that grips the dusty stadium is so inappropriate and out of place that it takes the subsequent geyser of blood frothing out of Eugene Cooney's cleanly dismembered neck, as the headless body drops puppetlike—first to its knees, then to its belly, landing in a heap as lifeless as a pile of shed skin—to suddenly elicit shouts of outrage.

Up in the crow's nest, behind panes of grimy glass, a wiry figure springs to his feet. The Governor gapes down at the infield, teeth clenched, hissing: "What. The. *Fuck?!*"

For a long, dreamlike moment, it seems as though a strange paralysis grips each and every person within the confines of the press box and across the stands. Gabe and Bruce move in toward the glass, clenching and unclenching their fists. The Governor kicks his folding chair behind him, the metal contraption banging against the back wall.

"Get down there!" The Governor points at the tableau on the field—the dark amazon with her sword poised, the circle of cadavers reaching for her—and he screams at Gabe and Bruce: "Rein those biters in and GET HER *THE FUCK OUTTA MY SIGHT*!" Liquid rage courses through him. "I swear I'm going to kill that bitch!"

Gabe and Bruce stumble toward the door, tripping over each other to get out.

Down on the field, the woman in the cloak—nobody has yet bothered to even learn her name—unleashes her controlled fury on the ring of walking dead circling her. It begins almost as a dance.

From a crouch, she spins and simultaneously swings the sword at the first walker. The sharp edge whispers through mortified neck cords and gristle, effortlessly taking off the first head.

Blood and tissue bloom in the artificial light as the head falls and rolls in the dust, and the body collapses. The woman spins. Another head jettisons. Fluids fountain into the air. The woman spins again, zinging through another putrefied neck, another cranium flying off its ragged, bloody mooring. Another spin, another decapitation . . . another, and another, and another . . . until the dust is running black with cerebrospinal fluids, and the woman gets winded.

By this point—unbeknownst to the crowd or the woman in the center of the infield—Gabe and Bruce have reached the bottom of the stairs and are racing around the corner of the gate toward the track.

The crowd starts braying—odd donkeylike barking sounds mingling with boos—and to an undiscerning ear it would be hard to tell whether they are angry, scared, or excited. The clamor seems to fuel the woman on the infield. She finishes off the last three reanimated corpses with a graceful combination of grand plié, jeté, and deadly pas de pirouette, the sword detaching crania silently, the dance a baptismal bloodbath, the earth flooding with deep scarlet-black fluids.

Right then, Gabe has crossed the warning track, followed closely by Bruce, and the two men charge toward the woman, who has her back turned. Gabe reaches her first, and he literally dives at her, as though he's got one chance to tackle an errant running back before the player scores.

The woman goes down hard, the sword flying out of her hands. She eats dust as the two men pile up on her. A gasp forces its way out of her lungs—she has said maybe ten words since she arrived in Woodbury—and she writhes on the ground under their weight, letting out huffs of anguished breath as they shove her face against the dirt. Little plumes of dust puff off the ground, kicked up by her angry breath. Her eyes glaze over with rage and pain.

The audience is struck dumb by all this—absorbing it on a deeper level by now—and the onlookers react again in stunned silence. The hush returns to the arena and presses in on the place until the only sound is the huffing and gasping of the woman on the ground, and a faint click coming from the crow's nest above the stands.

The Governor emerges, drunk with rage, fists clenching so hard that his fingernails begin to draw blood.

"HEY!"

A deep female voice—tobacco cured and coarsened by hardship—calls out to him from below. He pauses on the parapet.

"You son of a bitch!" The owner of the voice is a woman in a threadbare smock, sitting in a middle row between two waiflike boys in tattered clothes. She gazes up angrily at the Governor. "What the hell was *that* shit?! I don't bring my boys out here for that! I bring them to the fights for good clean fun—that was a goddamn massacre! I don't want my boys watching fucking *murder*!"

The crowd reacts, as Gabe and Bruce wrestle with the amazon, dragging her off the infield. The audience voices its disapproval. Mutterings rise and meld into angry shouts. Most of the people concur with the woman but something deeper drives the gathering now. Almost a year and a half of hell and starvation and boredom and intermittent terror come pouring out of some of them in a volley of shrieks and howls.

"You've traumatized them!" the woman cries out between the shrieking noises. "I came here looking for some broken bones, a few missing teeth—not *this*! This was way too much! ARE YOU LISTENING TO ME?!"

Up on the parapet, the Governor pauses and gazes down at the crowd, the rage flowing through him like a brush fire gobbling every last cell, making his eyes water and his spine run cold, and deep in the folds of his brain, a part of him breaks apart . . . *control . . . control the situation . . . burn the cancer out . . . burn it out now.*

From the bleachers, the woman sees him walking away. "Hey, goddamnit! I'm talking to you! Don't walk away from me! Get back here!"

The Governor descends the stairs, oblivious to the catcalls and boos, making his departure with hellfire and vengeance on his mind.

Running . . . hurtling headlong . . . lost in the darkness, night-blind . . . they plunge through the woods, frantically searching for the safety of their camp. Three women . . . one in her fifties, one pushing sixty, and one in her twenties . . . they flail at the foliage and tangled branches, desperately trying to get back to the circle of campers and mobile homes that lie in the darkness less than a mile to the north. All these poor women wanted to do was pick some wild blackberries and now they're surrounded. Pinned down. Trapped. What went wrong? They were so quiet, so stealthy, so nimble, carrying the berries in the hems of their skirts, careful not to speak to each other, communicating only in hand gestures . . . and now the walkers are closing in on them from all directions, the stench rising around them, the chorus of watery snarling noises like a threshing machine behind the trees. One woman screams when a dead arm bursts out of a thicket, grabbing at her, tearing her skirt. How did this happen so quickly? The walkers came out of nowhere. How did the monsters detect them? All at once the moving corpses block their path, cutting off their escape, surrounding them, the women panicking, their piercing shrieks rising up now as they struggle against the onslaught . . . their blood mingling with the dark purple juice of the berries . . . until it's too late . . . and the woods run red with their blood . . . and their screams are drowned by the unstoppable thresher.

"They came to be known as the Valdosta Women," Lilly says with a shiver, sitting on Austin's fire escape with a blanket wrapped around her as she tells her cautionary tale.

It's late, and the two of them have been sitting there for almost an hour, lingering on the platform long after the lights of the arena had begun to sequentially wink out and the disgruntled townspeople had started the long trudge back to their hovels. Now Austin sits next to her, smoking a home-rolled cigarette and listening intently to her strange story. His gut clenches with huge emotions that he can't quite parse, can't quite understand, but he needs to process it all before he makes his case, so he says nothing and just listens.

"When I was with Josh and the others," Lilly goes on in a voice drained of emotion, stretched thin with exhaustion, "they used to say, 'Be careful . . . and wear a sanitary napkin at all times during your cycle, and dip it in vinegar to mask the smell . . . or you'll end up like the Valdosta Women.' "

Austin lets out a thin, mortified breath. "One of them was having her period, I assume."

"You got it," Lilly says, lifting her collar and pulling the blanket tighter around her shoulders. "Turns out the walkers can smell menstrual blood like sharks . . . it's like a fucking homing beacon."

"Jesus."

"Lucky for me, I've always been as regular as clockwork." She shakes her head with a shiver. "The twenty-eighth day rolls around after my last period and I make sure I'm indoors or at least somewhere safe. Since the Turn started, I've tried to keep meticulous track of it. That's one reason I knew. I was late and I just knew. I was getting sore and swollen . . . and I was late."

Austin nods. "Lilly, I just want you to—"

"I don't know . . . I don't know," she murmurs as though not even hearing him. "It would be a big deal any other time but now in this crazy shit we're in . . ."

Austin lets her trail off, and then he says very softly, very gently, "Lilly, I just want you to know something." He looks at her through moistening eyes. "I want to have this baby with you."

She looks at him. A long beat of silence hangs in the chill air. She looks down. The pause is killing Austin. He wants to say so much more, he wants to prove to her that he's sincere, wants her to trust him, but the words escape him. He's not good with words.

At last she looks up at him, her eyes filling up. "Me too." She utters this in barely a whisper. Then she laughs. It's a cleansing laugh, a little giddy and hysterical, but cleansing nonetheless. "God help me . . . I do too . . . I want to have it."

They wrap their arms around each other in a bear hug, embracing like that for a long moment on that cold, windy precipice outside Austin's back window. Their tears come freely.

After a while, Austin reaches up to her face, brushes her hair from her eyes, wipes the tears off her cheeks, and smiles. "We'll make it work," he murmurs to her. "We have to. It's a big fuck-you to the end of the world."

She nods, caressing his cheek. "You're right, pretty boy. When you're right, you're right."

"Besides," he says then, "the Governor's got this place under control now. He's made this place safe for us . . . a home for our baby." He tenderly kisses her forehead, feeling a certainty he's never felt before in his life. "You were right all along about him," Austin says softly, holding her. "The man knows what he's doing."

FOURTEEN

Footsteps echo down the lower corridor under the sublevels. They close in hard and fast, coming down the stairs two at a time, moving at an angry clip, getting Gabe's and Bruce's attention in the darkness. The two men stand outside the last stall, in the shadows thrown by bare bulbs, trying to catch their collective breaths from the struggle to put the black gal back on ice.

For such a skinny little thing, she puts up quite a fight. Welts are rising on Gabe's ham-hock arms where the lady scratched him, and Bruce nurses a sore spot just below his right eye where the bitch caught him with an elbow. But none of it compares with the whirlwind presently coming down the narrow corridor toward them.

The figure throws a long shadow as it approaches, back-lit by the cage lights, pausing with fists balled up tight. "Well?" the thin man says, standing thirty feet away, voice echoing, his narrow face veiled in shadow. "She in there?" His voice sounds wrong—twisted and strangled with emotion. "Did you get her back in there? Is she tied up? WELL?!"

Gabe swallows hard. "We got her back in there, man—but it wasn't easy."

Bruce still breathes hard from the exertion, holding the delicate sword in his huge hand like a child holding a broken toy. "Bitch is crazy," he murmurs.

The Governor pauses in front of them, all blazing eyes and stiff-armed bluster. "Whatever—just—I just—*GIVE ME THAT FUCKING THING!*"

He snatches the sword away from Bruce, who instinctively jerks with a start. "Sir?" he says in a low and uncertain voice.

The Governor huffs and grits his teeth, pacing, with the sword clenched white-knuckle tight in his hand. "Where does that bitch get off?! I *told* her—told her I'd go easy on her—just needed her to do me a fucking favor—just this one fucking favor! ONE FAVOR!" His booming voice practically pins the two other men to the wall. "She agreed to help me! SHE AGREED!!" Temples pulsing, jaw clenching, neck cords prominent, lips curling away from his teeth, Philip Blake looks like a caged animal. "Fuck! Fuck! FUCK!" He turns to the two men. He snarls with spittle flying. "We. Had. An agreement!"

Gabe speaks up. "Boss, maybe if we—"

"Shut up! SHUT THE FUCK UP!"

The corridor echoes. The silence that follows could freeze a lake over.

The Governor gets his breath back. He settles down, inhaling and exhaling, holding the sword up in a strange display that looks, at first, just for a moment, as if he's about to attack his men. Then he murmurs to them, "Talk me out of walking in there right now and slicing her open from cunt to collar with this thing."

The two other men have no reply for him. They are out of ideas.

The silence is glacial.

At that moment, another pair of footsteps—heavy, urgent, and furtive—move through the warren of underground service bays and leprous corridors beneath the racetrack. In the musty stillness of the infirmary, these footsteps—which are approaching from the south end of the arena—are still far enough away to go unheard.

In fact, right then, in the makeshift clinic, in the moments before the troubling turn of events becomes known, the overhead fluorescents pulse and waver with faltering current from the generators on the upper level. The waxing and waning of the light, as well as the incessant droning noises, are beginning to make the man named Rick nervous.

He sits on a gurney in the corner, watching Dr. Stevens wash up at the sink. The frazzled physician takes a deep breath and stretches his weary back muscles. "Okay," the doctor says, taking off his glasses and rubbing his eyes. "I'm going home to take a nap, or at least try to. Haven't really slept much in days."

Across the room, Alice comes out of a pantry with a hypodermic needle in one hand, a vial of Netromycin—a strong antibiotic—in the other. She preps the needle and gives the doctor a look. "You okay?"

"Yeah, fine . . . fine and dandy . . . nothing a fifth of Stolichnaya won't fix. Alice, can you just come and get me if something big comes up?" He gives it more thought. "If you need me, that is."

"No problem," she says, nudging Rick's sleeve up and rubbing alcohol on the site. She injects another fifty cc's into him, still absently talking to the doctor. "You go get some rest."

"Thanks," the doctor says, walking out and shutting the door behind him.

"So . . ." Rick looks at her as she holds gauze on his upper arm, sealing the injection site. "What's with you two? Are you guys . . . ?"

"Together?" She smiles wistfully, as though amused by a private joke. "No. I think he wishes we were, and honestly, he's a nice man. Very nice, actually. And I do like him." She shrugs, dumping the used vial into a waste receptacle, lowering Rick's sleeve. "But I don't care if it *is* the end of the world . . . he's too old for me."

The man's face softens. "So you're . . . ?"

"Single?" Alice pauses, giving him a look. "Yes, but I'm not looking for anyone and you've got a ring on your finger, so . . ." She stops herself. "Is your wife still alive? I'm so sorry that I—"

"She is." He sighs. "It's okay. And don't worry, I'm just trying to make conversation. I'm sorry if I sounded like I was . . ." Another sigh. "So you're a doctor, too? A nurse? Paramedic? Something like that?"

She goes over to a cluttered desk, which is pushed up against the wall. She writes something in a log. "Actually, I was going to college to become an interior designer when the biters—walkers, whatever—made other plans for me. I didn't really know any of this stuff a few months ago."

"But now? How did you learn this stuff?" The injured man seems genuinely interested, if only in an idle-chatting-around-the-coffee-urn kind of way. "Did Dr. Stevens teach you?"

"Mostly, yeah," she says with a nod, still writing notes on inventory, medicine dispensed, supply levels. In Woodbury, every commodity is limited—especially medicine—so Stevens has instituted a meticulous record system, with which Alice religiously keeps up.

In the pause that follows, the oncoming footsteps have reached the corridor outside the infirmary. Still distant enough to be inaudible to Rick and Alice, they approach quickly, purposefully, urgently.

"I've always been a quick learner," Alice is saying. "Ever since I was a little girl. To be honest, I really just have to watch him do something once—maybe twice—and I can pretty much do it."

Rick smiles. "Well, I'm impressed."

"Don't be." She gives him a flinty look. "I don't consider *paying attention* to be something *special* just because most other people *don't* do it." She pauses and lets out a sigh. "Did that sound mean?

Did it make me sound like a bitch? I do that a lot. Sorry about that."

"Think nothing of it," Rick says, his smile lingering. "I didn't take it that way. And you're right, by the way." He looks down at his thickly bandaged stump. "Most people don't pay attention . . . to anything." He looks at her. "They just cruise through life worrying so much about their own bullshit they don't even notice the things that are happening around them." He glances back down at his injury and lets out a dry little grunt.

She looks at him. "What is it?"

"I miss my wife," he says softly, gazing down. "I just . . . I can't stop thinking about her." A long pause . . . and then: "She's pregnant."

Alice stares. "Really?"

Rick nods. "Yeah. She's due in a couple months. Last time I saw her . . . she was . . . she was doing fine." He swallows hard. "Thing about the baby, though . . . I don't know if—"

Across the room, the door bursts open, cutting off his words. "Rick—get up! NOW!"

The man barging into the infirmary wears a faded bandanna, carries a high-powered rifle, and has muscular arms protruding from his sleeveless shirt, which is stained under the arms with flop-sweat. "Come on—we've got to go!" the man urges as he hurries over to Rick, grabbing him by the arm. "RIGHT NOW!"

"Wha—? What the fuck are you doing?!" Rick rears back, pulling himself away from this crazy person. Alice backs away, too, wide-eyed.

Martinez drills his gaze into Rick's eyes. "I'm saving your life."

Rick blinks. "What do you mean? How are you saving my life?!"

"I'm getting you out of here! I'm helping you escape! C'mon!"

"Let go of me, goddamnit!" Rick yanks his arm away, heart racing.

Martinez raises his hand in a gesture of contrition. "Okay. Look, I'm sorry. Okay. It's just that we need to hurry. It's not going to be easy getting you out of here without anyone noticing. Listen to what I'm saying. I'm gonna get you outta here but I can't steal a vehicle—we only keep a couple gassed up and they're too hard to get without being detected."

Rick and Alice shoot panicked glances at each other, and then Rick looks back at Martinez. "Why are you—?"

"If they notice you're gone before we're far enough away, they'll be able to run us down. We gotta get out of here without anyone knowing it for a long time." Martinez looks at Alice, then back at Rick. "Now c'mon—let's go!"

Rick takes a deep breath—a barrage of contrary emotions slamming through him—before giving the man a terse, reluctant nod. He looks at Alice, and then back at Martinez, who turns and starts toward the door.

"Wait!" Rick grabs Martinez on the way out of the room. "They told me there are guards posted at the door! How are we gonna get past *them*?"

Martinez almost smiles in spite of the adrenaline. "We already took care of them."

"We?!" Rick follows him out the door at a fast trot, plunging into the corridor.

Left alone inside the room, Alice gapes at the open doorway.

Creeping cautiously down the central corridor, avoiding pools of light from hanging work lamps, descending stairs to the next level down, and making two quick turns, Martinez silently prays nobody sees them. Only he and the Governor know about this whole scam, and people like Gabe and Bruce are partial to shooting first and asking questions . . . well . . . *never*. Martinez silently raises his hand in a warning gesture as they approach one of the stalls. The two men pause in front of a security door.

"I think you've met my associate," Martinez whispers to Rick, quickly opening the metal door.

Inside the dim enclosure, a pair of bodies lie sprawled unconscious on the cement floor. They are a couple of the Governor's men—Denny and Lou—both of them bruised and battered but still breathing shallow breaths. A third figure, in riot gear, stands over them, fists balled, breathing hard, a nightstick in one hand.

"GLENN!"

Rick lurches suddenly into the room, and goes to the younger man.

"Rick, Jesus, you *are* alive!" The young Asian in the black SWAT-style body armor gives the other man a hug. With his round and boyish face, dark almond eyes, and short-cropped haircut, the young man could pass for a buck private in the army just out of basic training. *Or maybe a Boy Scout,* Martinez thinks to himself from the doorway, as the two men have their little tearful reunion.

"I thought you were dead, man," the younger one says to the older one. "Martinez told me he saw you but I don't know—I guess I didn't believe it until now." The kid looks at Rick's stump. "Jesus, Rick, there was so much blood—"

"I'm okay," Rick says, looking down, holding the bloody streaked bandage against his midsection. "I guess I'm lucky this is the *only* thing that freak took from me. What about you?" He pats the kid's Kevlar shoulder pad. "They told me they let you go—that you told them everything about the prison, and they were going to follow you there."

The kid lets out a burst of nervous laughter, which sounds more like a hyperventilating dog to Martinez. "Man—they never even *asked* me any *questions*." Something changes in his face. Eyes narrowing, jaws clamped tightly, he looks down. "Rick, I spent a day locked in a garage next to another garage with Michonne in it." Another pause here, the boy's eyes watering with repulsion. "Rick—"

The young man pauses again, looking like he can hardly draw a breath, let alone explain what's been going on. From across the room, Martinez soaks it all in. This is the first time he has heard the black woman's name, and for some reason the sound of it— *Mee Shaun? Meeshone?*—makes him nervous. He can't understand why exactly.

Rick pats the young man's shoulder. "It's okay, Glenn, we're gonna get her and us outta here."

"Rick, I love Maggie," the kid finally says, looking up at the older man through wet eyes. "I don't want to put anyone in danger—but the things I heard—the things they must have done to Michonne." He stops again. He looks at Rick and says in a quavering voice, "I think I might have told them anything to make them stop." He sniffs back the shame. "But they never even *asked*." Pause, anger flaring. "It's like they did it all just to *fuck* with me."

It's time for Martinez to step in and get this fucking show on the road. "That sounds about right," he says, his voice going low and grave. He gives both men a sullen look as he continues, "Philip—the Governor—whatever you want to call him—he's been slowly going over the edge for a while now. I've been hearing about the shit he's been doing, whispers, rumors . . . didn't want to believe it was true." Martinez takes a deep breath. "You kinda choose to ignore that stuff—keeps you from having to do anything. After seeing you"—he gives Rick a nod—"I suspected the 'accident' that took your hand was related to him."

Across the room, Rick and Glenn give each other a look. Something unspoken passes between them, and Martinez notices it but doesn't react.

"He asked me to fill in for his guards," Martinez goes on in a lower voice, "watch the garage he was keeping Glenn in. I didn't know he was keeping prisoners in here. I mostly work security— all my time was spent on the fences." Another breath. He looks at the two men across the room. "I couldn't let it go on—I had to help put a stop to this fucking insanity." He looks at the floor. "We're still human, goddamn it!"

Rick is thinking about it, licking his lips pensively, the lines on his face deepening. He looks at Glenn. "My goddamn clothes." He looks at Martinez. "My clothes!" He shakes his head. "We were wearing riot gear and when the doctor was working on me . . . someone *had* to see what I was wearing underneath." He shakes his head slowly, looking at the crumbling mortar walls, the arteries of rust or blood veining the corners. "*Christ*," he utters.

The younger man looks at him. "What do you mean?"

"The jumpsuit, the orange jumpsuit," Rick mutters. "*That's* how he knew about the prison. How could I be so fucking stupid?"

"Come on!" Martinez has heard enough; the clock is ticking. "We've got to get out of here."

Rick nods at Glenn, and the younger man flips down his visor.

And then the threesome slip out of the room and start down the corridor toward the ramp.

For almost ten excruciating minutes now, in the lowest level of the subbasement, Bruce and Gabe haven't budged from their places against the gritty cinder-block wall adjacent to the holding chamber.

The Governor paces in front of them, wielding the katana sword, moving in and out of pools of dirty light from hundred-watt safety bulbs, mumbling to himself, his eyes glassy with rage and madness. Every few moments, the muffled voice of the woman—barely audible behind the rolling door of the service area—murmurs cryptically. Who the hell is she talking to? What kind of malfunction is rotting this lady's brain?

Bruce and Gabe await their orders but decisions are not exactly forthcoming: The Governor looks as though he's battling his own demonic voices, trying to cut both the air and his problems to shreds with the saber, every once in a while snarling a garbled, enraged, "Fuck . . . fuck . . . how could . . . fuck . . . how the fuck could this . . . ?!"

At one point, Gabe ventures a suggestion: "Hey, boss, why don't we focus on them prisons down by Albany? There's a bunch of them over by—"

"Shut the fuck up!" The Governor paces. "I've got to round up new biters for the fights now! I've got to find new fighters! FUCK!"

Bruce chimes in: "Boss, what if we—?"

"FUCK!" He swings the sword at the air. "That fucking bitch!" He turns to the garage door and slams his boot as hard as he can against the rusty metal panels. The thing booms, leaving a dent the size of a pig belly. Gabe and Bruce jerk at the noise. "FUCK!—FUCK!—FUCK!—FUCK!" The Governor turns to them. "OPEN IT UP!!"

Bruce and Gabe exchange a quick, heated glance, and then Bruce goes to the door, kneeling and grasping the lower edge in both hands.

"I want to see her fucking guts spill out all over the ground, damn it," the Governor growls. The door squeals up and the Governor twitches, as though a bolt of electrical current is coursing through him. "STOP!"

Bruce freezes with the door half up, his big hands welded to the edge. Both he and Gabe twist around and gaze at their boss.

"Close it," the Governor says, his voice back to normal as though a switch has been thrown.

Bruce looks at him. "Sure, boss . . . but why?"

The Governor rubs the bridge of his nose, rubs his eyes. "I'm going to . . ."

The men wait. Another fleeting glance exchanged. Bruce finally licks his lips. "You okay, boss?"

"I'm sleeping on this one," he says softly. "I don't want to do anything I'll regret later." He exhales a long breath, stretching his neck muscles. Then he turns and starts walking away. "I gotta go over all the angles," he mutters as he departs, not even looking at them. "I'll be back in a few hours."

He vanishes around the corner at the end of the corridor, passing out of the gloomy light like a phantom.

"WAIT!"

The voice pops out of the shadows behind the escapees, from the depths of the corridor, and at first Martinez is sure they're busted and his plan has gone all to hell before they even had a chance to take a single step outside.

"Please stop!"

The three men jerk to a stop near two intersecting tunnels, the back of Martinez's neck prickling. They whirl around one by one—Martinez, then Rick, and then Glenn—each man breathing hard, hearts pumping, trembling hands going for the grips of their firearms and weapons. They squint to see who it is, a shadowy figure approaching quickly, passing under a yellow cone of light.

"Hold on," the young woman says, the light illuminating the crown of her head, the shimmer of blond hair in a French braid, the tendrils hanging down across a girlish face. Her lab coat positively glows in the dull light of the passageway. She approaches, out of breath.

Rick speaks up. "What is it, Alice? What do you want?"

"I was thinking about it," she says in a shaky voice, catching her breath in the murky, airless tunnel. Somewhere not far from there, one level up, outside the vestibules, the wind hums through empty bleachers and gantries. "If you're going," she says, "I want you to take us with you. Dr. Stevens and me."

The men share tense glances, but nobody offers a response.

Alice looks at Rick. "Wherever you're living has got to be better than this . . . and with your wife pregnant, I'm sure you could use us."

Rick chews on this for a moment. Then he proffers her a thin smile. "I'm not arguing with that. We'd love to have you. In fact—"

"Okay, guys and gals," Martinez breaks in, his voice as taut as a piano string. "We need to go now."

They hurry down a branching tunnel and then down a long ramp, the clock ticking. They end up in the fetid darkness of the subbasement. Glenn has a sketchy memory of where Michonne is being kept—he's thrown off a little by all the garage doors that look alike, the maddeningly similar scars of ancient grease and grit—but he remembers being dragged around this sublevel. They eventually find the last narrow warren of service bays and pause.

"I'm pretty sure it's just around this next corner," Glenn whispers as they huddle in the shadows of two intersecting tunnels.

"Good," Rick utters softly. "We get her, and we get the doctor, and we go." He looks at Martinez. "What's the distance to the doc's place and then to the fence? Is there an easy way out?"

"Hold it!" Martinez thrusts a gloved hand in the air, his voice a loud stage whisper. "Hold on . . . *quiet*. Stay back." He cautiously peers around the corner, then looks back at the group. "I'd be shocked as all hell if the Governor didn't put a guard where he's got your friend."

Rick starts to say, "Why don't we—"

"Running up there ain't the best of ideas," Martinez cautions. "Unless you want to get shot. Everyone here knows me. I'll go on—then call you guys up when I finish."

Nobody argues.

Martinez takes a deep breath, brushes himself off, and then walks around the corner, leaving the three outcasts to huddle together nervously in the darkness of the tunnel.

Glenn looks at Alice. "Hi, I'm Glenn."

"It's Alice," she says with a jittery smile. "Nice to meet you."

Rick barely hears their exchange. His heart beats in syncopation with the ticking clock in his head. They have one shot.

FIFTEEN

"Hey—what's up, Gabe?" Martinez approaches the last garage door with practiced calm, walking up to the stocky guard with a genial smile and wave. "He got you down here protecting the gold reserve or something?"

The portly man in the turtleneck—standing with his back pressed against the rolling door—gives Martinez a grin and a shake of the head. "Not exactly. That bitch who fucked up the fights is in there."

Martinez comes up and stands next to the burly man. "Uh-*huh*."

"She's a pisser, that one," Gabe says with a smirk. "Boss man ain't taking any chances."

Martinez returns the smirk with a lascivious grin of his own. "Think I could have a look? Just a peek. Didn't get a good look at her at the fight. Seemed *hot*."

Gabe's grin widens. "Oh yeah—she *was* hot. After the beating the Governor threw her, though, she—"

The blow comes out of nowhere—a swift, hard knuckle-punch to the portly man's Adam's apple—and it shuts off Gabe's air passage as well as his voice. The stocky man doubles over, gasping for air, shocked senseless.

Martinez finishes the job with the butt of his .762 caliber Garand rifle. The blunt end of the stock strikes Gabe squarely on the back of the skull, making a wooden smacking noise.

Gabe collapses facedown, a trickle of blood from the back of his head already forming in the cement. Martinez calls out over his shoulder, "ALL CLEAR!"

From the shadows at the end of the tunnel, they all come trotting up with eyes wide and adrenaline pumping. Rick takes one look at Gabe, and then turns to Martinez and starts to say something, but Martinez is already crouching by the base of the garage door.

"Help me get this door open—it's all dented—not opening," he says with a grunt, laboring at the bottom edge of the door with his gloved hands. Rick and Glenn come over and crouch next to him, and it takes all three of them to force the thing up. Hinges squeak and complain as they inch the thing halfway open.

They duck under the sprung door, and Rick takes a few steps into the dark, fusty-smelling mortar chamber . . . freezing in his tracks suddenly, paralyzed by the sight of his friend . . . instantly aware on some cellular level in his brain, like a synapse firing, that a war has already begun.

The woman on the floor of the dark holding cell, her arms pinioned to the wall, doesn't recognize her friends at first. Long braids hanging down, chest rising and falling with pained, shallow breaths, blood trails fanning out from her spot across the concrete, she tries to raise her head and gaze through catatonic eyes.

"Oh God . . ." Rick approaches her cautiously, barely getting the words out. "Are you—?"

She levers her head up and spits at him. He jerks back, instinctively shielding his face. Dehydration and shock and exhaustion have dried her saliva to sawdust. She tries to spit again.

"Whoa, Michonne! *Hold it*," Rick says, crouching down in front of her. "It's me." His voice softens. "Michonne, it's Rick."

"R-rick?" Her voice comes out in a withered, faint, husky whisper. Her eyes struggle to lock onto him. "Rick?"

"Guys!" Rick rises to his feet and turns to the others. "Help me get her untied!"

The other three hurry over to the ropes. Alice gently loosens one ankle, while Glenn kneels by the other and struggles with the slipknot, muttering to the woman, "Christ—are you okay?"

Another strangled wheeze comes out of the woman. "N-no . . . I'm not . . . not even close."

Rick and Martinez each take a wrist, and they start tweezing the knots open.

Contrary emotions flow through Martinez as he works on the rope, smelling the poor woman, feeling the fever radiating off her ravaged body. The air reeks of despair—a mixture of body odor, festering wounds, and the spoor of violent sex. The woman's pants are tied around her waist with strapping tape, the fabric torn and mottled with wet spots of every description— blood, tears, semen, sweat, urine, spittle—from days of torture. Her flesh looks scourged, as though somebody applied a belt sander to her arms and legs.

Martinez fights the impulse to confess everything to these people, to give up the ruse. His vision blurs. He feels light-headed, nauseous. Is all this worth a little security for this shit-heel town? A minor tactical advantage? What in God's name did this woman do to deserve this? For a moment, Martinez imagines the Governor doing this to *him*. Martinez has never been this confused.

The ropes finally come off and the woman collapses to the floor with a gasp.

The others stand back as Michonne writhes for a moment on the floor in a prone position, her forehead pressed against the cement. Rick crouches down by her as she struggles to get a breath, to lift herself up, to get her bearings. He says to her, "Do you need—?"

The woman on the floor suddenly pushes herself up, rising to her knees. She sniffs back all the agony in one stubborn, loud snort.

Rick and the others stare at her. Mesmerized by her sudden reserve of energy, they stand silently around her, not knowing what to say or do. How are they going to get her out of here? She looks like a paraplegic laboring to get out of her wheelchair.

All at once she rises to her feet, moving on pure rage now, balling her slender hands into fists. She swallows all the pain and looks around the room. Then she looks at Rick, and her voice takes on the sound of a phonograph playing a scratchy recording. "Let's get the fuck out of here."

They don't get very far. Barely making it out of the subbasement, and up a single flight of stairs, they are approaching the end of the main corridor—Michonne in the lead now—when the black woman suddenly shoots her hand up in a warning gesture. "Stop! Someone's coming."

The others freeze, pressing in behind her. Martinez shoves his way past the others and steps up beside Michonne, whispering in her ear, "I can handle this. People don't know what I'm doing yet—I'll keep them from seeing you."

From around the corner, a shadow looms, a pair of footsteps approaching.

Martinez steps out into the shaft of light spilling down on the junction.

"Martinez?" Dr. Stevens jerks with a start when he sees the man in the bandanna. "What are you doing down here?"

"Uh, Doc—we were on our way to get you."

"Is there a problem?"

Martinez gives him a hard look. "We're leaving here—this town. We want you to come with us."

"What?" Stevens blinks and cocks his head and tries to compute what he's hearing. "Who's *we*?"

Martinez shoots a glance over his shoulder, and he waves the others over. The doctor stares. Rick and Michonne and Glenn, and finally Alice, come sheepishly forward, out of the shadows, and stand in the harsh light of the work lamp. They all stare at the doctor, who stares back at them, processing all this with a somber look on his face.

"Hey, Doc," Rick says at last. "What do you say? You with us, or not?"

The expression on the doctor's face goes through a subtle transformation. His eyes narrow behind his wire-rimmed glasses, and his lips purse thoughtfully for a moment. He looks, just for an instant, as though he's diagnosing a particularly complex set of symptoms.

Then he says, "I just need to gather some supplies from the infirmary and then we can go." He gives them his patented sardonic smile. "Won't take a minute."

Outside the crumbling gates of the arena, they hurry across the parking lot, avoiding the stares of errant citizens wandering the side streets.

The night sky opens up above them—a riot of stars veiled by thin wisps of clouds, and no moon in sight. They move single file, quickly, but not so quickly as to make noise or to attract undue attention or to give the appearance of escape. Some of the passersby wave to them. Nobody recognizes the strangers—Rick and Glenn—but some of the wanderers do double-takes when they see the woman in dreadlocks. Martinez keeps them moving.

One after another, they hop the railing on the west side of the arena and cross a vacant lot, moving toward the main drag. The doctor brings up the rear, clutching his satchel of medical supplies.

"What's the fastest way out of here?" Rick asks, already winded and breathing hard as he and Martinez pause to catch their breath in the shadows of the mercantile building. The others push in behind them.

"This way." Martinez indicates the deserted sidewalk on the other side of the street. "Just keep following—I'll get us out of here."

They hurl across the street, and then plunge into the shadows of the unoccupied sidewalk. The walkway extends at least four blocks to the west, running under awnings and overhangs, shrouded in darkness. They hurry single file through the shadows.

"The less we're out in the open like this, the better," Martinez comments under his breath to Rick. "We just need to make it to an alley—then get over one of those fences. They're not guarded as much as the front gate. This shouldn't be hard."

They cross another half a block when the sound of a voice rings out.

"DOCTOR!"

This throws everybody off their stride and raises hackles on the back of Martinez's neck. Everybody staggers to a halt. Martinez turns and sees an unidentified figure coming around the corner of a building behind them.

Quickly, instinctively, not even looking, Martinez moves his fingertip toward the rifle's trigger pad—ready for anything.

A nanosecond later, Martinez breathes a momentary sigh of relief, releasing pressure on the trigger, as he sees one of the town's matrons approaching. "Dr. Stevens!" she calls out in a voice weak with malnourishment.

Stevens whirls. "Oh—hello, Miss Williams." He gives a nervous little nod to the middle-aged hausfrau coming toward him. The others slip deeper into the shadows, out of the woman's eyeline. The doctor blocks her path. "What can I do for you?"

"I'm sorry to bother you like this," she says, hurrying up to him. Dressed in a shapeless, frayed shift, with short-cropped hair, she looks up at him through huge, downtrodden eyes. The thickness of her middle and the jowls on her face belie her once youthful beauty. "My son, Matthew, he's got a slight fever."

"Oh . . . um—"

"I'm sure it's nothing but I don't want to take any chances."

"I understand."

"Do you have any time later?"

"Of course. I—I just—um," the doctor stammers, and it makes Martinez crazy. Why doesn't he just fucking get rid of her? The doctor clears his throat. "Just . . . uh . . . bring him by my office later today . . . if you could . . . I'll see him then. I'll be—I'll make sure to fit him in."

"Sure, I'll—Are you okay, Dr. Stevens?" She glances at the others lurking in the shadows behind Stevens, and then gives the doctor a quizzical look with those big sad eyes. "You seem upset."

"I'm fine—really." He clutches the satchel tighter to his chest. "I'm just—I'm in the middle of something right now."

He starts to back away from her, which sends a wave of relief down Martinez's midsection.

"I don't mean to be rude," Stevens says to the woman, "but I must be going. I'm sorry." The doctor turns and joins the others.

Martinez leads the group around a corner and pauses on the edge of the sidewalk for a moment, adrenaline surging. For a brief instant, he considers cutting Stevens and Alice loose. They know too much, and they're too tied into the community—they could be a huge liability. Worse than that, they may know Martinez a little too well. They could easily see through his gambit. Maybe they have already. Maybe they're just playing along.

"Doctor?" Alice goes over to Stevens and puts a hand on his shoulder. Stevens looks crestfallen, rubbing his face. Alice speaks softly. "That woman's son . . . ?"

"I can't think about that right now," the doctor mutters. "It's just too—I just can't. We have to get out of here—we may not have another chance." He takes a girding breath, looking down, shaking his head. "These people—they'll just have to get along without us."

Alice looks at him. "You're right. I know. It's going to be okay."

"Hey!" Martinez hisses an urgent whisper at them. "Save it—we don't have time for this right now!"

He gets them moving again—down a boardwalk, across another road, and down a side street toward the mouth of an alley two hundred yards to the south.

The hush that has fallen over the town bothers Martinez. He can hear the hum of generators, the rustling of branches against the wall. Their footsteps sound like pistol shots in his ears, the beating of his heart loud enough to lead a marching band.

He picks up the pace. The passersby have dwindled away. They're alone now. Martinez increases his stride from a trot to a steady run, the others struggling to keep up. A moment later, he hears the one named Michonne make a strange comment to somebody behind him.

"Stop looking at me like that," she says between heaving breaths as she runs. "Don't worry about me."

Glenn's voice is barely audible over the noise of their churning footsteps and heavy panting. "Okay—sorry."

"Keep it down!"

Martinez hisses a breathless whisper at them over his shoulder as they approach the mouth of the alley. Shooting his gloved hand up, he brings the group to a stop and then leads them around the corner of an adjacent building and into the litter-strewn darkness.

The alley is bound in thick shadows, sticky with the stench of garbage cans lined along one wall, a single flickering emergency light at the far end providing the only illumination. The beating of Martinez's heart kicks up a degree. He quickly surveys the area. He sees the sentry at the far end of the alley.

"Okay—wait here a minute," he says to the others. "I'll be right back."

Now Martinez faces another grand performance—a role within a role within a role—as he sniffs back his nerves and starts toward the end of the alley. He can see the young gang-banger on the lift platform thirty yards away, his back turned, an AK in his arms as he stares over a temporary barricade of riveted steel panels.

On the other side of the barricade lies the dark outskirts and freedom.

"Hey—hey, kid!" Martinez approaches the sentry with a ge-nial wave. He keeps his voice casual but authoritative, as if giv-ing a pet cat an order to get off the dinner table. "I'm taking over for you!"

The kid flinches with a start, and then he turns and looks down. Hardly out of his teens, with a spindly body decked out in hip-hop regalia, a headband drawn around his Jheri curls, he looks as though he's playing cops and robbers on the perch. He also looks slightly stoned and more than a little paranoid.

Martinez comes closer. "Hand me that rifle and run along. I'll cover the rest of your shift."

The kid starts climbing down with a shrug. "Sure, man—whatever." He hops to the pavement. "But, uh . . . why you doin' this? You need me somewhere else or somethin'?"

Martinez reaches for the AK in the kid's arms, again with that pet owner tough love in his voice. "Don't ask any questions. I'm doing you a favor here. Hand me the gun, thank me—and enjoy your time off."

The kid stares at him, handing over the firearm. "Uh . . . sure."

The kid walks away, heading back down the alley, mumbling

to himself. "Whatever . . . whatever, man . . . it's your show . . . I just work here."

The others huddle behind the adjacent edifice until the sentry has emerged from the alley and sauntered off into the night, muttering an off-key version of some obscure rap tune. They wait until the kid vanishes around a corner. Rick then gives Glenn a nod, and they slip into the alley—one by one—quickly traversing the length of dark, reeking, garbage-stained pavement.

Martinez is waiting for them on the lift perch, gazing down at them with businesslike fervor. "Come on!" He motions them over. "We get over this wall and we're home free."

The group gathers at the base of the barricade.

Martinez looks down at them. "This worked out better than I thought it would—but we still need to hurry. One of the Governor's goons could walk by any minute."

Holding his stump, Rick looks up at him. "Right, right . . . and you think we're not in a hurry to get out of here?"

Martinez manages a tense smile. "Yeah, I guess I see your point."

Behind Rick, a voice murmurs something that Martinez doesn't catch at first.

Rick starts, spins, and looks at Michonne. Glenn does the same. In fact, they all turn and look at the black woman, who stands in the shadows, looking grim and stoic as she stares off at the night.

"I'm not leaving yet," she utters in a voice so cold and committed it could be a declaration of name-rank-and-serial-number.

"What?!" Glenn gawks at her. "What are you talking about?!"

Michonne stares at the young man through bottomless dark eyes. Her voice is as steady as a cleric delivering the holy writ. "I'm going to visit the Governor."

SIXTEEN

The mute silence that follows Michonne's declaration seems to hold the entire group rapt for endless moments, as the implications of her pronouncement spread from person to person, from awkward glance to awkward glance, like a disease transmitted by eye contact. It goes unspoken what she has in mind for Philip Blake—although no one dares to contemplate the specifics—and that's the part that hits people first. But as the silence lengthens and turns uncomfortable in that reeking dark alley, it becomes clear to Martinez, who is gazing down at this transaction from the lift platform, that Michonne's unstoppable trajectory speaks to something darker than mere vengeance. In these brutal new times, the act of revenge—albeit a lower, baser instinct during the normal course of human events—now seems to take on an apocalyptic inevitability, as natural as shooting a walking corpse in the head or watching a loved one turn into a monster. Infected appendages are quickly severed and cauterized in this horrible new society. Evil people are no longer a thing of legend and forensic cop shows. In this new world, they are like sick cattle that simply need to be separated from the herd. They are defective parts that need to be replaced. Nobody standing at that wall that night could blame or even be surprised at Michonne's sudden and inexorable decision to circle back and find the cancerous cell festering in that town—the man who desecrated her—but that doesn't make it easier to watch.

"Michonne, I don't think—" Rick starts to object.

"I'll catch up with you," she says, cutting him off. "Or I won't."

"Michonne—"

"I can't leave without doing this." She augers her gaze into Rick's eyes. "Go ahead." Then she turns and looks at Alice. "Where does he live?"

At that moment, on the other side of town, nobody notices two figures slipping into the dark maw of an alley just beyond the S-curve on Durand Street—about as far away from the commotion of the racetrack and the central business district as you can get and still be within the safe zone. No guards stray this far south of Main Street, and the outer concertina-wire fences keep errant biters at bay.

Bundled in denim, with blanket rolls under their arms, the two of them move side by side, staying low. One of them hauls a long canvas bag on a sling over his shoulder, the contents clanking softly with each bump. At the end of the alley, they squeeze through a narrow gap between a semitruck cab and a railroad boxcar.

"Where in God's name are you taking me?" Lilly Caul wants to know, following Austin across a vacant lot veiled in darkness.

Austin gives her a mischievous chuckle. "You'll see . . . trust me."

Lilly steps gingerly over a patch of thorny milkweed and smells the odor of decay emanating from the adjacent forest, about fifty yards beyond the outer perimeter. The back of her neck bristles. Austin takes her arm and helps her over fallen timber and into a clearing.

"Be careful, watch your step," he says, treating her with the kid gloves of an old-school father-to-be, which, to Lilly, is at once annoying and kind of adorable.

"I'm pregnant, Austin, not an invalid." She follows him into the center of the clearing. It's a private place, sheltered by foliage and deadfall branches. There's a hollowed-out crater in the ground, scorched and petrified, where some previous visitor had dug a fire pit. "Where did you learn about prenatal care? Cartoons?"

"Very funny, wise guy . . . sit down."

Two ancient tree stumps provide perfect—if not exactly comfortable—places for a couple to sit and talk. The crickets roar all around them as Austin sets his bag down, and then takes a seat next to Lilly.

The sky above them twinkles and pulses with the kind of starry heavens only seen in rural areas. The clouds have dispersed, and the air—for once—is clear of walker stench. It smells of pine and black earth and clear night.

Lilly feels for the first time since—well, since as far back as she can remember—like a whole person. She feels as though they might actually have a chance to make this work. Austin is no dream father, nor is he the perfect husband by any stretch of the imagination, but he has a spark to him that touches Lilly's heart. He's a decent soul, and that's enough for now. They have a lot of challenges ahead of them, a lot to work out, a lot of dangerous terrain to navigate. But she believes now that they will survive . . . *together*.

"So, what's this mysterious ritual you dragged me out here for, anyway?" she says finally, lifting her collar and stretching her stiff neck. Her breasts are sore, and her tummy's been complaining all day. But in a strange way, she has never felt better.

"My brothers and I used to do this thing every Halloween," he says, indicating the canvas bag. "Came up with it when we were high, I guess . . . but it makes sense right now for some reason." He looks at her. "Did you bring those things I asked you to bring?"

She gives him a nod. "Yep." She pats her jacket pocket. "Got 'em right here."

"Okay . . . good." He stands, goes over to the bag, and unzips it. "We usually make a fire to throw the stuff into . . . but I'm thinking tonight we'll try to avoid attracting the attention." He pulls out a shovel, goes over to the pit, and starts digging. "Instead we'll just bury the stuff."

Lilly pulls out a couple photographs she found in her wallet, a bullet from one of her Ruger pistols, and a small object wrapped in tissue paper. She lays the bundle in her lap. "Okay, ready when you are, pretty boy."

Austin sets down the shovel, goes back to the bag, and pulls out a plastic one-liter bottle and two paper cups. He pours dark liquid in each cup. "Found some grape juice . . . we don't want to be drinking wine in your condition."

Lilly grins. "You're gonna drive me crazy with this Jewish mother routine."

Austin ignores the comment. "Are you warm enough? You need another blanket?"

She sighs. "I'm fine, Austin . . . for God's sake stop worrying about me."

He hands her a cup of juice, and pulls a small baggie from his pocket.

"Okay, I'll go first," he says. Inside the Ziploc are half an ounce of marijuana, a little metal pipe, and some rolling papers. He looks wistfully at the paraphernalia and says, "Time to put away childish things." He raises his cup. "Here's to a lifelong love affair with weed." He looks at the bag. "You got me through a lot of rough shit but it's time to go."

He tosses the pot in the hole.

Lilly raises her cup. "Here's to sobriety . . . it's a bitch but it's for the best."

They drink.

"I can't believe she just left us like that," the young man named Glenn says after climbing up the wall. His body armor creaks as he stands in the wind on the edge of the lift platform, helping Alice scale the wall. The nurse is having trouble—her upper body strength not what it could be—and she labors to pull herself onto the perch. Glenn grunts with effort as he pulls her over the precipice. "Should we help her? I'm not crazy about that guy either."

Rick stands on the platform behind Glenn, watching Martinez reaching down to Stevens, hoisting the doctor up the side of the barricade. "Trust me, Glenn," Rick says softly, "we'd probably just slow her down. Our safest bet is getting out now while we can."

The doctor struggles up the wall and cobbles onto the platform to join the others.

Martinez makes sure everyone is okay. They all take deep breaths, turning and gazing out at the wasted landscape on the other side of the rampart. They can see the neighboring woods through a narrow gap between two derelict buildings. The night wind swirls litter across empty dirt roads, the crumbling ruins of train trestles in the distance like fallen giants. The moon has risen full and high—a lunatic's moon—and the milky light puts an exclamation point on all the dark crevices, shadowy alcoves, and snaking ravines that could potentially contain biters.

Rick takes another breath and gives Glenn a reassuring pat on the back. "Michonne can take care of herself," he says in a low voice. "Besides, I get the impression this is something she'd want to do alone."

"Ladies first," Martinez says to Alice, indicating the far edge of the platform.

Alice takes a tentative step toward the ledge, filling her lungs with breath.

Martinez helps her find a foothold, and then he lowers her down the outer wall. "There you go," he says, his hands gripping her under the armpits. He accidentally brushes the sides of her breasts. "You're okay. Almost there."

"Just watch the hands," Alice says, scuffing and grunting down the side of the wall, until she finally hops down to the dirt road, raising a small cloud of dust. She crouches instinctively, looking around the danger zone, her eyes wide and her hackles up.

Martinez lowers Glenn down next, and then the doctor. The two men land next to Alice in the dirt, raising more dust. The silence is broken by their heavy, tense breathing—and the drumming of their hearts in their ears—as each of them turn and survey the dark road ahead of them, which leads out of town and into the black oblivion of night.

They hear the scuffling sounds of Martinez coming down the wall. The tall man lands with a thump, the weapons slung over his back rattling, and then he gazes back up at the parapet. "Okay, Rick . . . let's go."

Up on the platform, Rick tucks his bandaged stump against his sternum. "This ain't going to be easy," he murmurs. "You guys got me?"

"We got you, brother." Martinez reaches up for him. "Just ease on down."

Rick starts awkwardly lowering himself down the outer wall with one hand.

"Jesus," Alice says, watching. "Don't drop him. Be careful!"

Martinez catches the hundred-and-eighty-pound man with a grunt, easing him to the ground. Rick exhales a pained breath and looks around.

Across the dirt clearing, Dr. Stevens stands in the shadows of an abandoned storefront, a weather-beaten sign hanging by a thread, with the words MCCALLUM FEED AND SEED. He lets out a sigh of relief and checks his satchel for any damage. The glass vials of antibiotics and painkillers remain intact, the instruments in good order. "I just can't believe we made it out of there so easily," he mumbles, checking the last of the bag's contents. "I mean, the walls aren't exactly meant to keep people in . . . but . . ."

Behind the doctor, a shadow moves in the depths of the ramshackle doorway of McCallum's. Nobody notices it. Nor does anybody hear the clumsy, shuffling footsteps faintly crackling over detritus and packing straps, moving toward their voices.

"I'm just so damn relieved," Stevens is saying, snapping the satchel shut.

The figure lurches out of the doorway—just a blur of teeth, ragged clothing, and mottled fish-belly skin in the darkness—and clamps its jaws down on the closest human flesh in its path.

Sometimes the victim doesn't even see it coming until it's too late, which is maybe, on some fundamental level, the most merciful way for things to go down.

The creature that sinks its teeth into the nape of Dr. Stevens's exposed neck is enormous—probably a former field hand or stock clerk accustomed to loading sixty-pound bales of fertilizer or cattle feed into truck beds all day, day in and day out—and it latches down on the doctor's jugular so firmly, a crowbar couldn't loosen its jaws. Clad in moldy bib overalls, its thinning hair reduced to spidery wisps on its veined white skull, it has eyes like yellow pilot lamps and makes a watery, garbled coughing sound as it roots its rotten incisors into live tissue.

Dr. Stevens stiffens immediately, arms going up, eyeglasses knocked off his face, satchel flying, a horrid shriek bursting out of him in complete involuntary shock. He can't see or detect the agent of his demise—only the Day-Glo red shade of hot agony snapping down over his gaze.

The suddenness of the attack catches everybody by surprise, the group bristling in unison, reaching for weapons, scrambling backward.

Alice lets out a scream—"DR. STEVENS!!"—and she sees the weight of the massive biter, combined with the doctor's involuntary writhing and staggering, pull Stevens backward, off balance, and onto the ground.

Stevens lands on top of his assailant with a wet grunt, the blood washing over and baptizing the giant biter underneath him in a torrent of fluid as black and oily as molasses in the darkness. In a strangled, insensate voice, the doctor jabbers, *"What—? What is it? Is it—? Is it one of them? Is it—? Is it a biter?"*

The others lunge toward him, but Alice has already reached for the sentry's AK, which dangles on its strap over Martinez's shoulder, her voice booming, "GIVE ME THAT!"

"Hey!" Martinez can't tell what's happening, the tug on his shoulder accompanied by voices yelling all around him, and the other men pushing past him.

Alice already has the AK up and aimed, and then she's pulling the trigger—thank God the kid on the wall keeps his weapon locked and loaded, the safety off at all times—and the gun barks.

A bouquet of fire sparks and flickers out of the short muzzle as the shell casings fly, and the tracers burst a chain of holes in the biter's temple, cheek, jaw, shoulder, and half its torso. The thing twitches and wriggles in its death throes beneath the wounded doctor, and Alice keeps firing, and firing, and firing, until the magazine clicks empty, and the slide snaps open—and she keeps firing.

"It's okay . . . it's okay, Alice."

The faint sound of a male voice is the first thing that penetrates her ringing ears and her traumatized brain. She lowers the gun and realizes that Dr. Stevens is addressing her from the blood-soaked heap of a funeral bier on which he lies.

"Oh-God-Doctor—DR. STEVENS!" She tosses the assault rifle to the ground with a clatter and goes to him. She drops to her knees, and reaches for his neck, getting her fingertips wet with his arterial blood as she feels for a pulse, trying to remember the CPR lessons he provided her, the trauma unit protocols, when she realizes he is tugging at her lab coat with his blood-spattered fingers.

"I'm not . . . dying . . . Alice . . . think of it . . . *scientifically*," he utters around a mouth filling up with blood. In the darkness, his face looks almost serene. The others press in behind Alice and look on and listen closely. "I'm just . . . evolving . . . into a different . . . a *worse* . . . life form."

The horror spreads from person to person hovering over him, from face to face, as Alice fights her tears and strokes his cheek. "Doctor—"

"I'll still exist, Alice . . . in some way," he utters in barely a whisper. "Take the supplies, Alice . . . you'll need them . . . to take care of these people. Use what I taught you. Now go . . . go . . . go on."

Alice stares as the doctor's life drains out of him, his intelligent eyes going glassy, and then empty, gaping at the nothingness. She lets her head loll forward but no tears will come. The desolation in her core won't allow tears to come now.

Martinez stands over her, watching all this with nervous intensity. A fist of contradictory emotions grips his insides. He likes these people—the doctor and Alice—regardless of their hatred of the Governor, their petty betrayals, their scheming and gossiping and sarcasm and disrespect. God help Martinez—*he likes them*. He feels a weird kinship with them, and now he's groping for purchase in the dark.

Alice rises to her feet, picking up the satchel of medical supplies.

Martinez touches her shoulder, and softly says, "We gotta move."

Alice nods, says nothing, stares at the bodies.

"People in town will think the shots were just the guard taking out biters that got too close to the fence," Martinez goes on, his voice hurried and taut with tension. He glances over his shoulder at the other two men, who stand by, looking rattled.

Martinez turns back to Alice. "But the sound will attract more biters—and we need to be gone before they get here."

He looks at the doctor's slack face, stippled with blood, frozen in death.

"I—He was a good friend," Martinez adds finally. "I'll miss him too."

Alice gives one last nod, and then turns away. She nods at Martinez.

Without another word, Martinez grabs the AK and gives a hand gesture to the others, and then leads the three survivors down a side road—and on toward the town limits—their silhouettes swallowed within moments by absolute, unforgiving, implacable darkness.

"Damn it, honey—*eat it!*" The Governor lowers himself to his hands and knees on the foul-smelling carpet of his living room, holding a severed human foot by its big toe in front of the dead little girl. The Japanese sword lies on the floor close by—a treasure, a talisman, a spoil of war that the Governor hasn't let out of his sight since the debacle at the racetrack—its implications now the furthest thing from his mind. "It's not completely fresh," he says, indicating the gray appendage, "but I swear this thing was walking not two hours ago."

The tiny cadaver jerks against its chain eighteen inches from his hand. It emits another little growl—a broken Chatty Cathy doll—and turns its frosted-glass eyes away from the tidbit.

"C'mon, Penny, it's not that bad." He inches closer and waves the dripping, severed foot in front of her. It's pretty big, hard to tell if it's male or female—the toes are small but all natural, no remnants of polish—and it has already begun to turn blue-green and stiffen up with rigor mortis. "And it's only going to get worse, you don't eat it now. C'mon, sweetie, do it for—"

An enormous thud makes the Governor jerk with a start on the floor.

"What the fuck!" He turns toward the front door, across the room.

Another massive thud rings out. The Governor rises to his feet.

A third impact on the door results in drywall dust sifting down from the lintel, and a faint cracking noise along the seams of the deadbolt.

"What the hell do you want?!" he calls out. "And don't beat on my goddamn door so hard!"

The fourth impact snaps the deadbolt and chain, the door swinging open so hard it bangs into the adjacent wall in a burst of wood shards and dust, the knob embedding itself into the wood like a dowel.

The inertia drives the intruder into the room on a whirlwind.

The Governor tenses in the center of the living room—fists balling up, teeth clamping down in a tableau of fight-or-flight instinct. He looks as though he's seeing a ghost materialize next to his secondhand sofa.

Michonne tumbles into the apartment, nearly falling on her face from all the forward momentum.

She skids to a halt three feet away from the subject of her quest.

Getting her balance back, she squares her shoulders, fists also clenching, feet planted firmly now, head tilted forward in an offensive posture.

For the briefest of moments, they stand facing each other. Michonne has put herself together on the way over—her jumpsuit straightened, her top tucked in, headband tightened around her lush braids—to the point where she looks as if she's ready to begin a workday or possibly go to a funeral. After an unbearable pause—the two combatants staring each other down in an almost pathologically intense manner—the first sound emitted comes out of the Governor.

"Well, well." His voice is low, flat, cold, with zero affect or emotion. "This should be interesting."

SEVENTEEN

"My turn," Lilly says, her voice barely audible above the din of crickets and the breeze that is rattling the branches around the dark clearing. She finds a snapshot taken on a disposable camera of her and Megan at a bar in Myrtle Beach, both of them completely baked, their eyes glazed over and red as cinders. She stands and goes over to the hole in the ground. "Here's to my BFF, my gal pal, my old friend Megan, may she rest in peace."

The photograph flutters and falls like a dead leaf into the fire pit.

"To Megan," Austin says, and takes another sip of the sugary juice. "Okay . . . next up . . . my *bros*." He pulls a small, rusty harmonica from his pocket. "I'd like to drink to my brothers, John and Tommy Ballard, who got killed by walkers in Atlanta last year."

He tosses the harmonica in the pit. The little metal apparatus clunks and bounces off the hard ground. Austin gazes down at it, his eyes growing distant and shiny. "Great musicians, good dudes . . . I hope they're in a better place right now."

Austin wipes his eyes as Lilly raises her cup and says softly, "To John and Tommy."

They each drink another sip.

"My next one's a little strange," Lilly says, finding the little .22

caliber slug and holding it up between her thumb and index finger. The brass gleams in the moonlight. "We're surrounded by death, every day; death is everywhere," she says. "I'd like to fucking bury it . . . I know it doesn't change anything but I just want to do it. For the baby. For Woodbury."

She tosses the bullet in the hole.

Austin stares at the little metal round for a moment, then mutters, "For our baby."

Lilly raises her cup. "For our baby . . . and for the future." She thinks for a moment. "And for the human race."

They both stare at the bullet.

"In the name of the Holy Spirit," Lilly says very softly, staring down at the hole in the ground.

A fight—the spontaneous hand-to-hand kind—comes in many varieties. In the East, the business of fighting is Zenlike, studied, controlled, academic—the opponents often coming at each other with years of training behind them, and a sort of mathematical precision. In Asia, the weaker opponent learns to use the adversary's strengths against them, the mêlées settled promptly. On the other end of the spectrum, in competitive rings around the world, freestyle battles can last for hours, with many rounds, the final outcome resting upon the physical stamina of each pugilist.

A third kind of fistfight occurs in the dark back alleys of American cities, during which opponents engage in a wholly different kind of battle. Fast and brutal and unpredictable— sometimes awkward—the common street fight is usually over within seconds. Street fighters have a tendency to shotgun their blows at each other, willy-nilly, driven by rage, and the whole fracas usually ends in a draw . . . or worse, with somebody finally pulling a knife or a firearm to bring things to a quick and mortal conclusion.

The battle that ensues in the Governor's foul-smelling, dimly lit living room that night encompasses all three styles, and spans a grand total of eighty-seven seconds—the first five of which involve very little fighting at all. It begins with the two opponents planted where they stand, staring into each other's eyes.

Quite a lot of nonverbal information is exchanged during those first five seconds. Michonne keeps her gaze welded to the Governor's, and the Governor stares back at her—neither adversary giving the other so much as a blink—and the room seems to crystallize like a diorama seized up in ice.

Then, right around second number three, the Governor averts his gaze for a scintilla of a moment to the floor on his right flank.

He makes note of both the child and the sword, each of which lie within his grasp. Penny seems oblivious to the human drama unfolding around her, her livid, pasty face buried in the bucket of entrails. The sword gleams in the dull light of an incandescent bulb.

The Governor tries his hardest, over the course of that split instant, *not* to register any panic, or any outwardly visual concern for his little dead girl's safety, or the idea forming in his mind—the human brain can formulate complex notions in the smallest soupçon of time, in less time than it takes a synapse to fire—that he just might be able to grab the sword and conclude matters quickly.

In the space of that single second—the third in a series of eighty-seven—Michonne also flicks her own gaze toward the girl and the katana saber.

Second number four finds the Governor snapping his gaze back up to Michonne's smoldering glare. In that time, she has also glanced back at the Governor.

Over the duration of the next one and a half seconds—number four and a portion of number five—the two enemies read each other's look.

The Governor knows now that she knows what he's thinking, and she knows he knows, and the next half second—the rest of number five—recalls the end of a countdown. The engines fire and the thing explodes.

It takes six seconds for the next phase of the encounter to unfold.

The Governor dives for the sword, and Michonne lets out a booming cry—"NO!"—and by the time the Governor's shoulder hits the carpet three feet from the blade, and his outstretched hand has approached the general vicinity of that magnificent handle with its scaly serpentine pattern, Michonne has also moved in with the suddenness of a thunderclap.

She instinctively delivers the first blow of the conflict at second number eleven. Her leg comes up and she kicks out at him. The hard edge of her boot strikes the side of his face below the temple just as he is grasping the sword's handle.

The sickly crack of hard leather fracturing a human mandible fills the room—a sound not unlike a celery stalk snapping—and the Governor winces backward in agony, a thread of blood flinging from his mouth. He falls onto his back, the sword unmoved.

The next eight seconds are a mishmash of explosive movement and sudden stillness. Michonne takes advantage of the Governor's punch-drunken stupor—he has managed to roll over onto elbows and knees now, his face leaking blood all over the place, his lungs heaving—by darting quickly toward the fallen sword. She snatches it up and whirls back around in less than three seconds, and then spends the next four seconds marshalling her breath and preparing to deliver the killing blow.

By this point, exactly nineteen seconds have elapsed, and it looks as though Michonne has the advantage. Penny has glanced up from her feeding trough and softly growls and sputters at the two adversaries. The Governor manages to rise on his wobbly knees.

His face, without him even being aware of it, takes on an expression of pure unadulterated bloodlust, his mind a TV screen at the end of a programming day—a blank wall of humming white noise—blocking out all extraneous thought other than killing this fucking bitch right this instant. He instinctively lowers his center of gravity as a cobra might coil itself before striking.

He can see the sword in her hand like a divining rod absorbing all the energy in the room. He drips blood and drool from his mouth. Michonne stands only five feet away from him now, with the sword raised. Twenty-seven seconds have transpired. One well-placed strike with that beveled razor's edge and it will all be over but that doesn't even faze the Governor now.

At thirty seconds, he lunges.

The next maneuver on her part covers a total of three seconds. One, she lets him get within inches of her, and two, she unleashes one of her patented groin kicks, and three, the blow immobilizes him. At this proximity, the steel-reinforced toe of her work boot connects with such extreme results that the Governor literally folds in half, all the breath forced out of him, the mixture of blood, snot, and saliva in his mouth spewing out in a spray across the floor. He lets out a garbled grunt and falls to his knees before her, gasping for breath, the pain like a battering ram smashing through his guts. He flails his arms for a moment as though trying to hold on to something, and then falls to his hands and knees.

Bloody vomit roars out of him, splashing the carpet at her feet.

At forty seconds, things settle down. The Governor wretches and coughs and tries to get himself together on the floor. He can feel her standing over him, gazing down at him with that eerie calm on her face. He can sense her raising the blade. He swallows the bitter taste of bile in his throat and closes his eyes and waits for the whisper of hand-forged steel to kiss the back of his neck and end it all. This is it. He waits to die on his floor like a whipped dog. He opens his eyes.

She hesitates. He hears her voice, as smooth and tranquil and cold as a cat purring: "I didn't want it to be this quick."

Fifty seconds.

"I don't want it to be over," she says, standing over him, the blade wavering.

Fifty-five seconds.

Deep in the recesses of the Governor's brain, a spark kindles. He has one chance. One last shot at her. He feigns another cough and doesn't look up, coughs again, but ever so subtly he blinks and peers at her feet—those steel-toed boots spread shoulder-width in front of him—only inches away from his hands.

One last chance.

At the sixtieth second, he pounces at her lower region. Taken by surprise, the woman tumbles backward.

The Governor lands on top of her like a lover, the sword flying across the floor. The impact knocks the wind out of her. He can smell her musky scent—sweat and cloves and the copper-tang of dried blood—as she writhes beneath him, the sword only about eighteen inches away on the carpet. The gleam of the blade catches his eye.

At second number sixty-five, he makes a play for the sword, reaching for the hilt. But before he has a chance to get ahold of it, her teeth sink into the meat of his shoulder where it meets his neck, and she bites him so hard, her teeth penetrate flesh and layers of subcutaneous tissue, and finally down into muscle.

The searing pain is so sudden and enormous and sharp that he shrieks like a little girl. He rolls away from her—moving on instinct now—clutching at his neck and feeling the wetness seeping through his fingers. Michonne rears back and spits a mouthful of tissue, the blood running down the front of her in thick rivulets.

"Fuh—FUH-KING!—BITCH!" He manages to sit up, stanching the flow of blood with his hand. It doesn't occur to him that she might have very well breached his jugular and he's already a dead man. It doesn't occur to him that she's going for the sword. It doesn't even occur to him that she's rising up over him again.

All he can think about right then—at seventy-three seconds into the fight—is stopping all the blood from leaking out of his neck.

Seventy-five seconds.

He swallows the metallic taste in his mouth and tries to see through his watery eyes as his blood soaks the ancient carpet.

At seventy-six seconds, he hears inhaling sounds as his opponent takes a deep breath and rises up over him again and mutters something that sounds a little like, "Got a *better* idea."

The first blow of the sword's blunt-ended handle strikes his skull above the bridge of his nose. It makes a loud clapping noise in his ears—the brunt of a Louisville Slugger hitting the sweet spot of a hardball—and pins him to the floor.

Ears ringing, vision blurring, pain strangling him, he makes one last attempt to grab her ankles when the iron-hard handle comes down again.

Eighty-three seconds into the confrontation, he collapses, a dark shade coming down over his vision. The final blow to his skull comes eighty-six seconds in, but he barely feels it.

One second later, everything goes completely black and he's floating in space.

In the moonlit darkness of the clearing, in the rushing silence of night, Lilly carefully unwraps the last object to be tossed into the mouth of the fire pit. The size of a peach pit, it lies nestled in a handkerchief. She looks down at it, a single tear tracking down her cheek. She remembers all that the little nodule means to her. Josh Hamilton saved her life. Josh was a good man who didn't deserve to die the way he did, a bullet in the back of his head, fired by one of Woodbury's thugs, the man they called the butcher.

Lilly and Josh journeyed many miles together, learned to survive together, dreamt of a better time together. A gourmet cook, an executive chef by trade, Josh Hamilton had to be the only man who traveled the roads of the apocalypse with an Italian black truffle in his pocket. He would shave flakes off the thing to flavor oils and soups and meat dishes. The nutty, earthy flavor was indescribable.

The thing in Lilly's lap still gives off a pungent aroma, and she leans down and takes a big whiff. The odor fills her senses with memories of Josh, memories of first coming to Woodbury, memories of life and death. Tears well up in her eyes. She has a little grape juice left in her cup and she now raises it.

"Here's to an old friend of mine," she says. "He saved my life more than once."

Next to her, Austin bows his head, sensing the importance of the moment, the sorrow being exorcised. He holds his cup tightly to his chest.

"Hope we meet again someday," she says and goes over to the pit.

She tosses the little black node into the hole with the other symbolic objects.

"Amen," Austin says softly, taking a sip. He goes over to Lilly and puts his arm around her, and for a moment, they both stand there in the darkness, staring down at the jumble of artifacts in the hole.

The ambient drone of crickets and wind accompanies their silent thoughts.

"Lilly?"

"Yeah?"

Austin looks at her. "Have I mentioned that I love you?"

She smiles and keeps looking at the ground. "Shut up and start shoveling, pretty boy."

Out of the void of absolute night—the darkness at the bottom of the Marianas Trench—a nonsensical phrase floats in the opaque blackness like a ghostly sign, a message meaning nothing, a blip of coded electrical energy crackling across a wounded man's mind-screen with neon intensity:

WAY UP AND SOLD!

The wounded man doesn't understand. He can't move. He can't breathe. He's fused to the dark. He's an amorphous blob of carbon floating in space . . . and yet . . . and yet . . . he keeps sensing the presence of this message meant only for him, an urgent command that makes no sense whatsoever:

WAIT UP AND ROLL!

All at once he feels the physical laws of the universe returning very slowly, as though he's a vessel in the deepest part of the ocean righting itself, feeling the weight of gravity through the mists of paralyzing pain, acting on him—first on his midsection, and then on his extremities—a tugging sensation from below and from each side of him, as though the moorings holding him prisoner in this black sensory deprivation tank are tightening.

He senses the existence of his own face, sticky with blood, hot with infection, a pressure on his mouth, and a stinging sensation in his eyes, which are still sightless but are beginning to absorb a glowing, nebulous light from somewhere above him.

In his midbrain, the neon message being transmitted to him slowly becomes clear, either through sound or some other inchoate telepathic means, and as the message jerkily comes into focus—a crude imperative clicking into place like tiles on a puzzle box—his fractured psyche begins to compute the deeper meaning of it.

The angry command currently being directed at him triggers a warning alarm that shatters his courage and weakens his resolve. All his defenses crumble. All the blockades in his brain—all the heavy-duty walls and partitions and compartments—come tumbling down . . . until he is nothing . . . nothing but a shattered human being groping in the dark, horrified, tiny, fetal . . . as the coded words are slowly decrypted in his mind:

WAKE UP, ASSHOLE!

The voice comes from inches away, a familiar breathy feminine voice.

"Wake up, asshole!"

He opens his encrusted eyes. *Oh God, oh God, no-no-no—NO!* A voice deep in his subconscious registers the horror and the true nature of his situation: He is tied to the walls of his own foul-smelling living room, which now serves as a perfect doppelganger for the torture chamber under the speedway in which he kept Michonne.

A single overhead safety lamp in a tin shade shines down on him. Michonne must have brought it in. The upper half of the Governor's body is battered and bruised, torqued so severely by the ropes that his shoulders are nearly dislocated. The rest of him—which he now realizes with no small measure of horror is completely nude—rests with his legs bent at the knees and awkwardly splayed outward against a wooden panel hastily nailed to the carpet beneath him. His cock stings, stretched at an odd angle beneath him, as though glued to the floor in a puddle of coagulating blood. A strand of thick, viscous, bloody drool dangles off his lower lip.

The weak, mewling voice deep inside him pierces the noise in his head: *I'm scared . . . oh God I'm scared—*

—SHUT UP!

He tries to push back the voice. His mouth is as dry as a lime pit. He tastes bitter copper, as if he's been sucking on pennies. His head weighs a thousand pounds. He blinks and blinks, trying to focus on the shadowy face right in front of him.

Gradually, in bleary, miragelike waves, the narrow face of a dark-skinned woman comes into focus—she crouches right in front of him, only inches away—burning her gaze into him. "Finally!" she says with an intensity that makes him jerk backward with a start. "I thought you were *never* going to wake up."

Dressed in her dungarees and headband and braids and boots, she rests her arms on her haunches directly in front of him like a repairwoman inspecting a faulty appliance. How the fuck did she do this? Why didn't anyone see this bitch skulking around his place? Where the fuck are Gabe and Bruce? Where the fuck is Penny? He tries to maintain eye contact with the woman but has trouble keeping his half-ton head aloft. He wants to close his eyes and go to sleep. His head droops, and he hears that awful voice.

"You passed out a second time when I nailed your prick to the board you're on. You remember that?" She tilts her head curiously at him. "No? Memory a little messed up? You with me?"

The Governor starts to hyperventilate, his heart kicking in his chest. He senses his inner voice—usually buried deep within the remotest cavities of his brain—bubbling to the surface and taking over and dominating his stream of consciousness: *Oh God I'm so scared . . . I'm scared . . . what have I done? This is God paying me back. I never should have done those things I did . . . to this woman . . . to the others . . . to Penny . . . I'm so damn scared . . . I can't breathe . . . I don't want to die . . . please God I don't want to die please don't make me die I don't want to die oh God-oh-God—*

*—*SHUT THE FUCK UP!!*—*

Philip Blake silently howls at the voice in his head, the voice of Brian Blake—his weaker, softer self—as he stiffens and cringes against the ropes. A sharp dagger of pain knifes up his midsection from the mutilated penis, and he lets out an inaudible gasp behind the tape clamped over his mouth.

"Whoa there, cowboy!" The woman smiles at him. "I wouldn't do much moving if I were you."

The Governor lets his head droop, and closes his eyes, and lets out a thin breath through his nostrils. The gag holds tight on his mouth, a four-by-four-inch hank of duct tape. He tries to moan but he can't even do that—his vocal cords strangled by the pain and the war going on inside him.

The "Brian" part of him is pushing its way back up through the layers . . . until it insinuates itself again in the Governor's forebrain: *God please . . . please . . . I did bad things I know I know but I don't deserve this . . . I don't want to die like this . . . I don't want to die like an animal . . . in this dark place . . . I'm so scared I don't want to die . . . please . . . I beg you . . . have mercy . . . I will plead with this woman . . . I will plead for my life for mercy for my life please please-please-please-please-please-please-OH-GOD-please-GOD-please—*

Philip Blake winces, his body convulsing, the rope digging into his wrists.

"Easy there, sport," the woman says to him, her glistening brown face almost sanguine in the shifting light of the gently swaying lamp. "I don't want you to pass out again before I get a chance to begin."

Eyes slamming shut, lungs erupting with fire, the Governor tamps down the voice, swallows it back, shoves it back into the dark convolutions of his brain. He silently roars at his other self: *STOP YOUR FUCKING WHINING YOU LITTLE WEAK-WILLED FUCKING BABY AND LISTEN TO ME, LISTEN, LISTEN, LISTEN—YOU ARE NOT GOING TO BEG AND YOU'RE NOT GOING TO FUCKING CRY LIKE A LITTLE FUCKING BABY YOU LITTLE BABY!!!*

The woman interrupts the clamor: "Calm down for a second . . . and stop jerking around . . . and listen to me. You don't have to worry about the little girl—"

Philip Blake's eyes pop open at the mention of Penny, and he looks at the woman.

"—I put her in the front room, just inside the door, where you had all this junk. What are you doing? Building a cage for your little sex slave? Why do you have her here, anyway?" The woman purses her lips thoughtfully. "You know what . . . don't even answer that. I don't even want to know."

She rises up, and stands over him for a moment and takes a deep breath. "I'm anxious to get started."

Now the storm raging in Philip's brain suddenly ceases as though a fuse has blown. He gazes up at the woman through tunneling vision—she has his undivided attention now—and he gapes at her as she turns and ambles across the room, moving with a kind of casual authority, as if she has all the time in the world.

For a single instant, he thinks he hears her whistling softly as she goes over to a large, grease-spotted duffel bag on the floor in the far corner of the room. She bends down and rummages through a phalanx of tools. "I'll begin with some show-and-tell," she mutters, pulling a pair of pliers from the duffel. She stands, turns, and displays the pliers to him as though asking for a bid at an auction. *What can I get as an opening bid on these fine Craftsman titanium pliers?* She glares at him. "Show-and-tell," she reiterates. "I'm going to use everything here on you before you die. First up—these excellent pliers."

Philip Blake swallows acid and looks down at the blood-soaked wooden platform.

Michonne puts the pliers back into the duffel, then grabs another tool and shows it to him. "Next up, a hammer." She waves the hammer cheerfully. "Already used this puppy on you a little bit."

She puts the hammer back and digs some more through the bag's contents, while Philip stares at the stained platform and tries to get air into his lungs.

"LOOK AT ME, MOTHERFUCKER!" Her roaring voice yanks his attention back across the room. She holds a small cylindrical device with a copper nozzle. "Acetylene torch," she says with a sort of righteous expression, her voice suddenly calm again. "Feels almost full, too. And that's good. You used this for cooking." She manages another icy smile. "I will too."

Philip Blake's head droops again, the white noise in his brain crackling.

The woman across the room finds another implement and pulls it out of the bag. "You're really going to like what I do with this," she says, holding a bent spoon up into the light so that he can get a good look at it. The concavity of the spoon gleams in the dim room.

Dizziness courses through the Governor, his wrists blazing with pain.

Michonne rifles through the duffel for another object and finally finds it.

She holds the apparatus up for him to see. "Electric power drill," she says. "Must have just charged it recently . . . the battery's full."

She walks toward him, pulling the drill's trigger, revving its motor. The noise recalls the whirr of a dental instrument. "I think we'll start with this."

It takes every last shred of strength for Philip Blake to look up into her eyes as the drill bit whirs and slowly comes toward the sinewy part of his left shoulder where the arm meets the torso— the place where all the nerves live.

EIGHTEEN

During the normal course of a small town's ebb and flow of daily life, a muffled scream in the wee-hour dark of night would raise not only suspicion but also sheer terror among those minding their own businesses slumbering with their windows open to let in the pleasant breeze of a spring evening or dozing at their third-shift cash registers at all-night convenience stores. But right then, at exactly 1:33 A.M. Eastern standard time, in Woodbury, Georgia, as the keening emanates from the second floor of the Governor's building, the noise dampened and muffled by layers of mortar, concrete, and glass—as well as the duct tape suppressing the screams—the course of daily life is anything but normal.

The men working the late shift on the north, west, and south walls have started abandoning their posts, flummoxed by their supervisor's absence. Martinez hasn't checked in for hours—a bizarre development that has most of the guards scratching their heads. Bruce and Gabe have already discovered the deserted infirmary—the doctor and Alice nowhere to be found—and now the two men are discussing whether or not to bother the Governor with the news.

The strange calm in town has also roused Bob from a restless sleep, and caused him to struggle to his feet and take a drunken walk in the night air to try to clear his mind and figure out why things seem so strangely still and quiet. In fact, Bob Stookey may be the only resident who actually hears the faint sounds of screaming at that moment. He is staggering past the front façade of the Governor's building when the high-pitched shrieking—masked by the duct tape gag, as faint and yet unmistakable as a loon calling out over the dark reaches of a still lake—echoes behind one of the boarded windows. The sound is so eerie and unexpected that Bob thinks he's imagining it—the hooch will sometimes play tricks on him—so he continues weaving down the sidewalk, oblivious to the import of the strange noises.

But right then, inside said building, at the end of the second-floor corridor, inside the airless living room of the largest apartment, in the jaundiced light of a hanging work lamp, which now sways gently in the air currents, there is nothing imaginary about the pain being inflicted upon Philip Blake. The pain is a living, breathing thing—a predator—chewing through him with the ferocity of a wild boar rooting for bloody nuggets in the nerve bundle between his left pectoral and deltoid muscles.

The drill sings as the bit digs deeper and deeper into his nerve tissue, throwing a wake of blood and human particulate into the air.

Philip's scream—filtered behind the duct tape, almost to the point of sounding like a warbling car alarm—is constant now. Michonne pushes the spinning bit down to the hilt, the delicate mist of blood blowing back into her face. Philip lets out a feral moan—which sounds something like "MMMMMMMMMMMMMMMGGGHHHHH!!!"—as the drill buzzes and whirs. Michonne finally lets up on the trigger and unceremoniously yanks the bit out of the pulp of Philip's shoulder with a violent jerk.

The Governor shudders in agony between the two ropes that creak noisily with every twitch.

Michonne drops the drill on the floor with little concern for its well-being, cracking the housing. Tendrils of gristle and matter cling to its bit in a bloody tangle. Michonne gives it a nod.

"Okay," she says, speaking more to herself than to her subject. "Let's take care of that bleeding and make sure we keep you awake."

She finds the roll of duct tape, snatches it up, pulls a strip clear, bites it off with her teeth, and wraps it around the bloody, wounded shoulder with very little tenderness. She would practice more care if she were dressing a turkey for Thanksgiving dinner. She closes off the wound as though securing a leaky pipe.

Meanwhile, Philip Blake feels the curtain of darkness closing down over his line of vision. He feels the world separating like two panes of glass sliding apart underwater, forming a double image, which fades and fades, until his head lolls forward and the cold spreads through him, and he mercifully starts to pass out again.

The slap comes out of nowhere, hard and fast, to the side of his face. "WAKE UP!"

He heaves back against the ropes, eyes fluttering back open to the horrifying sight of the black woman's steadfast, baleful expression. Still bearing the scars and the purple scourge marks of her own torture, the woman's face furrows with contempt and fixes its unyielding glower on the Governor. Her smile is a clown's grin of madness and hate. "The last thing you want to do is pass out again," she says calmly, "you'll miss all the *fun*."

Next come the needle-nosed pliers. She procures them from the duffel, and comes back whistling that maddening tune that makes the Governor's flesh crawl. It feels like a hive of wasps humming in his ears. He fixes his hot gaze on the pointed tips of those pliers as Michonne reaches down and grabs his right hand, which dangles loosely from its bound wrist. Whistling absently, she carefully holds his index finger up between her thumb and forefinger as though she's about to give him a manicure.

It takes some effort, but she wrenches off his fingernail quickly, like ripping a Band-Aid off a sore. The searing pain corkscrews down his arm, strangles him, ignites his tendons with molten lava. His ferocious groan—suppressed by the gag of tape—sounds like a cow being slaughtered. She moves to the middle finger and tears off the nail. Blood drips and bubbles. Philip hyperventilates with agony. She does the third finger and then the pinkie for good measure.

"That hand is just ruined now," she says as matter-of-factly as a manicurist offering grooming advice. She drops the pliers, turns, and searches for something across the room. "Just ruined," she mutters, finding her sword.

She comes back and very swiftly—without hesitation—she winds up like a major league batter about to swing for the fence and brings the sword down hard and fast on the joint of his right arm just above the elbow.

The first sensation that smashes into Philip Blake—before the burning, unbearable pain—is a slackening of pressure as the rope tumbles away with the severed arm attached. His penis detaches from the board and blood fountains from the ragged stump as he falls sideways now, loosened from the east wall. He hits the floor hard, gaping at the remains of his right arm with uncomprehending horror—way down in the center of his eyes, in the pupils, in the cores of the irises, the apertures closing down to pinpricks that burn like diodes—and he lets out a grotesque sound behind the muzzle of duct tape that recalls a strangled pig.

The blood has bathed him by this point, making the wooden platform as slimy as an oil slick. Profound cold engulfs him, turning his flesh to ice.

"Don't worry," Michonne is saying to him, but he can hardly hear a thing she's saying anymore. "I'm pretty sure I can stop the bleeding." She pulls a Zippo from her pocket. "Where's that torch?"

In the surreal passage of time before she comes back with the torch, lying on the floor in his own blood, the cold spreading through him, he senses the other voice way down in some far-flung cavity of his brain, sobbing and choking on its anguished plea: *God please don't let me die like this . . . please . . . save me . . . don't let it end . . . not like this . . . I don't want to die like—*

ENOUGH!

ENOUGH!!

Deep down in the core of his soul, Philip Blake turns a corner, the revelation traveling up his spine and exploding in his brain.

In syrupy slow motion, Michonne approaches with the torch, lighting the nozzle with a WWWWHOOMP, but the sight of her no longer troubles him, no longer alarms him. She is fate on two legs and he finds his true character then. He watches her lowering the arcing flame toward his ragged stump of an elbow. He gazes at her with that one eye—peering through dangling strands of his greasy hair—and he has his greatest epiphany yet.

It's time, he thinks, flinging his thoughts at her through the beacon of his feverish gaze. *Go ahead. I'm ready. Get it over with. I dare you. Go ahead, bitch. I'm fucking ready to fucking die. So kill me . . . do it now . . . KILL ME! I'LL BET YOU DON'T HAVE THE FUCKING GUTS! GO AHEAD AND KILL ME NOW YOU FUCK-ING BITCH!!*

She burns the stump with the blue flame, cauterizing blood and pulp and tissue, making horrible crackling noises in the silent living room, spuming smoke and sizzling marrow, and sending the worst pain through Philip he has ever experienced . . . ever.

Ever.

And unfortunately for Philip Blake—AKA the Governor—the process does not kill him.

And the woman named Michonne has only just begun to work on him.

————

On the other side of town, under the stars, as the ubiquitous droning of crickets and other rustling night sounds continue unabated, the first spadeful of earth gets dumped on top of the fire pit. The sandy, dark-brown Georgia dirt lands on the photograph of Megan with a soft thump. Austin scoops another shovelful and dumps it. And another. And another. And the dirt begins to cover the pile of precious objects with the finality of a graveside burial.

At one point, Austin pauses in his shoveling and glances over at Lilly, who stands nearby, wrapped in a blanket, watching. She holds it tightly around her neck, and she lets the tears build until they run down her cheeks and soak the edge of the blanket.

Austin hands her a shovelful of dirt, and she drops it on the pit.

Neither one of them says it aloud, but the sense passing between them is one of letting go.

They are letting go of their grief, their fear, their past. They have a future now. They have each other, and they have a tiny ember of new life growing inside Lilly like a silent promise. Lilly smiles sadly, wiping her face. Austin smiles back at her. They finish filling up the hole, and Austin puts down the spade.

Then they go back over to the tree stumps and rest their weary bodies in the dark silence.

"Oh, you're awake again . . . good."

The light has gone all gauzy and dreamy in the terrible living room as her voice floats like a beautiful moth hovering in the air behind him. He can't see her anymore—only her shadow rippling across the floor beside him—but he can hear her back there near his ass. He realizes he's been repositioned, and is now lying prone, his face pressed flat on the platform, his rear-end elevated. All his sensory organs now absorb the environment slowly, blearily—a camera whose lens has been knocked askew.

The cold hard edge of the spoon enters his rectum hard and deep.

He nudges forward with a jerk as the implement sinks as far as his sacrum. For a fleeting moment, the horrors of having the one prostate exam he ever had come flooding back to him, the doctor in Jacksonville—what was his name? Kenton? Kenner?—chatting idly about the Falcons' draft picks the whole time. He imagines himself laughing at that private little joke but instead he gasps.

She shoves the spoon all the way down to his sacral vertebra and turns it with a vengeance—as though she's trying to scoop out his entire coccyx and intestines—and he screams. Naturally the tape muffles his scream, and all he hears with his own ears is a series of infantile moaning noises. The fire in his abdomen blazes out of control as she starts to struggle a little bit, the spoon caught on some part of his internal anatomy.

He is about to once again sink into the quicksand of unconsciousness when she yanks the bent spoon from his anus with a wet smacking noise. "There," she says. "Gonna be sore for a while down there."

She rises and strolls around the front of him so that he can glimpse her in his feverish peripheral vision. She holds the bloody spoon up.

"And I thought getting it *in* was hard," she comments wryly as the blinds close down, once again, ever so mercifully, on the Governor's vision, taking him back to that blessed, empty, cold darkness.

The experts know how to keep a person awake and conscious during "enhanced interrogation"—CIA spooks, third world goons, KGB ghosts, drug cartels, et cetera—but this amazon with the Medusa dreadlocks has no questions in mind and has no apparent experience in the art of keeping a person conscious during this kind of slapdash, improvised torture. All she has, as far as the Governor can tell, is her innate sense of justice and a little street sass to keep her going and keep the Governor awake. The Governor realizes all this every time he snaps back awake and finds his level of comprehension corrupted and distorted even further through the surreal lens of his hellish pain.

This time, he awakes to the feeling that a piano has fallen on his head. He feels the massive impact, cracking the side of his skull, concussing him, sending particle-bombs of agony down the bridge of his noise. He hears the atonal clang of all eighty-eight keys of the piano, all at once, inside his head, and his ears sing an off-key aria, the ringing so loud he can't even breathe.

Michonne stands over him. She slams the sole of her boot down on his head a second time.

The heel cracks his jaw, and all at once, the Governor is only half awake . . . not wholly conscious, and not really unconscious.

He lolls and moans and giggles behind the tape in a sort of neurological fog, the higher functions of his brain shutting down and going to the default program: *his primal self.* He feels as though he's a little boy in Waynesboro, and he's sitting on his dad's lap at the carnival. He smells the popcorn and horseshit and cotton candy. He hears the calliope playing a comical little tune, and the star of the show—the Dark Warrior Woman from Borneo—slowly circles him, slowly circles his seat on his dad's lap in the front row.

"I think I kicked you too hard," she says in her funny little voice. The audience claps and laughs. "It looks like something ripped."

He wants to laugh at her funny joke but somebody—his daddy, maybe?—holds a hand over his mouth. Which makes everything seem even funnier. The Dark Warrior Woman from Borneo kneels down really close to his face. He looks up at her. She looks down at him and grins a funny grin. What is she going to do with that spoon? Maybe she'll do her greatest trick yet!

She holds the spoon near his left eye and murmurs, "Don't pass out on me—we're not done yet."

The edge of the spoon is cold as she begins to shovel out his eyeball. It reminds him of the time the dentist had to drill into a cavity way in the back of his mouth—it hurt so, so, so, so, *soooooooooooo* bad—and he got a lollipop afterward, which made him feel a little better, but *this* time there's no lollipop, and it hurts worse than he thought possible. He even hears the yucky sounds—like when his mama pulls a chicken apart for dinner— the snotty, wet smacking noises. As the Lady from Borneo digs out his eyeball, the thing eventually uncorks from its socket.

He feels like clapping for this amazing dark lady who manages to leave the eyeball lying halfway down his face, hanging on strands of nerves and icky red stuff like wet party streamers.

His vision now goes completely haywire and it's like he's on a thrill ride—like when his daddy took him and his brother Brian to the Heart of Georgia State Fair and they rode the Zipper—and everything is spinning. He can still see—kind of—out of the hanging eyeball. And he can still see out of his other eye. And what he sees right then makes him feel bad for the Great Wild Warrior Woman from Borneo.

She's crying.

Tears roll down her brown, shiny face as she crouches in front of Philip, and Philip feels sad *himself* all of a sudden for this poor lady. Why is she crying? She's staring at him like a lost child, like a little girl who has just done something very bad.

Then something else happens that gets Philip Blake's attention.

A loud knocking on the door brings him back to the here and now. He blinks his one good eye, and the lady blinks away her tears, and they both hear the deep, angry, male voice outside the door.

"GOVERNOR! YOU IN THERE?!"

All at once, the calliope music stops and little Philip Blake is no longer at the carnival.

Michonne grabs her sword, stands, and faces the doorway—paralyzed with indecision. She hasn't completed her masterpiece, the most important piece of the puzzle about to be put in place, but now the whole thing may have to be—on many levels—*cut short*.

She turns to the grotesque remains on the floor—the man barely clinging to life—and starts to say something to him when the voice booms outside the door.

"YO!—PHIL! OPEN UP! THE CRAZY BITCH IS GONE, MAN! THE DOCTOR AND ALICE—AND THE OTHER TWO AS WELL!" The creak of wood, a snapping noise.

Michonne looks down at the Governor as an enormous thud reverberates. She extends the tip of the katana sword toward his groin.

Gabe's voice—unmistakable in its gravelly, heavily accented bark—rises an octave outside the door: "WHAT THE FUCK HAP-PENED TO YOUR DOOR, MAN?! WHAT'S GOING ON?! SAY SOMETHING, SIR! WE'RE COMING IN!"

Another massive thud—perhaps both Gabe and Bruce putting their shoulders into it, or perhaps a makeshift battering ram out there—the hinges already cracking, raining down dust, threatening to burst where Michonne had hastily nailed them back up.

Michonne holds the sword centimeters from the Governor's flaccid penis.

"Looks like what's left of that thing could possibly heal if you survive this," she says softly to him, her voice so low now she could be talking to a lover. She has no idea whether he can even hear her, or comprehend her. "And we wouldn't want that."

With a single flick of her wrist, she expertly severs the man's penis at its base, the blood bubbling and percolating as the organ flops lifelessly to the wooden flooring next to the man.

Michonne turns and darts out of the room, and she has already traversed the length of the apartment, thrown open a window, climbed out, and made it halfway down the fire escape when the door finally gives way.

Bruce lurches into the apartment first. Bald head glistening, eyes wide and hot, he nearly stumbles to the floor. Gabe lunges in behind him, fists clenched, eyes quickly scanning.

"FUCK!" Bruce whirls when he hears the tiny snarling voice of the dead child. "FUCK!" He sees Penny chained up for safekeeping across the foyer. "FUCK!—FUCK!—FUCK!" He smells the heavy stench of bodily fluids and the blood of an abattoir in the air. He looks around. "FUCK!-FUCK!-FUCK!-FUCK!-FUCK!— FUCK!!"

"Look out!" Gabe shoves Bruce aside when the little dead girl reaches for them, stretching her chains, snapping her tiny black teeth at the air near Bruce's torso. Gabe hollers, "Get away from her!"

"Oh fuck . . . fuck," Bruce utters suddenly when he turns toward the archway into the living room. He sees the gruesome remains of Penny's meal. "Governor! Oh—fuck!"

In the calm, pristine darkness of the clearing, under the vast rural sky, Austin Ballard finally breaks the silence. "You know what? I just realized . . . I can build a little nursery in that sun room in the back of my apartment."

Lilly nods. "That would be nice." She thinks about it. "I saw a cradle in the warehouse nobody's using." She thinks some more. "Call me crazy but I think this is going to work out."

Austin reaches over to her, and pulls her into a soft embrace. They sit on the same stump now, holding each other. Lilly kisses his hair. He smiles and pulls her tighter. "Woodbury's the safest place we could be right now," he says softly.

She nods. "I know . . . I get the sense the Governor's got things under control."

Austin squeezes her tenderly. "And Stevens and Alice can deliver the baby."

"Good point." She smiles to herself. "I think we're in good hands."

"Yep." Austin stares at the night. "The Governor's gonna keep us safe." He smiles. "This is the best situation in the world to start a new life."

Lilly gives him another nod. Her smile could power an entire city. "I like the sound of that—a new life—it has a nice ring to it."

For the first time in her life, she actually feels like everything's going to be okay.

Gabe and Bruce plunge into the torture chamber of a living room and all at once they see the evidence of Michonne's handiwork—the bloody tools, the duffel bag, the severed arm, the tissues and blood smudges fanned out across the wooden platform like hellish demonic wings sprouting from the body. They take another few steps toward the remains.

Their minds swimming with panic, they try to stay calm and talk to each other.

Gazing down at the body, Gabe says, "What about the black chick?"

Bruce gapes. "Fuck her. She's probably outside the safe zone by now—she ain't got a chance."

"Jesus," Gabe mutters, looking at what's left of his boss, the remains eviscerated, scorched, scourged, and contorted, one eye dangling by strings of tissue on the side of the man's face. The body twitches. "Is he—Is he dead?"

Bruce takes a shallow breath and goes over to kneel by the Governor.

A faint sound whistles from the man's nostrils.

Bruce can't even find a place to feel for a pulse, the body is so mangled. He carefully peels the tape from the man's lips.

Then Bruce leans down and brings his ear close to the man's bloody mouth.

Signs of a faint breath reach Bruce's ear but he can't tell if it's a death throe—

—or if the man is clinging to a twilight world on the cusp of death.

Under a canopy of twinkling stars, Austin touches Lilly's face as though caressing the beads of a holy rosary. "I promise you, Lilly, everything is definitely going to take care of itself." He kisses her. "Everything's gonna be great." He kisses her again. "You'll see."

She smiles. God help her, she believes him . . . she believes in the Governor . . . she believes in Woodbury. Everything *is* going to be okay.

Her smile lingering on her lips, she puts her head on Austin's shoulder and listens to the eternal night continue to churn and drone its ancient cycle of destruction and regeneration.

Thank you, God.

Thank you.

extracts reading groups
competitions books new
discounts extracts extracts
competitions discounts
books new events
events extracts discounts
reading groups books reading groups
events books
extracts
new titles reading groups
interviews events
events extracts extracts books
discounts events
new books events interviews
events new new extracts
discounts extracts discounts

www.panmacmillan.com

extracts events reading groups
competitions books extracts new
books